EVEN IF
THEY FAIL

David Holbrook

EVEN IF
THEY FAIL

a novel

BREESE
BOOKS
LONDON

First published in Great Britain by
Breese Books (A division of Martin Breese International)
164 Kensington Park Road, London W11 2ER, England

ISBN: 0 947 533 958

The characters in this novel are entirely fictional and have no
resemblance to any person living or dead.

Typeset in 10½/12½pt Palatino
by Ann Buchan (Typesetters), Middlesex.
Printed and bound in Great Britain by
Itchen Printers Ltd., Southampton.

For Margot
who, to my relief,
liked it

For a moment Paul Grimmer thought he would have to abandon the whole thing. It would be the first time he had ever failed in such a session. Perhaps it was foolish to begin like this? Perhaps it would be better simply to revert to formal instruction? Perhaps his dogged stance, sitting there and waiting for his students to talk about a poem, was foolish? Would they take it as a confession of his own stupidity? Perhaps they supposed he had nothing to say? Were they correct, that he was letting them down by his methods? Had things altered so much, since the sixties and seventies? Was he too old for the work, at fifty-seven? He was overcome by a quite uncharacteristic sense of his own ignorance and lack of experience. He was terrified of failure.

The taut silence after he read aloud the poem for discussion seemed unlikely ever to be broken. But then the discomfort of it proved too much for Joel Aschenberg, the Jewish boy whose dark eyes glanced nervously around at his fellow students, before he ventured to speak, with an odd, but charming smile on his lips.

"I'm interested in the theme of space in the poem," he said. "There's the hole being dug, the bubbles, the bubble-ideal of the colonel, the ditch . . ."

"Is that the kind of thing we are supposed to discuss?"

Poppy Beldon was bridling, flushed, her eyebrows going up further than seemed physically possible. But she had a handsome body, he thought: her cotton frock of striped colours hung prettily over her shapely legs. From the set of her jaw, however, he knew what a bully she could be.

"Supposed?" said Paul, in spite of himself. "Supposed by whom?"

"By the English faculty."

"I don't know what the faculty expects us to discuss," he said, rather annoyed. "And I don't care. I want *us* to read this poem and say what *we* think about it."

"You're a rum sort of Director of Studies," said a cross, gangly boy with a pale face, Brian Butley, "if you don't know what the faculty wants."

Always, Paul growled inwardly, they refused to go in for straight cooperation. They would always challenge the procedure, like maddening MPs raising points of order. But he kept as positive an expression on his face as he could, waiting.

"Let's get back to this poem," said Aschenberg. "I'm interested — what is this theme of space doing in it? Is it about the emptiness he sees in his world?"

"Well done, Joel," another man said.

Well done, indeed, thought Grimmer to himself: Aschenberg has thrown me a lifeline. He had given up any hope that the seminar would "go" this time, and was appalled at the implications. Joel was simply prepared to play the game. Grimmer thanked God for that Jewish intelligence, and that kind of glad acceptance of culture, as a priority in life.

"Space," said Aukland, with his slightly *fin-de-siècle* air, as of a dilettante, "Space has a kind of phenomenological connotation . . . it may be a manifestation of a vacancy of consciousness . . . or a spiritual yearning . . . Bachelard explores the symbolism of space as an analogue of the mother's body . . . he's the philosopher of *surréalisme*, and don't we detect a surreal element in this poem?"

"I can't see," said down-to-earth Poppy, "how an earth-digging machine making an underworld garage can be anything to do with surrealism. He's just a conservationist, who doesn't like historical places being dug up."

She tended to say "oop".

"But it is bizarre," declared Aukland. "The bubbles of the television screen, the statues being eroded: reality is being eaten away."

"What does the Latin mean?" asked Bo Dibbans from the shadows, where she had insisted on squatting on the carpet.

Somehow, the women tended to be so literal: it was the men who were willing to explore the more mysterious meanings. But Paul Grimmer, relaxing, found with delight that he was now listening to the individual comments being made by students on the meaning of the poem. The seminar was beginning to work, and they were forgetting to be suspicious. Their natural intelligent interest in their subject was beginning to emerge. Aschenberg was going strong. "In a way, it's a very nihilistic poem. He can't find solidity in any of the objects in the foreground — the statehouse is sinking, even the monument is undermined: the statues don't seem to stand for any intrinsic values."

"How can a statue have an 'intrinsic' value?"

Rhees was scathing, looking round for approval for his scepticism.

"Well, I mean a value that's really embodied in that symbol. All his symbols are menaced by the threat of emptiness: 'Space is nearer' — that's what he means."

"And the atom bomb is the biggest emptiness of all — it's the last ditch."

Paul Grimmer checked the individuals against the names on his list to see who had turned up to his weekly seminar. There was Daniel Rhees, with a pale freckled face, glasses and sandy hair, a fiery youth whom Grimmer noted down to himself as "Comrade Ossipon". The boy had a thin, gawky figure and wore old patterned pullovers and grey flannel trousers. He was a state school product. Paul thought he was sensitive and intelligent under the somewhat scowling "radical" front. Peter Aukland was a typical public schoolboy from Stowe, elegantly dressed in a grey suit with a dark blue cravat, long thin hands, a prominent Adam's apple, and was utterly incoherent. There was the dark Jewish man, Joel Aschenberg, with deep brown suspicious eyes and a pale earnest face. He wore black shoes and a conventional dark blue suit. Poppy Beldon was a plump girl with highly coloured cheeks and a fixed expression of hauteur: her permanent expression, with eyebrows raised by careful work with the tweezers, made her look continually as if someone had just said something outrageous to her. She wore frocks in pastel colours, rather well chosen and pleasantly feminine. But Paul detected a stubborn dogged will under the surface with her and expected trouble.

Bo Dibbans was a small dark girl who wore suits, had dark eyebrows and eyelashes and kept well out of sight, smouldering in a dark corner of the room. She was very much a cat that walked by herself, and as she and Paul discussed her work he could see that she was privately thinking differently and was determined to do everything in her own dogged way, whatever he said. There was a pale pretty girl, very intelligent, from a state school in Essex, Rosie Nicols, who seemed to him perhaps the most tormented of all his students, though very sympathetic. Next to her sat Pointer, a sharp-faced young man, extremely intellectual, and nervous: he knew him to be a devotee of his predecessor, Mrs Petula Weekles, a research fellow who had been doing what she could to help out with the college's English students in the interregnum before he was appointed. Perhaps she ought to have had his job, Grimmer thought? So he was careful what he said to Pointer who seemed keenly critical of everything he proposed, as the new director of studies. This young man was whispering behind his hand to Peter Brown, a first year boy whom Paul found very sympathetic, not least because, like him, he too had come up from a state school and found it very hard to make ends meet: also, he seemed very critical of Cambridge while responding with enthusiasm to the kind of literature Paul enjoyed. Then there was Brian Butley who seemed quite mad: Paul couldn't understand how he had ever got into the place. Though the man was bright enough, his grasp of everything seemed utterly eccentric and he was completely unable to express himself clearly. Poor Butley was liable to fall into sudden paroxysms of incoherent rage, and Grimmer feared he might wreck any teaching session if he was in the mood for it.

Grimmer already had some kind of thumbnail sketch of them all, from his interviews with them at the beginning of term. They are all still children, he said to himself inwardly, guardedly. But the recognition opened a chasm in which he perceived his own sentimental paternalism: let us act as if they were adults, he warned himself.

He liked the atmosphere of his new room. It had elegant

proportions, and handsome ceiling mouldings, with three long Georgian sash windows looking on to a lawn and rose-trees. He had tried hard to make the room sympathetic: it had white walls and a dark green carpet, and he had found some simple dark grey armchairs. On the walls he had hung some of his own holiday paintings and some early prints of the college. He had standard lamps to make pools of light. The gas fire hummed gently: they ought to feel at home, he thought. But it was clear they didn't.

The silence had become a silence of dull resentment. "I've walked into a lion's den," he thought to himself. "Is a lion's den worse than a hornet's nest?" He needed all the power or ironic and comic detachment he could summon, for since taking up his post, he had been confronted, to his amazement, with a persistent inexplicable hostility.

The sun was shining in through the big curtained windows and the students sat awkwardly, rather tense and stiff, despite all his assurances that the seminar would be relaxed and informal. In this weekly seminar he brought all three "years" in English together, and he wanted to treat them like adults, reading poems in relation to their experience of life. He had many experiences of evening class and classes of teachers all over the world — East Anglia, Australia, Illinois — of adult students taking part in such an exercise. They would grasp the opportunity to discuss literature gratefully, all attention, trusting the tutor not to waste their time, but to provide a stimulating work which they would describe as "something to get your teeth into". By contrast the Pemning students seemed to want not to be there at all. They held themselves stiff on the chairs, whispered to one another and squirmed awkwardly as if they could not wait until they got out of the room.

Afterwards, as they filed away, after an hour and a half, Grimmer thought it had all been somewhat ragged — but still something had "gone". Perhaps he should have done more to hold it together? How many there got nothing out of it at all? There were some, he noticed, especially Bo, who had hardly spoken.

*

Later the same afternoon his attention at a supervision was broken: the moon-faced Poppy Beldon brusquely interrupted.
"I don't like Wordsworth," she declared. "Moreover, he is not in the period I'm doing."
"How do you mean, 'doing'?" Grimmer responded. "You're taking Part I, aren't you?"
"Yes, but I'm not doing Paper 3."
"You're going to offer a dissertation instead of that paper?"
"Yes."
She looked cross and defiant.
"But my task is to give you a perspective on English literature from 1300 to the present day over the whole stretch of it. That's how I interpret Faculty policy. There are some works, some writers, you *must* know surely?"
No answer. The scowl deepened on the girl's plump face. He reflected on his own inconsistency: at the first seminar he had said he didn't care what the Faculty wanted.
"Irrespective of which papers you're taking . . . you don't suppose you can consider yourself educated in English without taking some notice of Wordsworth, who is one of the most important figures of all?"
"I don't *like* Wordsworth."
"Why not?"
"He's . . . sentimental . . . and . . . silly."
He laughed, exasperated rather.
"You must have had a bad experience of him: *Daffodils*, I suppose?" he ventured.
She made a disagreeable face, and murmured,
"He's . . . wet and soppy."
"Hardly the terms for *Margaret* and *Michael*," he said. "Have you read those?"
"I refuse to read Wordsworth."
He stared at the round-faced girl as if he was seeing her for the first time, and as he reached this degree of detachment, he saw himself, as if he were elevated some feet above his own head, examining his own predicament. He was invested with all the authority of College Director in his own subject, and

here was this girl student whom he had had no hand in selecting. What was she doing here then? And what was he doing? He had never come across anything like it. She was wearing a white T-shirt and tight blue jeans today, with soft white shoes. She had longish fair hair held back in a ponytail. Her face was pale and freckled but she had pink spots on her cheeks and these easily deepened if she became angry. Her face wore a perpetually petulant look with those plucked eyebrows, and whenever she confronted Paul at least, she displayed that expression of defensive hauteur: it could easily become just a rude stare. For no good reason that he could think of, she seemed inclined to be bitterly critical of everything he did or proposed. He'd never quarrelled with her or crossed her over anything: it was all projection. She had some bee in her bullying little bonnet about him. She seemed to divine that if he had been involved in admissions, he would never have given her a place. Why had someone chosen her? Despite all his intentions to make himself agreeable she detects, he reflected, with her female intuition, that I don't like her much. When she did get her degree, what would she do? She was enthusiastic about books for children: he could see her contemplating a teaching job in the primary school: but then he supposed she was more likely to settle for a job in advertising.

He stared now dismally at her, sitting in her disgruntled way in his armchair. She was somewhere between a school child, a school girl, in revolt, and a woman — her tight jeans and her emblazoned T-shirt decorating her sexuality that seemed to be turned now into a smouldering hostility.

"But," he protested, "you *must* do Wordsworth. How can anyone read for an Honours degree, not having read Wordsworth?"

"I hate him," she declared.

She made a brusque movement with her legs, establishing, as it were, a position in body language, to make it plain she would not read Wordsworth, ever.

"You can't surely consider yourself educated in English unless you read all the major authors?"

She stared at him balefully.

"You don't seem to be on our side."

"Your 'side'?" he asked, baffled.

"Well, surely, the important thing is that we should do well in the exam."

"The important thing is you should be educated."

He gave a kind of sardonic humourless laugh. He could only shrug and mutter that he would have to think about it. He really didn't know what to do. As she left, without any kind of farewell, he shook his head. He wasn't enjoying this new job at all.

Later in the week, another woman student also refused to read Wordsworth: she tipped a miserable scrap of paper through the letterbox of his room: "I have nothing to say about Wordsworth: I hope I may be excused this week's supervision." Preposterous, he said to himself: I am her Director of Studies. But then he thought he was being as pompous as Dogberry:

"And one that hath had losses," he mused, aware of his own pride, "and a good fellow enough, go to!"

But these girls who refused to read Wordsworth were not the only problem. Protests came all the time now: even Peter Brown protested at being asked to read *Sons and Lovers* — it was a long book to read in their first term he said. Rhees declared that T.S. Eliot was not worth their attention: he had never read *The Waste Land* and didn't intend to. And when Paul presented a poem by Sylvia Plath at the next seminar they all declared that he was trying to trick them. It was "The Night Dances", and he chose it because it was so difficult even to see what the poem was about.

"Trying to trick you?" he exclaimed. "Whatever into? What trap do you suppose I'm setting?"

There was a hostile silence. At last Butley spoke with his rather dark troubled brows, unwillingly.

"Into making fools of ourselves."

"As if I would!"

After a while they worked out for themselves that the poem was about a baby and its movements in its cot. He congratulated them. But they remained unconvinced, and still seemed angry.

It was the continuing hostility and suspicion that disturbed him deeply. He had assumed that he was walking in, as the new Director of Studies, to bat on a wicket that could be no better. These students were the cream of the nation's sixth forms, after all. They would be grateful, he had supposed, for his direct and open human approach, open to human interests and problems.

On the contrary, he found himself the butt of all manner of projections. He felt at times as if he were living inside some shell formed by other people's images of him around him: the real self became invisible within. The students scrutinised him intensely and minutely, ready to pounce on the least sign of his inadequacy. Now, he realised, he had to take another turn. He had to win. He must not fail — for *their* sakes. As a professional he had to be responsible for them: they had got it wrong. He had to bear it, and still do his best for them, for the subject, for the art. He had to dig down to his own resources, and re-establish confidence in himself, to reassure himself he was capable of teaching his subject, and of being a reliable teacher and adviser to his own students. Whatever his theories, his abstract grasp of his professional work, he was having to start, in the reality of his situation, from the beginning again, from the absolute bottom.

So, in the small house, he would dig, dig, dig into his inner confidence, and by degrees find his own authority in himself. Yes, he did know what to select, how to present the material, how to listen to their responses, to criticise their presentations, to choose teachers for them. It was not true that he was unsympathetic or unreliable.

Until, one dim morning, at dawn, he reached a point which had he been more suspicious, he might have reached much earlier. All this strange labyrinthine web of difficulty had not come from his mind, even his own deepest and most troubled psyche — he could see that. One thing that especially struck him was how cruel the students were being. Young people, he knew, are not naturally cruel.

It suddenly came to him, that pale grey dawn: young people like that are simply not capable of being as hostile and hurtful as his present group were being: *someone was setting them on.*

It must come from someone else, or some group of people. He burst out between the sheets into a damp sweat, in recognition that someone was stirring up some kind of conspiracy against him. At first he rejected the thought as paranoia: he got up, poured himself a glass of orange juice and made himself a coffee downstairs in the kitchen. But the conviction stayed, and as the dawn moved towards sunrise, and he went over all the strange things the students had said to him, he realised more and more clearly that they would not have come to their conclusions alone, could not have developed such attitudes towards him by themselves. They were too young, too nice, too innocent. They were only schoolchildren, after all. *They were being used.*

Who was it?

He felt at once outraged, and his first impulse was to raise it with the college.

But with whom?

It was like Councillor Mikulyn's question to Rasumov in *Under Western Eyes*: "Where to?" He could even feel something of Rasumov's moral isolation. No-one would believe him.

He didn't want to discuss it openly with anyone yet, though he had talked to the senior tutor about the refusal of two girls to read Wordsworth. The man was a dark, tough, down-to-earth engineer.

"Silly little bitches" the man exclaimed: but it was rather left in the air, as to what to do about it. No-one wanted to make it a confrontation. Having suffered a good deal in the days of the student revolt, the older dons, he found, were not anxious for a fight. Wilkinson, the senior tutor, was solemn about the matter and briskly sympathetic: but Paul could see that he felt it was a problem he must solve himself. He thought he didn't really understand what was happening — and in any case had plenty on his own plate.

He talked one day to Petula Weekles, who was their Research Fellow in the Arts, writing a thesis on angels in Mediaeval Literature. She was a small woman, dark and physically slight. He wondered how much he would share of her views on literature.

So many academic people puzzled him. One had to respect the great energy they put into their work. But he already had an odd sense that nothing these new professional types ever said to one about literature ever gave off any sympathetic glow. They walked across the grass of the main court together. He recalled the wine party she had given his students at the beginning of term, at which he became uncomfortably aware they knew her better than they knew him. She had done what she could to help the college through the patch last year during which there was no-one in charge: and they seemed more at ease with her than with him, which made him a little envious and unhappy. But he felt he ought to be grateful to her, for carrying the job, before he arrived to take over.

"They don't seem very happy," he said. She moved rather jerkily and nervously. He sensed that she didn't really like him, and belonged to a different generation — was across a gulf that it would be impossible to bridge. How unfortunate this was, he inwardly sighed. But she was intelligent, and seemed to know a great deal about her subject.

"Well, they've had a rather bad spell, you know, with no-one giving them direction. I expect they'll settle down."

"I hope so."

"They ought to, with someone mature like you, a kind of father figure. I think that's exactly what they need."

He looked carefully at her. There was no sign of sarcasm. But there was something wrong about the way she said it, a kind of false fulsomeness, beneath which he detected the hint of an edge, and beneath that a shadow of criticism.

And later in the day he met her in the corridor.

"What do you think?" he asked. "Poppy Beldon tells me she doesn't want to do anything written between 1700 and 1830 because she's avoiding Paper 3 by doing a dissertation on it."

Her face put on a professional studiousness.

"I should think that's a good idea."

"Good idea!" he exclaimed. "But they're supposed to cover

all periods. How can you have a student leaving out the whole of the eighteenth century?"

She began to nod at him and almost admonish him, even in a school-mistressy way.

"Well, you must think of the best use they can make of their time and resources. There's so much to get through."

"But it's surely faculty policy, that they should be taught the whole period 1300 to the present day. We must educate them, surely, across all English literature, otherwise . . ."

"Yes, but everybody . . ."

She shrugged her shoulders.

"But do you advise them like that? I mean, do you advise them to ignore faculty policy, then?"

She had turned pale and angry, and he began to see a different Petula from the woman who had been so ingratiating while they were crossing the grass.

"I think you should think carefully about what is in the students' best interests," she said, disdainfully.

He was too angry to speak and turned his back, diving away into the stationery room where the Xerox machine was kept. What an extraordinary state of affairs! Here was this woman, who taught his students their mediaeval texts, and had their confidence, leading them on to buck the system, and avoid being properly educated, so as to try to get a good degree, by cheating, virtually — by what seemed to him dishonest manipulations, by avoiding any period or subject they didn't like.

On reflection, he had a strange sense of a dogged and persistent opposition, as she stood there in her brown skirt and jacket, with a dark blue blouse that didn't go well with the earth-coloured material, her eyes bright with annoyance. He, on his part, had raised his voice, and the angry sound had, he knew, been picked up in the office, and everyone would soon know there was a crisis in the college English Department, if you could call it that.

He took it, however, to be a simple difference of opinion, as to how the work should be organised for the students. And yet the way the students continually challenged him seemed to point to something more complex. A day or two later Mark

Pointer, the exceptionally bright student from Northumberland, stopped him outside his staircase.

"Excuse me, Mr Grimmer, but I'd like to say something to you."

"Yes?" said Paul, warily, suppressing a sigh.

"I'm not happy about my supervisions, with you."

"What's wrong?"

"Well, this week you were dealing with some poems by Traherne. Now, Traherne's poetry is much influenced by Augustinian theology, and you didn't say anything about Augustinian theology at all."

Paul reflected that he had read the same chapter in the book in the library, too. The young man was an exceptionally bright one: but, yet again, he had a sense that this was not a conclusion he would have come to himself: he was being used. Who put him up to this rubbish about Augustinian theology?

"There's not much point in going in for Augustinian theology or whatever, unless people can read the poem. What I was trying to do is to get students to 'possess' the poem, by good reading."

Pointer looked contemptuous.

"I'm not sure I know what that means."

He gave a funny little wriggle, as he often did when he was advancing an argument. But, Paul reflected, the trouble was that Pointer was always off on a theory, but when you tried to pin him down, to what this line or that line meant, he wasn't very forthcoming. He was a potential for the Structuralists, Grimmer reflected, and would probably go that way, sailing away into some tenuous theory when he still couldn't read attentively. But he felt hurt, that Pointer wasn't prepared to give him a chance.

"Well, what do you want to do?"

"I thought I'd arrange some supervisions with Tom Butcher instead."

Paul really sighed this time. Butcher was one of those struggling hangers-on in the Cambridge scene, teaching on the fringe, a hack, really. He knew little of the man's work, but what he had seen he had not been impressed by, while some students had told him Butcher didn't read the texts to keep up with them. He had been told the man was critical of the Cambridge establishment, but there was a lot of that among the crammers who did supervisions for a pittance, and whom the university exploited. Well, if Pointer felt like that, let him go to the devil in his own way, Augustinian theology and all. He was exceptionally intelligent, but there was a strange lack of warmth in him, a deficiency of sensibility, which Grimmer had hoped to help improve. But now the man was quitting him. Watching Mark Pointer's rather nervous eyes, Paul thought he saw that he was trying to remember what Butcher had said to egg him on to raise difficulties with his Director of Studies. How many people, he thought to himself, are getting at me? What is this? There must be quite a party of them, out there, who think I ought never to have been given this job.

"Well, do," he said.

"And Mrs Weekles," said Pointer, his pale, rather spotty face intent with disaffection. "She is a very painstaking and effective supervisor, for whom I have the greatest respect."

Why did he say that, with such emphasis?

Paul nodded, and Pointer walked away, his trousers too tight and his socks showing. Presumably he would no longer come to him: the one man in his year who might be expected to get a first. He had more or less directly declared that Paul Grimmer was useless to him, to his face. Yet he had no cause to say so: he hadn't even time to know what kind of use Paul's teaching could be to him. He hadn't given it a chance. By now Grimmer was quite clearly aware of other voices behind the postures of his own students: as they uttered astonishingly unkind things to him, when they were too young and naive to know how sharp they were being or what hurt they were causing him. They were being used by someone behind the scenes, who thought he shouldn't be there.

*

He tried the problem out on one or two of the senior fellows. They were cautious but he could see that they, too, thought it all too likely. They were weary of conspiracies in the English Department: so, they didn't heap coals on the fire of Paul

Grimmer's disquiet. It was all very embarrassing: but there was enough agreement to make it clear to him that he was not merely being paranoid. Someone, or some group, was stirring things up. It made him very uncomfortable to know that every day someone was working on his own students and on others, in energetic secret hostility, to demonstrate that he was incompetent, and, if they could, to generate a situation in which he could even be seen to be ineffectual, if the students could be brought to distrust him. It seemed to him the most wicked thing to do: to undermine the confidence of students in order to wreck their relationship with their university teacher. He had heard, too, that at least two people telephoned the college to protest against the appointment. But he had no evidence. Only he was aware that they were waiting for a false step — whereupon they would exploit it.

*

At home, he tried to explain it all to his wife Frances. It seemed such a waste, he said, for people to become involved in childish conspiracies, over nothing. How absurd it was, that the intellectual life should be so affected by such manifestations of petty spite! Yet, of course, in the event the mischievousness was not childish — it was real enough, and could do such harm, when the capacity of the young to learn depended so much on trust and goodwill.

"You seem astonished," she said, smiling and laying a comforting hand on his arm, "that the world of dons is as full of mixed-up personalities and bitches as the outside world."

"Oh, worse," he protested. Frances knew the university better than he did: she had been in charge of its accommodation office for ten years. She was a small Welsh woman of great energy and feeling and, he had to admit ruefully to himself, more intelligent than he was. She grinned at him reassuringly with her green eyes.

"But I deal with loonies all the time. Every mathematician who comes in to the office is a looney. And there was a man today who turned down two rooms because there wasn't a desk or table which would fit *The Times* laid flat, open at a double spread."

"Yes, but for so much hatred to be directed at one!"

"This morning Mrs Jennings rang me to say, 'If you don't get that young man out of my lodgings my 'usband says 'e'll *kill* 'im!' "

Paul sighed.

"So much for the life of enlightened mind," he exclaimed.

"Landladies were never supposed to represent 'mind'," she warned.

Their circumstances had been completely changed by his appointment and they felt themselves borne along by a new tide. After years trying to sustain himself as a self-employed writer, and failing, there was a chance now he could pay his debts and even look forward to a small pension when he retired.

"I always wanted you to have a place in the university," said Frances, "so you could have some sort of recognition."

"Humph," he said, looking at her with irony. "Bit of a mixed blessing, don't you think, after these first two weeks?"

She looked as if she were wondering whether she ought to say what was in her mind. Then she ventured:

"It's rather like you, though, isn't it, to start a new job with a bit of a stir?"

He looked angry.

"It isn't *my* stir, is it?" he asked sharply. "Or do you think I bring these things on myself?"

There was still a radical uncertainty in him, and from time to time it reminded him of the moment when he had been given a research fellowship at Prince's long ago: the dreadful months when he wondered whether he could live up to it. In the end the book was written, and was what he had wanted to do. Now, he had promised other books, but it seemed to get harder all the time. Had developments passed him by? he couldn't understand Structuralism and Deconstructionism: and he didn't like what he could understand. He had done his own explorations in his own way and would stick to them. But there was the teaching itself: he had never had full charge of a college English Department, and it still remained to be seen if he was any good at it: not least because the students were so hostile and truculent, and because some person or persons were actively gunning for him. Some university teaching officers clearly thought he should never have been appointed to the job, and others were waiting for him to make a mistake and exploit it. His perceptions drew out of him his touch of paranoia, and his dread of failure. So, he was still in two minds about the new post. He sighed.

"I suppose I could give it all up and go back to being an independent writer again."

"And what would you live on?" asked Frances scathingly, "bread and cheese?"

"*I'm* not keeping you any longer," she said firmly.

They had ceased to talk about money, since she had been landed with paying all the bills and his debts. He had to cling to a dream that one day he would become self-supporting: well, in a way he had gained something, since his published works had landed him the job after all. In the age of the triumph of television over reading, he had found his dream of sustaining himself by writing books impossible to fulfil. So, there had been this radical failure at the heart of their married life. Whenever money came up in conversation he felt like Hamlet, acting a part, since his contribution was minimal. His only way to deal with such matters was to adopt a jokey cynicism — but then he began to feel even more disgustingly like Harold Skimpole. "The butterflies are free. Mankind will surely not deny to Harold Skimpole what it concedes to the butterflies?" He hated the character of Skimpole: for him it was too near the bone.

Frances was determined it should never happen again, the descent into crippling debt such as they had experienced in the sixties. She loved Paul and respected his work: but she was a realistic and business-like woman and needed to make herself secure for their retirement. She was putting a large proportion of her salary into a pension fund and insisted that he did the same now he had one.

They had both been scholarship students. His parents could never have paid for him to go on to higher education without a grant. Her father who was a lawyer in Wales, died when she was eleven, and left her mother with only modest means. As a student, and, indeed, as a young wife and mother, she had led a life of comparative poverty with this struggling writer with his half-time jobs in teaching and adult lecturing, and his pitiful earnings from writing.

"The trouble is," he said to Frances, "we grammar school people . . . we were given a taste of the delights of culture, but not the power and money to go with it."

"You mean, you should have been born a country gentleman?" she said, scathingly.

"No, for God's sake," he said. "I'm not going to be trapped by that concept of 'being a gentleman': nor do I envy the gentry, who have to turn their houses into funfairs to survive. No — but I mean there's a contradiction between the aspirations one is given even, say, by reading about the delightful times of the Wordsworths, or *The Prelude* and one's actual predicament: one would like to please oneself like that, but one doesn't have William's railway shares."

"Well," she said, with realism, "the academic world is not a bad solution: you give something to the community, and you get your portion of culture for it. After all, it's one of the big problems nowadays: how to *pay* for art and study."

"Well," he said, "we're certainly up against it nowadays, as the universities cut back. I've been talking to some of the English graduates. Roberts has been refused a grant for his other art course at the Courtauld: Jackson, our other research fellow will have to go next year because his research grant comes to an end."

His wife groaned.

"Even the Vice-Chancellor has spoken out against this penny-pinching government and the way they interfere with matters they don't understand."

Frances was still much more politically radical than he was: she still voted Labour, while he wavered around the SDP. "They have a point I suppose — the arts have to have a base in manufacturing and industry to pay for them. But a country that doesn't cherish its universities jeopardises its future."

"You can argue that culture is a primary need," he said. "It's a fundamental human need, like hunger and the need to be free to walk about."

He blushed, feeling he was talking like Harold Skimpole again.

"But it upsets people, doesn't it? Art can't be said to cement the fabric of society or whatever. Some of the polticians hate culture, because it gives people aspirations and makes them ask awkward questions."

"Does art have any effect on life at all? I assume it does, but sometimes I wonder. Look at Aschenberg — he sits there sometimes, pale and tense, as if his life depended on it, whether or not an author is ultimately trustworthy or not."

"Ah, how lucky you are, though," she said. "To be involved in such arguments with them! For that to *be* your work!"

It was true: as so often, she brought it home to him, when he tended to be discontented. Now and then he resented being burdened with the students and their sometimes maddening needs. But then he felt they should understand what the university could do for them: how, as an invisible atmosphere of the mind, even, it drew people into new perspectives, on their own suffering and difficulties — but, even more so, on human possibilities.

"What you've always said is right," Frances declared, for she had put up with his unrewarding life because she believed in his work. "If art is to be of any use to us, it should illuminate the here and now, the mundane. You used to say that in your adult class lectures and I used to go with that."

"If we can't find meaning in ordinary mundane existence, then we are lost — yes I believe that," he said. "But you don't like it sometimes when I write in that vein."

"I don't like all that about 'small hopes' and 'little apples', " she said, pouting. "You might celebrate our relationship a bit harder."

"Oh, bugger!" he said. "But that's it, I'm trying not to idealise it. We had enough of that. I'm not going to brow-beat myself with idealism again."

They were silent, remembering the time when they had both willed their marriage to be perfect, among the apple-blossom and the willows of their mediaeval house in a village in Hertfordshire in the sixties. They knew now that it was because of the intensity of the dream that the reality was often full of pain and distress. Gradually, they had learned not to seek to impose idealisation on themselves: and in consequence had found joy and peace. That was something at least, he thought, sighing. Now, Frances had found them a house to rent with a garden and a vegetable patch, near Midsummer Common, right in the centre, within walking distance of the colleges.

"What we have to do," he said, "is to establish some kind of an island of integrity, a true picture of reality. I don't want to belabour the world and waste time in hating it: but all the same, it is insane. You noticed how thoughtful I was over the weekend?"

"Yes, I wondered what was up," she said.

"It was a broadcast about the bombs at Hiroshima and Nagasaki: about some of the things they have in the museums — a man's hands melted into a glass jar: banknotes turned to ashes inside a bank vault. And descriptions of roasted people. There are thousands of these weapons now that could do that to all of us, targeted on us every day. And then, when I spin the dial of the same radio, there is endless triviality and manic drivel: and if you listen to some of it, it is insane. It is actually insane, about sex, drugs, and violence."

"One could be terrified," she said, gravely. "But it wouldn't do to rage against it."

"I can escape from it with my students: if we're 'into' *Mansfield Park* or *Nostromo* or *Antony and Cleopatra*, we can draw in great draughts of gravity into our consciousness, or we can at best," he asserted. "They save my sanity, really," he added. "Maddening though they are at times."

She sniffed, critically.

"Ah, the *Puritano Frenetico!*" she said wryly.

Like most women, Frances was down to earth. She admired her husband's idealism and relished being his inspiration, but she resented some of the secrets he revealed about their marriage in his writing, and she thought he was a fool about money, as she often told him.

And then, of course, he had no tact: it would never enter his head to consider the effect of what he was saying in public on other people, including me, she reflected. Once before, because of his work doing supervisions for Pemning, some years ago, Paul was invited in to talk about a more permanent post there. The same week he blasted off in a letter to *The Times* about the distortion of resources represented by Concorde. The Master at that time happened to be the leader of a team commending Concorde to the government. When she upbraided him Paul shrugged.

"One can't not speak one's mind about such a menacing intrusion into aviation policy," he asserted. "One mustn't compromise."

"Unfortunately," she said bitterly, "you can't *eat* moral purity."

She was convinced that he had made so many eccentric and uncompromising pronouncements that no institution would have anything to do with him. So, she gritted her teeth, and supposed she would simply have to go on being the bread-winner.

Though Frances was small in stature, she had great determination and courage. She was still a beautiful woman at 55, but in the fine petite bone-structure of her face the ancestral Pen-y-waun chin (as the family called it) showed with its forceful thrust. Her green eyes had those little specks of orange flame in them, and her mobile mouth was agile with feeling and intelligence. She and Paul were still very much in love and in greater harmony than ever: they renewed their love enthusiastically at weekends, from islands of quietness they guarded fiercely against distraction. Evenings in the week were given up to Paul's need to catch up on his reading, and her need to write minutes and agendas.

From time to time during the last ten years, Grimmer had applied for a regular job, but over the years little had ever come of these efforts — perhaps one interview a year. When he had applied for the post at his old college, he thought very little about it: he supposed it was simply a duty to apply, and that there would be little hope for a man of late middle age, when so many young academics were out of work.

Grimmer had had a plan of a kind, for his life: but it had all gone wrong. Well, not all of it had gone wrong. In his family life he felt more secure than ever: the days when the bottom seemed likely to drop out of that domestic world at any moment had gone. But the assumption had been that so long as he applied himself persistently to his writing work, this would be recognised. It was this assumption that was now shown to be far from realistic — not least because the conclusions to which it had led had proved unpopular. The world had changed: it had taken a path and an attitude he considered false, and said so. He had turned against the stream, and the stream didn't like it: so, it rolled on and studiously ignored him. By degrees, he became unreviewable, unmentionable, and, in consequence, largely unpublishable.

So now, at the age of fifty-seven, he still sent off manu-scripts to publishers and letters of application for academic posts with a sense of unreal detachment. Funds for universi-ties were being cut, and there were a hundred and fifty applications for every job advertised. Who would want a man near to retirement age, who had been out of teaching for fifteen years anyway, and who was so disastrously controver-sial? It seemed laughable even to apply.

To his great surprise, Grimmer was called for interview. And to his still greater surprise, the interview seemed more like a jolly dinner talk with old friends. He had supervised at Pemning for three or four years, some eight years before, and during that time had come to know several of those sitting round the table. Besides, they had brought in a member of the faculty to advise them, and he was a sympathiser with the *Scrutiny* movement, to which Paul supposed he belonged, and of which Pemning had been the centre. It was good to talk to them all and he was deeply astonished to find they actually read his books. When he returned home, exhausted and trembling, he was convinced it had all been too friendly.

"They only asked me out of politeness, I'm sure," he said to Frances. "They just went over everything out of charity, and will appoint a young Turk lecturer to the post. But they went through the motions with me, so I should not feel hurt."

He had met just one of the other short-listed candidates, a quiet and, he thought, cold young man in a neat grey suit, from Reading. He had been properly through the system, with a doctorate and everything. Grimmer knew he could not compete with that new kind of professionalism, and he felt he had none of the essential qualifications for the post: he didn't even have a PhD.

He had no interest in university politics and had never speculated about whether there were factions in the college for him or against him. He knew, of course, that old Leavis had left a trail of confusion, enmity and malice even, in his wake: the old man had even walked into the college hall a year or so before his death to remove his portrait on one occasion, during dinner. But how could this affect him? At his interview he had said,

"I hope I can emulate some of the seriousness of my distinguished predecessor — but avoid the prickliness."

Was that right?

But a few days later a hand-written note came through his door, from the Vice-Master, a Professor of Law, John Berry, who was an eccentric, quirky man whom Grimmer, being rather solemn and square, had never really been quite able to understand, though he liked him.

"The Fellowship Committee has unanimously agreed to put your name forward to the G.B. Which way that animal will jump is always anybody's guess. But unless things go seriously wrong our proposal should be accepted, and as far as I am concerned this will be one of the best things I have accomplished as Vice Master before I retire."

Paul Grimmer stared at the piece of paper puzzled. He had been ploughing on with his work in such isolation, he found it hard to understand why anyone else, especially someone in another subject, should care so much about him and his influence. What did it mean? One day he must ask. The trouble was, Berry always put things in such an eccentric way he couldn't fathom them.

In any case, he wondered whether he could face the reality of teaching work, if his application for the post succeeded. He hadn't taught for eight years: if he was appointed he would have some twenty students to supervise, at a time when English studies were in some turmoil in Cambridge, and competition was fierce. Would this prove just another failure

— his last and most catastrophic? He was known widely as a writer on the school teaching of English, and as a man with strong opinions about culture and literature: would all this now be shown up as so much empty wind? Was he up to the task? Would he be of any use to the young people of the day? Would he be a credit to the college? The questions in his mind filled him with foreboding.

At last, he was inducted as a Fellow and Director of English Studies, all ready for the Michaelmas term. Paul Grimmer would pause as he turned to push open the heavy oak door of his staircase, to look across the open space, across to the end of the college hall, with a deep sense of belonging. Each side of the wide stretches of grass ranged the main blocks, two-storey eighteenth-century buildings, symmetrical, faced with pinkish ochre Ketton stone, with a stone moulding along the eaves, and stone steps at each staircase entrance. The wide spaciousness of the college grounds was splendidly satisfying.

From the steps of his staircase one could imagine oneself back in the eighteenth century. The end of the hall was modelled on the lines of a Greek temple, by William Wilkins, with six fluted stone columns ending in rolled Ionic mouldings, supporting a plain lintel, all speaking in their proportions of the aspirations of classicism — "nothing in excess", of carefully reasoned conceptions and balance — brought by way of Italy from Ancient Hellenic Greece. The simple stone shapes gleamed against the dark foliage of the trees in the fellows' garden. The clean, orderly and beautiful forms spoke of an idea — the idea of a university, whatever recent decades might have done to it.

What fascinated him was the way the whole perspective of a day altered, as he walked into the wide expanses of the college grounds. The main buildings were erected about 1800, and consisted of sedate, urbane structures clad in warm yellow and pink stone, two storeys high, with classical eight-by-five sash windows. At the ends of the main ranges along the court were the classical porticos supporting an architrave and pediment of severe simplicity. The flat lawns, the stonework, the simple classical forms significantly altered the sky: the sky was turned by the architecture into that sky of an eighteenth-century watercolour. There were one or two black chimneys rising about the level grey roofs, but you could easily suppose yourself, standing in the court, to be back in the time of Pope, Jane Austen and Wordsworth. The effect was to generate a sense of peaceful timelessness, and it was this to which students today responded: perhaps indeed they yearned for the harmony and security of which the buildings spoke. Certainly, they appreciated the sense of continuity the college and its grounds conveyed: and this indeed, as he knew, was a real appreciation of what the buildings meant. He, of course, could recall the grim days when half of it all was given to trainee airmen who marched about the wide gravel paths: and, indeed, the cold nights of war when, above the roofs, small silver slivers were caught in the great X-shapes of searchlight beams. In those sparse days, he and others would come out of a sparse meal of spam and steamed potatoes, arguing about *Othello* or *Burnt Norton*, a poem which had just come out. Some of them were dead now — Winkler, Doyle — but others occasionally re-appeared, wizened by age. Yet throughout the decades the buildings went on standing for a faint memory of Augustanism, of the idea of the application of reason to truth, the brave investigation of the nature of reality: and the application of intelligence to experience.

But was it credible? Was it to be respected? Was one really able to serve it? Can the mind be applied successfully to experience, as the architraves implied? He often wanted to capture the forms in paint: the scene looked like a watercolour in itself, the sun on the stones with their definite forms, the dense green foliage, and the sky above which, within the grounds, transformed itself into that *aquarelle*, achieved by artifice, to match. The solid blocks of architecture seemed to sail on through eternity, as the clouds drifted or swept past, or the sun from a calm blue sky beamed down on the mellow walls though, of course, as Grimmer knew, the Domestic Bursar who had to maintain them, knew better and had a more ironic view.

*

Paul Grimmer was a grey-haired man with a slight stoop,

caused by sitting for so many hours at his desk. Though he was coming up for sixty, he was still lively in mind and body, he hoped. His green eyes were not so bright and looked anxiously over his depressed clericals, the half-moon gold-rimmed spectacles he wore, so he could both read the texts and look up at the faces of the students discussing them. His face was wrinkled like an actor's, because of so much effort in dramatizing the pages of plays and novels, in teaching sessions. One had to work so hard nowadays, to get students off the ground: they simply weren't trained, as he had been at school, to read, and to discourse upon one's reading, from the ages of eleven to eighteen, before ever coming up to the university. One even met students at interview who had never heard of Jane Austen, or who announced that their private reading consisted solely of " 'orrer!" as one had told him last week.

The previous English man at Pemning had simply departed suddenly in the middle of the previous year to a high administrative post, leaving the students and the college to fend for themselves as best they could. So, the undergraduates Grimmer took over had some feelings of resentment against the authorities: they were anxious about their future, their examination results, their job prospects, at a time when many graduates were out of work. In the interim, in the previous year, they had managed to fix themselves up with all kinds of odd supervisors, and had had to cope themselves with the regulations and the syllabus requirements. They had devised their own makeshift system, without much help. From the first they seemed to find it hard to appreciate Grimmer's approach, and out of their insecurity, they seemed to greet his introduction with defensive scepticism.

Grimmer's view of teaching English was a traditional one. His concern was simply to try to help them read better, and by this he meant to get them to respond to works of literature in what he called a "whole" way — to respond to it as art. It didn't matter what works one took — they could only be a selection anyway. He simply assumed the relationship between art and "life". He knew that in some universities the bright new factions, Marxist or Structuralist, had even made radical reconsiderations of such assumptions and had encouraged their students to sneer at lecturers with his kind of approach, involving "response". He had heard from one anguished colleague that he had retired early because his assumptions had been undermined in this way. Well, it was the only way he knew.

On the other hand, the students were obsessed with a superficial pragmatism — directed simply at passing the examinations, with the minimum of effort. They talked in narrow, practical terms about the syllabus, the "Renaissance paper", the "Literary Criticism paper". Far from preoccupying themselves with developing their own capacity to respond to texts, they sought to subject themselves to cramming: they sought about for "experts", experts in "Augustanism" etc, who could coach them in a carefully chosen selection of subjects, of which they had made their own cunning choice for each paper. They wrote neatly contrived essays for these crammers, and Grimmer had actually found a note by one of these part-time supervisors on a student's essay:

> You had better think how to condense this essay for the purposes of the examination. I suggest that you adopt the structure of this essay and produce numbered points under each heading: once you have done this you should be able to memorise the argument . . .

He snorted with contempt: yet, he had to recognise it was only their realism that drove them to such procedures. It was just for this kind of antic that students were given good degrees. Why should they drop such contrivances for the benefit of a broad general education — including all those bewildering and baffling topics on which they might never be examined?

So, he found he had to try to establish a middle course, between what the students were inclined to do — "shooting bull" as the Americans call it — and urging them to deepen their sense of the relevance of literature to life. He even found some who could not believe that a literary work had such relevance — one youth even scoffed at the possibility that *King Lear* had anything to do with him.

"It's a *fiction!*" he kept proclaiming, scornfully.

With others, there seemed now such a gap between their world and that of a century ago, while they seemed unable to make allowances for the imagination.

When it came to fixing his salary with the meticulous Bursar, Paul Grimmer was startled by its ampleness, although he knew that some well-qualified colleagues had told him they couldn't afford to apply for such an ill-paid job.

As time went on he began to feel more secure. He thought the faculty programme satisfactory on the whole — still influenced much by the tradition from "Q" to Leavis and the *Scrutiny* movement, in its choice of major texts, from *Sir Gawain and the Green Knight*, through Shakespeare to *Middlemarch* and *The Rainbow*. Of course, there wasn't time to do things thoroughly: how long it used to take him, to discuss one major novel, in adult evening classes! Four sessions of two hours at least. There wasn't scope for such close attention here, except in the dissertations that Raymond Williams had worked towards introducing. But there were some good lecturers, Laurel on Dickens, the Kale husband and wife on Coleridge and nineteenth-century women writers, together with some pyrotechnic displays by young Turks among the junior staff. And the faculty seminars on the set Shakespeare plays were rewarding. Most students, he found, went to only one or two lectures. He had established a team of painstaking people to supervise his own students, mostly on certain period papers, leaving him to tackle some of the major works. Things were beginning to come together, he thought.

*

Poppy Beldon and Peter Aukland were having trouble with Dickens one morning at a supervision. They were stuck on the decline of Richard in *Bleak House*, and the villainy of Vholes.

"There are two things I find it hard to stomach in Dickens," said Poppy. "One is the way people suddenly lose their fortunes . . ."

"Or gain them . . . gain it back like Mr Dorrit," said Aukland.

She nodded.

"The other is the way some characters are so evil, so selfish, so ruthlessly calculating, like Vholes himself."

"Well," said Peter, "Vholes has three daughters to bring up."

"Would it have been any better if they had been sons?" asked Poppy sharply.

"Having three daughters seems somehow the hallmark of respectability, I suppose," said Paul. "But what's the difficulty? Do you find it hard to believe there are people like that? People *do* lose their fortunes, and some people *do* destroy others."

Despite the haughty elevation of her eyebrows, Poppy looked fresh-facedly ingenue, unworldly this morning. Peter Aukland grinned in a young-man-of-the-world way.

Paul was aware of the distance between these young people and himself: I don't suppose they have ever lain awake in the night worrying about bills, as we have, night after night.

"There *are* people like that," he said. "You can read about them in the newspapers — like that man who extracted thousands from credulous Christians, to supply him with the cash to buy diabolic insignia or something — then he spent it all on women."

"But Vholes is respectable, too," said Peter, "he has a professional brief to destroy Richard."

Poppy looked grudgingly unwilling to allow wickedness to exist.

"Well, I suppose there are. . . ."

"Perhaps the point is that we all have a Vholes proclivity in ourselves."

"I can't imagine myself being like that at all," she said. I can, thought Grimmer to himself.

"You're too nice," said Aukland gallantly, grimacing with his handsome freckled face.

Grimmer was silent for a moment, amazed that Poppy, at least, was dropping her belligerent resistance to the kind of debate he wanted — and was revealing how young she was. They both looked so innocent, on this autumn morning, their faces so full of energy and brightness, their clothes so neat and informal, as they sat clutching their books and files. They were full of good will and wanted to deny the very existence of weakness and wickedness.

He thought to himself how he could undermine their attitudes, if he chose. He thought too of the college's own problems, which had come up at a recent governing body meeting, of losing some £20,000 in legal fees and delays over an action taken by a nightclub owner, who had used every legal trick to obstruct a building development. He thought too, of his own anguished moments when, every now and then, he seemed crushed by the failure of a publishing venture, as when, after Hampton Press had offered him £800 for a book, the firm went into liquidation the next week. Indeed, how every organisation he had ever had anything to deal with suffered some overwhelming catastrophe before long. But he said none of this. He only said,

"I assure you that Dickens does not exaggerate. Was it Santayana who said, 'When people say Dickens exaggerates, I sometimes think they have no eyes and ears . . .'?"

Would they be able to find Dickens' lengthy dramatic novels as having to do with the truth of experience now? He himself found the decline of Richard, with his obsession with the Jardyce suit, almost unbearable. It would never have entered his head to think of it as an exaggeration about life: he knew only too well how one could ruin oneself.

*

It was a relief for Grimmer, to escape from the obsessions of an author, engaged for so many hours in his solitary task, into the community of fellows. He soon found that the college fellowship was a genuine society, and it was refreshing for him to find himself living and working happily with so many normal individuals, behaving normally himself.

He was most impressed by the scientists, who flitted off from time to time to conferences in Venezuela or New Zealand, and took flying over the Pole to Japan in their everyday stride. Some risked the manipulation of dangerous pathogens: others did frightful things to mice, grasshoppers or cats. And while he was always puzzled by his own attempts to relate the lessons of literature to "life", he found the young scientists used their own rational techniques in the family household.

"We do it all scientifically," said Mark Brownjohn, the bearded young astronomer. "I calculated how many napkins the baby would require, and bought them in bulk. Plenty of room in the attic."

Paul laughed.

"You didn't need a computer for that."

"I never use a computer: I'd rather scribble on the back of an envelope. Except, of course, we need to use them to collate the signals from our telescopes. There are, you know, over seven million celestial objects for us to keep track of."

Grimmer felt daunted by the astronomer, because, as with so many of the researchers in science, there came a time, after a while, when the lay person could no longer follow. But he and Mark had had some lively talk about babies and birth — Mark's second had just been born by Caesarian section — and so he didn't mind exposing his ignorance. He liked the young man's clean efficient way of talking about his work, with his sound gleaming white teeth, appearing in his intensely black beard as he talked.

"The telescope at the Mullard Radio lab," he asked, "on the old Lord's Bridge railway line?"

"Well, it isn't on British Railway's line, I can tell you that: that was no good to us. We had to work to a hundredth of an inch."

"When I first used to come by there, there were just frames with wires on."

"That's right. Then we built the dishes, when we found that the idea worked. Of course, the first work was done at Jodderel Bank: that's the site with the big dish two hundred feet across. But to get a better resolution, we needed a telescope half a mile or a mile across, and you couldn't build such a thing. Sir Martin and his team worked out that if you put dishes along a railway line, and coordinated the signals by computer, you could produce a more accurate map. Now, of course, we're working on an even wider system."

"That's a map of the reception from those stars which emit radio waves?"

"Yes, they're caught in the dish and reflected into a receiver at the centre. With two or more discs at a mile or two apart you can focus as if you had a lens and reflector of that size, only this isn't light but radio emission."

"I used to have a strange feeling," said Grimmer, "years ago, driving past those aerials, when we were in the middle of our own child-rearing, when they were infants: I used to have a feeling that what they might see out there was something dreadful. I suppose," he sighed, "I had some kind of primitive fear of knowledge itself. But now I wonder what use this obscure knowledge is?"

"Since then of course they've got bigger and bigger. There are telescopes in the American desert, laid out on a 'y' shaped track system, twenty miles apart. And now we're coordinating telescopes all over Europe: and one day they will have telescopes in space hundreds of miles apart."

Paul carefully buttered himself a piece of toast.

"It won't answer anything, of course," he said. "As an arts man, it delights me, that you people spend so many millions on knowledge that is really useless."

"Oh, that's right," said Mark, with his big brown eyes wide. "Of course there are spin-offs: but it is pure knowledge we seek. We couldn't stop, though, could we? I hope not."

"Of course not: you must believe that, as a telescope designer. But what do you find out? *Are* there terrible things out there?"

"Well, that's a very subjective way of putting it. I don't think I feel like that — familiarity breeds contempt, I suppose. There are exciting things — for instance, if you compare images made by radio astronomy of the Crab Nebula, one made 10 years ago, and one made this year — you can see that this galaxy which exploded in 1530. . . ."

"That's the one the Chinese recorded?"

"It's still expanding at a tremendous rate: it's the one image in the sky that changes its shape. Then there are masses moving out at speeds of 2,000 miles or even 6,000 miles a second: spiral shapes of gas flaring out from the centre of galaxies, huge flares with shock wave patterns in them. Then, of course, there are the black holes: the bigger the telescopes, the closer we can get to the edge of the black hole at the centre of our own galaxy."

" '*Our* own'," said Paul, scathingly. He admired the young man's excitement and enthusiasm. "I tried to read about black holes and it made no sense to me at all: only I was glad it is such a mystery to the scientists, because our work is full of mystery, too."

" 'Mystery' — well I suppose that's the word to use. Only we must assume that it is just a question of understanding the laws."

"But then — some of the laws *don't* work: I mean, like the way some of these objects rotate round one another, at a rate at which they should not be able to rotate. Or there's now something about the echo of the Big Bang being too smooth — not *lumpy* enough!"

"That's true. There's a lot we don't understand. But I don't know if I'd call it a mystery."

"The mystery is that we can see it and understand it, or at least some of it. We can understand so much more 'out there' than we can understand in here."

He banged himself on the chest.

"Or rather, I suppose, in there," he corrected himself, tapping himself on the temple. "Where we think, 'our galaxy', God save us!"

He went on, being in full flow, excitedly.

"The consciousness that sees is much more mysterious than the universe itself. And then, besides, there's the wider philosophical questions — as to why it should be 'there' at all, and whether there's any life anywhere else and whether if there isn't, there's some special reason why we should be here to look at it at all. I think it's that kind of question that daunted me, and made me afraid, when I drove past the Mullard site."

Mark turned up his nose rather scathingly. "I don't see much point myself in all those metaphysical questions," he said, "because I'm so familiar with it all, I suppose. The distances and times are so immense that there's not going to be any sudden drama overtaking us — though it could. We're due, by the statistics of chance, for a collision with an asteroid, for instance. And there's no consideration for man, of course, among all the immense forces of collision, reaction, explosion and the rest that go on in the millions of galaxies. In a way, you lose the sense that there is anyone in this universe at all: it all seems just a great complex machine."

"But then, what's on the other side of the black holes? Is there an anti-universe, with time going backwards? I talk to our CERN man and he says the most incredible things nowadays."

"And a lot depends on what theory you take up: at the moment the Big Bang theory seems the only tenable one."

"Except for Fred Hoyle?"

"The Americans, the Russians and we British are all collaborating in astronomy now, you know."

"If only we could collaborate on the exploration of inner space, with the same energy and application!"

"That's your job," said Mark, laughing.

Walking home he looked at the stars, which were clear and bright, even appearing to hang in space in the clarity of the atmosphere. His mind quailed at the task Brownjohn had intimated, of trying to track them all, and make sense of it. Perhaps no-one would be able to make sense of it in the end, so that all the effort and expenditure was futile. All those millions of pounds — on nothing?

And if we knew where everything was, and what it was doing, and how it began and how it will end — would we have answered any of the great questions which are of importance to us? Of course, these questions must be pursued, but they would not be answered as he wanted to answer them. What dare I believe? he asked himself. And then he remembered that Mark was a Christian and had his children baptised. I must ask him how he reconciled his faith with his astronomy, he thought. But such conversations with the scientists reassured him largely because they turned out in the end to be in as big a mess as he was, philosophically, which at least was reassuring.

As he opened the gate in his garden, there was Frances, very Welsh, looking for the new moon with a silver coin in her hand.

"Oh, my superstitious little fool," he cried, embracing her tenderly.

*

The English Faculty Appointments Committee sat round a large table in the Old Library at Blair College. Through an immense gothic leaded window could be seen the stone pinnacles of the chapel. Before each member lay a piece of pink blotting paper and a pile of new white papers, with a typed agenda. At the Chairman's place were the Ordinances of the University, bound in blue cloth.

Although the men and women gathered around the table were neatly dressed and wore black gowns, quietly behaved and polite with one another, there was an air of anguished tension in the room. Everyone there knew that one of the items on the agenda required a decision that would be a painful embarrassment to them all. The names of two assistant lecturers had come up for consideration, for a possible extension of their term of appointment. One was clearly not to be renewed: with the other there were strong reasons for not renewing his appointment, but these were coupled with aspects of the case that were acutely embarrassing. The young man in question was an energetic theorist, a fanatical linguistic sociologist, deeply into Structuralism and more recent theories of Deconstructionism: he challenged everything, the existence of the author, the validity of the text, the nature of response. But all these energetic intellectual ploys made the committee, with their decent liberal inclinations, feel they should keep the man as a provocative goad to Socratic debate. The reason for letting him go was that he was not really interested in literature, at least not in the way that the English Faculty at Cambridge was: he was becoming more and more interested in film, but also included everything in his concept of "culture": "pop" numbers, advertisements, graffiti, videos, political pamphlets — and he dwelt on all this while refusing to confine himself to the approved works in the syllabus — at a time when there was a problem of simply covering these anyway, because students were less well read.

But, of course, since the various acts affecting unfair dismissal and such matters, an employer has to be careful. And O'Neill had another lecturer, a devotee, James Leith, watching his welfare. Leith was devoted to O'Neill, who was for him a subject of adoration. There was a strange symbiosis between them, an intense clinch as between prophet and disciple. Moreover, both of them were the kind of activists who knew every ordinance, and every procedural ploy, in committee work and administrative procedure. So, the appointments committee had an unwelcome task. What was really a routine matter threatened to become a *cause célèbre*.

Anton Drew, a professor who had written on Shakespeare, was Chairman and Peter Kale was secretary: both were shy men — with Kale it was sometimes impossible to get a word out of him in an hour's supervision, he was so reticent. Drew was tough, behind his thick glinting spectacles. He brought to the meeting profound doubts about O'Neill, naturally. But both approached the issue as if it were a booby-trap bomb, which in a sense it was. Yet they were desperately anxious to be fair and liberal.

At least they knew that no one on the appointments committee was a personal friend of O'Neill or Leith, likely to leak a report of the discussion. The members were all loyal "Cambridge" people, respectable and reliable: there was Marilyn Kale, Peter's wife, Mrs Bolton, Mrs Steel, and George Chaney, the eighteenth-century scholar. They all sat round gloomily in their gowns, trying to look as if this was all customary routine, but tense with an awareness of the momentousness of their considerations. The Chairman spoke quietly, but his blinks betrayed his anxiety.

"Ladies and gentlemen, we come now to the difficult question of the renewal or otherwise. . . ." he paused to let his implicit recognition of the problem sink in . . . "Of the Assistant Lectureships of Grey and O'Neill. With Grey the matter is I believe straightforward and we have no recommendation for renewal. With O'Neill perhaps the issue is a little more complicated."

A few frosty smiles greeted this, but most of the committee sat straight-faced and glum with their heads on one side.

"Grey first. You have the papers before you — I think they were sent round a few days ago, so everyone has had a chance to read them I hope?"

There was a pause as everyone turned over their papers and gazed at them gloomily.

"Does anyone here have anything to say?"

Mrs Kale looked up with her peaches and cream complexion.

"I think it is clear we do not wish to renew. However, I hope that when the secretary writes he will thank Dr Grey for the very special efforts he has made to supervise two of my students on the Gothic novel. He was very painstaking. I think he is a dull man with limited capacities and was not successful as a lecturer."

"Nobody went," declared Mrs Bolton, bluntly.

"But with a few students doing dissertations, he was most thorough and attentive."

"Perhaps Dr Bristol will write to that effect. It will lessen the blow."

There was a slight relaxation, at the rapid disposal of this. All right hands were raised a few inches above the table to dismiss Grey.

"Now O'Neill. Again, I think we would be reluctant to reappoint. But we must recognise that our decision will be scrutinised closely not only in the faculty, but throughout the university and beyond."

A sigh of exasperation came from Mrs Bolton.

"O'Neill has made himself into a proponent of advanced literary theory and writes in a lively way in the quality press."

"And he has a powerful following among radical students."

"Mr Chairman," said Chaney, "I don't think we must let that affect our decision in any way. Nor, indeed, are Dr O'Neill's opinions or interests relevant. The sole consideration, as with the last subject, is whether Dr O'Neill serves the faculty well enough to have his lectureship renewed, at a time when such re-appointments need to be under careful scrutiny and assessment."

"Exactly what I was going to say," said Drew mildly, inwardly annoyed that Chaney had taken the words out of his mouth. "And I think it is important that our vote on this issue should be unanimous."

"It would be true to say, wouldn't it," asked Mrs Steel, "that we're not very much in favour of promoting Dr O'Neill's tendency to use every cultural artefact as an instrument in the class war?"

"Well I think," said Drew, "that that kind of discussion of his views and position is not relevant. In short, his politics are not at issue, though of course we can't ignore the possible reaction."

"You mean the students might kick up a protest?"

"I rather wish," said Chaney, "that his politics hadn't been mentioned. If students want to discuss Structuralism, there should be experts in literary theory. But the question is whether he is giving us good enough value for us to keep him on?"

"I should have thought that too few students would have found him useful enough to wish to rally to his support."

"They'll do so if they think we are kicking him out for his political views."

"Yes," said Drew, looking unhappy. "Well, perhaps we should keep him on to prevent trouble."

"Oh, no!" declared Mrs Kale, turning red. "That's just what we mustn't do . . . you never know where that kind of policy leads. If he were a Catholic or just an academic with only uncertain humanistic views, we'd never have hesitated for a moment. Just look through these assessments we have asked people to make — they simply add up to the fact that his enthusiasms for film and the rest — 'pop' culture and so on — preclude him from teaching the literature we need him to teach."

"Well, then, we mustn't be diverted by the fear of the reaction," declared Chaney. "I only wish it were otherwise."

There was a pause, in which everyone sat dismayed, wishing they were not there.

"Are you ready to vote?" asked Drew sadly. "I think it is a great pity that we have had no-one who could make out a strong case for O'Neill's defence. However. . . ."

Right hands were gloomily raised — all of them — and

everyone had their eyes miserably turned down to the papers. They had the air of a doomed crew who had undertaken some fearful journey. Had they read the papers carefully enough? Had they discussed the matter enough? Had they been fair? They were unanimous, that O'Neill should go, or, rather, that they were not prepared to keep him on.

"Does anyone wish to say anything more about this matter?"

"Only," said Mrs Bolton, "that if we are asked by the press or anyone at all for that matter, I suggest we should say only that it has been decided that the lectureships of Dr Grey and Dr O'Neill are not to be renewed — and that's all."

Every hand was raised.

"Unanimously agreed."

"And nothing more. And that your letters, Mr Chairman, should say nothing more."

"Except that we are grateful for all the work they have done."

It was a quiet, discreet and polite committee, and the deed had been done: but the members realised that the minute would explode like a bomb, once it reached the streets, the student newspapers and then the London journals, as it was sure to do, whatever any of them said or did not say to the press.

On the way out, Drew murmured to Mrs Bolton, "I hear that Paul Grimmer has been appointed DOS at Pemning."

She grimaced, and gave a cold laugh.

"Let's get this crisis over before we look forward to another one," she said. "I can't think how we would deal with it, if he applies for a faculty post."

Drew looked loftily wise.

"Well, he just wouldn't get it, would he?" he said, with professional certainty.

*

Laurel Jameson, lecturer in English at Godwit College up the road from Pemning, was a fine-boned, tall and energetic young man, rather naive, yet capable of acute understanding. Yet despite his capacity for insight, he was unworldly, and the telephone call from *The Sunday Press* caught him completely off his guard. He was in his tall college room, lined with his many fine leather bindings in their handsome polished cases, and in the quiet seclusion he could suppose the conversation was discreet and confidential. At the other end it was being recorded, unknown to him.

The voice at the other end sounded sympathetic — a Cambridge man full of ironic nostalgia.

"How's old Bynne," he chirped. "Does he still wear that orange tie? I hear he's got a family?"

With a patronising laugh.

"Tried to read his poetry once. Oh, my God!"

Laurel blinked, and tried to give a considered answer.

"His early poems . . . I like the 'Backroom' poems."

"I got nowhere. I think he likes them obscure, don't you?"

Laurel said nothing, but licked his lips, rather nervous.

"Of course, I didn't telephone you to talk about Bertie, bless him. I've been detailed off to write something about this sacking in the English Department."

"Well," said Laurel, his voice going deep, as it did when he roused himself to deal with something that mattered seriously to him. He put out a demonstrative hand to the air.

"It isn't really a sacking — you see. . . ."

"Well, I mean, they're getting rid of O'Neill, aren't they?"

Laurel began to stammer a little, blinking behind his glittering gold-rimmed spectacles.

"I must be careful what I say . . ." he said, really to himself.

"Oh, I know, old boy," said the journalist. "Of course, I realise that. You're not on the Appointments Committee?"

"Oh, no!" cried Laurel. "I couldn't say anything at all if I had been."

He looked horrified, and took the telephone away from his face to look at it with outrage.

"Well, what *are* you going to say?" said the voice of the apparatus, commandingly.

There was a blunt pause. Laurel felt some alarm, that the poor man might not be able to write anything for his paper. Something ought to be said. It wasn't fair that Cambridge should be presented as a place where the English dons turned their minds against new ideas. He began to stammer again.

"The matter has been presented as if we here in Cambridge are afraid of the latest ideas."

"Well, it looks a bit like that, old man, you must admit."

"It's been made out like that," said Laurel, thinking of the fuss James Leith had been making. Leith was, Jameson thought, almost in love with O'Neill: a fanatical disciple, certainly. From the beginning he had challenged the decision not to renew O'Neill's post, as an attack on radical ideas. He had to believe that to protect his guru in his own mind.

"There's one lecturer here . . . who believes that — another left-wing Structuralist . . ."

"Oh, I've spoken to him!"

"Leith, yes."

Laurel was startled.

"Oh, have you? Well, you've got his side of the story then."

"He said Cambridge has always been like that: it's deeply conservative, and, of course, a centre of power, bourgeois power. They can't stomach criticism, and truly radical positions, and they're not going to have it. They're closing ranks. Sailing back into dull academism, old boy."

Laurel grasped the cream plastic receiver tightly, bending his head forward intently, as he did when he wanted to make a point.

"That's not true at all. Well, there are backwoodsmen here. But . . . mind you . . . I don't know all the facts . . . But it is possible . . . I don't say any more than that . . . it is *possible* that O'Neill may not have satisfied the faculty that his teaching was satisfactory."

There was a pause.

"They would say that, wouldn't they?"

"They haven't said anything. I'm only telling you what I've heard."

"What have you heard?"

Suddenly, Laurel was on his guard. He had heard that O'Neill was so eccentric that some students found him impossible. He had been told that with those who shared his Marxist structuralist views, he had a strong following. Entering the lecture room, he grasped people's hands with fervour and they gave an ardent welcome. He led them into discussions of film, pop song, pop art, ethnic music, protest life styles. But with any who disagreed with him or challenged his assumptions about culture, it was said, he was unhappy. Some had complained, and even refused to be taught by him. But he knew he must not tell of all this.

"I can only say that it is possible that the faculty did not find his teaching satisfactory. They may be wrong: it could be an excuse to get rid of him for political reasons, but I don't think so."

"You can't say any more about how he fell short as a teacher?"

"No," said Laurel quietly. He began to feel a little out of his depth with the smooth young reporter at the other end.

"Who's campaigning for him?"

"Oh, Ermintrude, I think, and probably Roger Evans from retirement. After all, they appointed him."

"It seems to be quite a row."

Laurel had pulled himself together and his face was sharp.

"It isn't . . . it doesn't appear from this end quite as it is being presented in the Sunday papers," he said quietly.

The story as it appeared on Sunday quite shocked him, especially where he was quoted.

"Cambridge row deepens," it said. "Opinion varied over the reasons for the sacking of controversial lecturer John O'Neill. A colleague, Laurel Jameson, of Godwit College, told me that it is possible the faculty were not satisfied with O'Neill's teaching capacities. He was said to be bigoted and authoritarian."

"But I didn't say that," he exclaimed to himself. "What can I do?"

O'Neill was never the kind of person to miss anything to do with himself, he knew. But Laurel was surprised all the same to receive a letter from a firm of solicitors later the same week.

> On behalf of our client Mr John O'Neill, it said, we have been asked to point out that he considers your remarks, as quoted in an article in *The Sunday Press* of 10 April last about his teaching abilities to be grossly

libellous and damaging and that legal action will be taken against you on these grounds.

"Well, you'll have to defend yourself, won't you?" said his friend Charles Hardy, the law don at Godwit, rubbing his hands. "It's all good business for the bar."

Laurel turned pale.

"Of course," Charles went on, "if you were asking me if you should start a libel case, I should have to say no. Damn fool's game — for you never know how it's going to go. It's a minefield. But once some fellow has his hook into you, you've got to stand up and fight."

"How much . . . I mean what damages ought a man to claim on a thing like that?"

Laurel seemed appalled at the development that had over-taken him.

"Well, he could claim you have so damaged his reputation that he couldn't get another job . . . I'd say he might claim twenty thousand . . . and of course you'd have to pay his costs which might be another five or ten before you'd finished!"

"And if I did nothing about it?"

"Pay up all the same old boy. Then of course there's your own costs to think of. Costs go up all the time," he added, with satisfaction. "You might have a bill for thirty thousand."

"But I don't *have* thirty thousand pounds!" exclaimed Laurel angrily, almost speechless with dismay.

Charles shrugged his shoulders.

"Well, I can't tell you, the way they'd go to work — your house, car, furniture — you'd have to go bankrupt."

He looked thoughtful. Once one knew anyone personally involved, the processes of the law did seem a bit ruthless.

"What about your colleagues? They must think it's pretty lamentable for one university lecturer to sue the other. I wonder if between you all you could say it was in the public interest?"

"I didn't even say what they quoted me as saying!" said Laurel, looking miserable.

Laurel, however, did nothing, and merely lived day by day in a haze and terror of a libel action.

A few days later Paul Grimmer's telephone went as he sat working in his study at home, overlooking Midsummer Common. It was the *Sunday Press* man, trying a new tack with another member of the faculty.

"I wonder if I could talk to you about this fracas in the English faculty at Cambridge?"

Grimmer had heard only that Laurel was being sued by O'Neill for libel. He grunted, suspiciously: but he was flattered to be asked, since he was so new.

"I can't of course telephone Dr Jameson."

"Why not?"

There was an awkward pause.

"Haven't you heard, old boy? He's being sued by O'Neill for what he said in an article in this paper. Libel action."

There was another pause. On the part of the newspaper man it seemed to indicate that he was conceding that Grimmer was unlikely to say anything.

"I'm . . . I'm not anything to do with the English Faculty," said Grimmer rather hesitatingly.

"Well, you're a member of it, old boy, says so in the listings."

"It's quite a complicated system . . . you see, the colleges have their own people . . ."

The conversation was sagging: although the man at the other end said nothing, Grimmer could hear he was frustrated and bored. He knew the dangers of dealing with the world of London journalism. He had given interviews and they had turned out grotesquely; some bitterly hostile and defamatory, though he always found out he could do nothing about it. His heart sank.

"But I mean," said the voice, the man obviously trying to devise a ploy, "this poor bloke Jameson — he'll be ruined won't he?"

Grimmer panicked.

"No comment," he said.

There was a gasp at the other end, genuine or assumed he couldn't tell.

"You're not going to put me off with that answer are you,

old man? I mean . . . I'm hoping to find someone to defend him."

"No comment," repeated Grimmer.

The man rang off.

"I'm a shit," Grimmer said to himself.

"No, that's not true. I like Laurel and I think it's terrible for him: but I'm not going to let myself into a catastrophe like that."

But he felt a deep sense of ill-ease and a suspicion of his own betrayal, all the same.

*

Aschenberg was significantly different from the others. Besides him only Rhees and Aukland had his qualities of operating from their own dynamism. With Aschenberg, it wasn't a case of needing to stir a man about until you got some kind of reaction out of him. He would come in pale and anxious, looking about himself with his dark brown eyes, and say,

"I can't make up my mind whether Conrad is being sincere or not . . . no, that's not right. It isn't a question of sincerity . . ."

"I'm sure," said Paul Grimmer, "that his sincerity is unquestionable."

"Well, what do I mean then?"

"This is *Under Western Eyes*?"

"Yes. It's the ending: 'The anguish of hearts shall be extinguished in love.' Does he leave you believing in love?"

"Is that a positive?"

"Or is it presented ironically? 'There was nothing in that task to become disillusioned about'."

"That's Conrad."

"About Tekla. But does he mean it? Does he mean us to accept that straight? Or is he being sardonic?"

"Conrad isn't ultimately nihilistic, is he? I mean, in *Victory* the victory is sparse, but there is a kind of triumph in the love that *has been*. In *Nostromo* . . . well, it's a long time since I read *Nostromo*, but even Nostromo isn't quite despicable for his ultimate duplicity. The ideals, the things people serve are not all rejected, despite their illusions."

Aschenberg thumbed through his copy, as if in desperation to find the answer.

" 'There are evil moments in every life. A false suggestion enters one's brain . . . how many would deliver themselves up deliberately to perdition . . . rather than go on living, secretly debased in their own eyes . . .' "

"Conrad suffered terribly writing that novel, you know. You know his father was involved in subversive politics, and his uncles were arrested and executed. Writing that brought it all up to confront."

Aschenberg, Paul had discovered, had been brought up a Roman Catholic by his parents, though they were Jewish. He himself was losing, perhaps had lost, his faith: so, he was in some turmoil, trying to find some kind of ground under his feet. At this moment Conrad disturbed him. What was left? Love? But was Conrad bitterly ironic about that? Was there authenticity in Conrad? Could you trust him? Or was he destructively sceptical?

"There's some kind of positive," Paul attempted, "in Miss Haldin's devotion, misguided though it is. And certainly there is a positive in Razumov's love of her, and his consequent self-immolation. He suffers a fate which is symbolic, like that of King Lear — symbolically he becomes deaf and a hopeless cripple, but because of his earlier expediency and compromise, his moral confusion. The symbolism of his deafness is like that of the blindness in *Lear*."

"His earlier courses of action are those, you mean, of a man caught in moral isolation?"

"Yes, and surely he learns, doesn't he? But then, the consequences of one's deficiencies do catch up on one. So, he is deafened for not *hearing* his own moral sense, as it were?"

"It's true, it's very positive, when he points to his own breast."

They looked more closely at the moment, as Paul read it aloud.

" 'His atrocious confession', Natalia calls it."

" 'He'll need all the devotion of the good Samaritan' — and

he gets it. But does he deserve it? Does Conrad believe in love in that way?"

"The thing is, surely, that in that confession he was at last true to something in himself that was above or beyond all ordinary considerations — call it authenticity, if you like. I can't think of a better word. That contrasts with Miss Haldin's yearning for 'the day when all discord shall be silenced'. I suppose if we could all be authentic, this ideal could come about. But I don't see the drama of all this as ironic — there's a lot that's positive in the way people are trying. The ideals may be presented ironically, but (to take Eliot's line) — Conrad says 'for us there is only the trying!' "

"It's true those people Conrad really dislikes are the indolent."

"And those who display moral turpitude — Verloc, Michaelis . . ."

For a moment Aschenberg lost his customary aspect of desperation. Indeed, he looked quite cheerful. Inwardly Grimmer supposed he would not do so very well in the Tripos — at least, he wouldn't do better than a good second, because he was too intelligent, too perplexed, too involved. He prayed the man didn't have some philosophical or emotional crisis the week before the examination. He heard the man was embarking on a wild love affair with a girl medical student: that, surely, should save him from the void? On the other hand, if it went wrong . . .

On reflection, he thought, in this teaching process, at this level, with young adults, what we are all involved in is love. The word bounced about his mind awkwardly, nervously, as if assailed by a chorus of hostile derision. But the truth was that the recent episodes had shown how easy it is to spoil love. Echoes of lines of poetry sounded: "love . . . The name . . . The intolerable shirt of flame . . ." He had looked forward to some kind of security and satisfaction as a teaching fellow: instead of which he now found himself suffering badly. At times, especially in the small hours, he wanted to opt right out of it all. He had even said to the Senior Tutor in a fit of annoyance, "If I can't sort this out, then I'll go back to being an independent writer, incapable of supporting myself as I may be!"

Being experienced at diplomacy and tact, the hard-headed engineer had said nothing. But for Paul Grimmer the situation looked like being the greatest crisis of his life, as it faced him with the possibility of failure.

And now — had he let Laurel down? Had he prevaricated? He knew he felt that for O'Neill to sue Laurel was an appalling act of spite. Ought he not to have taken a public stance? Wasn't he guilty of the very moral turpitude that Conrad had pilloried — and which he and Aschenberg had between them found to be so deplorable?

*

He lay awake a good deal in the night, pondering his position in the Laurel libel affair, and continuing to argue with Aschenberg over moral corruption. How grateful he was to Aschenberg, for his involvement in such issues! It was because he was Jewish, of course: Joel belonged to a whole cultural tradition of grave attention to truth and the numinous. But Aschenberg wasn't the only one: indeed, all of them became, at times, caught up in it and preoccupied with the application of literature to life. There were those blessed moments of attentive silence, in supervision hours and the seminar, when heads were bent over the meanings of words — and beyond the words, the perplexities of existence:

> Droll rat, they would shoot you if they knew
> Your cosmopolitan sympathies . . .

Often, as with that poem by Isaac Rosenberg, it was a question of tone, of listening to the exact quality of voice — so one could pick up the attitude to experience. The afternoon sunshine would fade to twilight, or perhaps dashes of rain would burst upon the panes, but out of that flux a momentary meaning would be held. He would look round the room, and note how the schoolgirls and schoolboys whom the college interviewed and admitted last year were already growing into women and men. They cast off the neat and respectable clothes of school, and displayed more dashing gear. They experimented with this or that role in a club or society, and with this or that responsibility, as secretary for this, or stage manager for that. He knew nothing of their private lives for the most part, except for the most serious family problems: two of the women and one of the men had lost their fathers recently, and he was only too aware of the clouds of grief that sometimes hung over them. But into this unfolding of maturity penetrated something of the poetry and the novels, and the texts of plays. Aukland had told him of taking Pointer to the Royal Shakespeare Company's *Antony and Cleopatra* and how the tears were flowing down both of their faces at the scene of Cleopatra's death: he knew the value of such an experience. And he knew how much their study of the verse together had contributed to the response. Yet his intense involvement with his subject also seemed to generate in him a kind of dread at times, as when he attended faculty meetings, or pondered the evidence of hostility somewhere behind the moves to sabotage his work, or reflected on poor Laurel's situation.

Of course, he heard from time to time about students' sexual escapades: Pointer falling out of a punt trying to seduce Poppy Beldon, who resisted vigorously. But that kind of puppy antic seemed hardly yet merged with the advancing depth of their perspectives on life.

But now he was anxious about his own capacity to learn from literature. Could he confidently claim to be committed to civilised values in his own behaviour?

In this mood next day he had to call for some examination scripts at the house of one of the faculty members, Mrs Steel. Her husband was a history lecturer and they were fellows in their respective colleges. They were on many committees and were, people said, pillars of the university establishment: sound and reliable. If one of the senior administrators in his own college had a problem about an arts subject he knew, they would defer to the Steels. They were *echt* Cambridge.

He arrived at their house at tea-time, as they were about to arrive home. He had to collect a parcel of scripts, only. The husband showed him in and asked if he would mind waiting: his wife had the car, and the parcel was in it. Paul sat on a handsome sofa and waited, then wandered round the room to look at the books. He was uncomfortable, because he felt from the way the man spoke to him and asked him how he was settling down at Pemning, that he disapproved of him. By a kind of intuition, he knew suddenly that the Steels were possibly two of the people who had telephoned the college, to protest at his appointment. They belonged to that Cambridge establishment that knows everything and felt absolutely sure they had the clue to everything and would know he was not quite . . . not quite . . . Well, not quite *"right"*: NQOC. Now, as he was in their house he had a sense of being softly strangled, by a kind of spiritual death. Everything about him was fine and handsome, well-arranged, neat, responsible, sound — oh, the Steels were utterly sound — but deathly. They reeked of the proper conduct of examinations, of academic judgement, of time-honoured time-serving. He was surprised by his feelings, but they were those which often came upon him in Cambridge society and he recalled poor Leavis's life-long struggle against it. The old man used to come into his supervision classes in 1941 looking as if he had seen a ghost, collapsing on his chair, panting.

"Excuse me a moment," he would pant. "I must have time to recover, you know. . . ."

His mouth gaped, his brown eyes looked full of alarm, his thin hands with their veins showing, trembling.

"My wife . . . saw Dadie Rylands walking past this morning . . . very strong reaction, you know . . . like a wave of Bloomsbury threatening me . . . I had to remonstrate . . . unnecessary expenditure of ener-gy. . . But . . . it brought back so much, from *Dusty Answer* and the black beetles of King's . . . and poor Lawrence . . . what did Eliot say? . . . 'rotting himself and rotting others'. . ."

It was all rather incoherent and dotty, and they hadn't understood any of it in 1941. But what they did pick up was an implacable hatred — of the atmosphere of King's, and of the entrenched "Cambridge" set, Bloomsbury, and the fashionable literary world and the domination of that Tripos exam process of "stand and deliver against the clock" against which Leavis never ceased to rail.

"Of course," Leavis would say, in his queer Fenland accent,

"one shouldn't, I suppose, trouble oneself with the third rate, the mediocri*tays* . . . But they have such assurance, you know: they are *it* . . . Vani-*tay* . . ."

One day he met Tillyard in the street, he said, and Tillyard advised him,

" 'There's a very good job going in South Africa, you know!' that's what he said. They were trying to get rid of me, because of what I said about Milton. It was outrageous, impermissible. . ."

His bushy eyebrows had gone up in histrionic disdain.

Mind you, thought Paul, there was a good deal of hate on his side, too: but the complacent, established Cambridge "set" had enraged Leavis — because it threatened death, to poetry and the word: to being and sensibility.

Now, in the Steel's house, he looked round at the air of solid academic establishment. He envied the atmosphere of deeply entrenched comfort, and compared it with his own absurd quixotic attempt to become self-supporting, and the dance he had led Frances over the years. Well, there was nothing intrinsically wrong with university lecturers being well paid. And he could not escape the feeling of a price having been paid: it all spoke of a monumental dullness — a dullness of the right thing being done, of duties properly carried out, of professional responsibilities adequately performed: but all dead. Anything adventurous, or tragic, or catastrophic, or desperate, had been absorbed into a comfortable and safe mass of complacent security.

"You're envious!" he told himself sharply. "You've only yourself to blame."

"But then," he reflected, "who are they to patronise me?"

He left the house in a turmoil of rage, not knowing quite why. He felt undermined, by the sense of safety and comfort: he yearned for the days when he didn't care what he said. He remembered reading the papers for the last faculty meeting, and had noted that Mrs Steel was on the appointments committee, which had refused to renew O'Neill's appointment. Now there were such nationwide repercussions, "Cambridge" would close ranks and everyone was supposed to be loyal.

"That's the trouble," he said to himself, "about belonging to an institution and having 'colleagues'. You don't speak your mind out of some kind of absurd group loyalty!"

At home, he sat down at once, and wrote a piece about O'Neill's libel action against Laurel, declaring that there were principles in the humanities, which implied that those who served them should be tolerant, and allow discourse, and openness — and not attack one another through the law for speaking out. He sent it at once to the *Sunday Press* and it appeared in print the next weekend.

He and Frances never took the Sunday papers, and he didn't tell her. Laurel rang him and told him it had appeared and thanked him for his support.

"I must say though," said Laurel, "you've jumped into this one with dynamite attached to both feet."

"Oh, lor'," said Grimmer wryly, "but I thought someone ought to say something."

There was a pause in which the awfulness of what he had done came creeping like an icy breeze down the back of his neck.

"Well . . . let me know if there are any repercussions."

Grimmer didn't show anyone the letter that arrived after a few days, from O'Neill's solicitors, in similar menacing terms to the one Laurel had received. He didn't tell Laurel and he didn't tell Frances. He just hoped the whole thing would go away.

*

To have love's pinnace over-fraught. . . .

Grimmer was trying to understand Donne's *Aire and Angels*: he hoped his students would help him. Bo Dibbans however, was in two minds about the poem altogether, and yet was unwilling to bring out the inward dialogue she was having with herself. She was dressed in a rather plain way, in a brown pullover and brown tweed skirt — rather playing down her femininity, about which she felt this morning rather vulnerable.

" 'Love's pinnace!' " she exclaimed to herself. Her wrists still ached from resisting the onslaught of one drunken McIlroy, after a drama club party. We are launched on a tide of booze at the beginning of term, she reflected, and it goes on like that. Some of these fools can't take it. Suddenly this ginger-haired natural scientist had appeared in her room, fuddled but resolute. He had virtually fallen on her, and had seemed like one of those oriental gods which are sculpted with ten arms. As soon as she wrenched one of his hands from where it was groping under her skirt, another appeared at her neck, trying to thrust itself down the neck of her blouse. It was neither playful nor amorous nor fun: it was simply insulting, and in the end she had hit him and he had punched her in the mouth.

Fortunately, her cries had alerted Rosie Nicols and Poppy Beldon from next door and between them they had managed to evict the youth, who had stumbled mumbling down the concrete staircase and out into the night, where he had attacked one of the new trees planted on the greensward.

She wasn't going to tell Grimmer. She knew him to be a married man who spoke happily about his wife, and she hoped she was safe with him, though, even though she was only twenty-two, she already had a fund of irony and distrust about every man she met, not least "old men" as she called them. But she liked the kind of sanctuary Grimmer offered, even his somewhat strait-laced gravity. A friend from school some four years older than her, had just told her, of her dismal experience with one of the English lecturers. Bo was appalled, but let it be a lesson to her: a woman could be exploited even at the heart of the academic establishment. But in P1 she felt safe.

She didn't, however, feel safe with John Donne. Oh, yes, she said to herself, I know he is supposed to be the greatest erotic poet, and there's that marvellous Elegie about "what covering needst thou but a man." But he made her uneasy, she told Grimmer, pointing to the page opposite:

> for I shall hate
> All women so. . . .

He seemed often to hate women: he was spiteful, she said:

Then thy sick taper will begin to wink. . . .

Even this noble courtier, she reflected, had something in him of the drunken McIlroy. It was here:

Some lovely glorious nothing I did see.

Grimmer ought to see it.

"Wait a minute," she said. "You're treating it as an intellectual exercise in poetry, him trying to find and grasp her image and so on. But he's *patronising* to her."

"Do you think so?" Grimmer was a little startled. He had always had a deep respect for Donne's attitude to women and had even idolised it a bit.

> "Just such disparitie
> As is twixt Aire and Angells puritie
> Twixt womens love and mens will ever be —

It's the men who are the angels and the women mere air: it's the woman who is 'some lovely glorious nothing'."

"Perhaps he's being playful?"

Between them, he felt, he and his students sometimes grasped the poem, sometimes not: English was an evasive subject.

"It all depends," she said, "whether he thinks the woman's substance is air and his, angels, or the reverse."

"Let's work our way through the metaphysics of it," he said. "Just as angels seek to take a form which is visible to us, so love needs a body to dwell in. So, he tries to give his love a habitation in her beauty. But this is too much: 'much too much,' because it is 'Extreme and scattering bright': that seems like a compliment, surely?"

Bo was deeply doubtful, still. She was still haunted by the previous night's brutality.

Grimmer ploughed on.

"So, he says, my love must find its sphere — its planetary

proper place, as it were — in her love, not in her bodily being. So, his love, like an angel adopting a form out of air (which is not as pure as the angel itself) can take shape in her love, even though her love is not as pure as his."

"But he's still discriminating," she proclaimed. "He's struggling for *mastery*. Love!" she suddenly said bitterly.

Grimmer was startled by the energy of her little explosion.

" 'The spider love' " he quoted, " 'which transubstantiates all/And can convert Manna to gall.' "

"I noticed that," she said. Then with a sad look. "Maybe here's something literature teaches us — Troilus, Romeo, Antony and Cleopatra: love always drags in hate."

Grimmer thought he should show some wisdom about experience.

"You can't ever be starry-eyed, merely — certainly not with Donne. It's clear he had a problem. All you can say is that he wanted to love, wanted to know love.'

"Wanted too hard," said Bo. "And when the women didn't come up to his idealistic scratch, he hated them."

It was the most she had ever talked in a supervision. Something has set her off, he reflected, and then noticed a bruise on her wrist. Her eyes met his as he dwelt on it, and for a moment they communicated without saying anything about it. She didn't want to reveal anything to him, because that would be betraying her generation who must fight their own battles. He didn't want to pry, to some extent because he was afraid that if he knew too much about their youthful struggles he would lose his sense of their goodness and charming naivety. He on his part, as we have seen, didn't want to mar their innocence.

But Bo was excited: she sensed something of a breakthrough in this discussion between herself and a man of a much older generation, on equal terms, as adults.

"You looked shocked," she said.

"I suppose I am," he confessed. "It's so good having women students — you learn new angles on writers from the woman's point of view."

She grinned at him, in a friendly way. She was not a high-flyer and she knew she'd never get more than a moderately good second. But she worked hard and was determined to do as well for herself in the world as she could. She was an attractive woman, knowing that she was a homely girl and that her charms were comfortable ones. She had been one of the first to stand out from the group's distrust of Grimmer, because she found him easy to talk to. She thought he respected students.

"Well, there's always 'women's problems', you know."

"You mean," he smiled, "like the ones the Victorians didn't warn their women sufficiently about?"

"Yes, but even though we don't get pregnant nowadays, we're still *targets* all the time. Come to think of it," she added, "Donne's women are targets."

"Targets," he laughed. "I had an extraordinary letter when I was appointed, from an Australian lecturer I know." Grimmer did his Strine voice. "Yew must take care, Paul cobber, some uv these young sheilas among the students — they'll troy to seduce yew to git a good mark!' "

"Can you believe it?" he added, laughing. "Fortunately, I'm not even involved in marking the Tripos."

Bo suddenly turned serious.

"Someone who was at school with me. . . ." she said, hesitantly, wondering whether she should go on.

Paul waited.

"Dixon took her out . . . made up to her . . . must have seduced her, or whatever you might call it. She said he 'fucked her up'. She only told me yesterday."

Grimmer — shocked by the phrase she used so bluntly — felt a mixture of disbelief, distaste and anger. Dixon was one of the lecturers, a sharp, cold unattractive man, only a few years younger than himself: very much of the new fashion, sharp and brilliant.

"I can't believe it," he exclaimed.

But his head swam, because he suddenly remembered encountering the man, who was grey, with a girl, having tea in Hobson's Pavilion. He disliked Dixon intensely, because of the way he wrote, even before he encountered him physically. He was one of those cursed knowers, who knew everything and respected nothing.

"Was she a dark girl with a rather pinched, unhappy face?"
Bo smiled.

"It sounds like her. She's had a terrible series of family
tragedies. Oh, she's forgiven him. She's actually become a
lesbian now. She's come out. . ."

Grimmer looked glum.

"I wish you hadn't told me."

"I'm sorry," said Bo. "I didn't want to make life difficult for
you. But, you see, I was angry when I found out, and . . . well,
it makes a woman a bit cynical, at the face some of these
people put on . . . The lecture list, for instance."

"Ah, the lecture list," he exclaimed.

"And Jack Porton," she went on. "He was supposed to have
been seen in a homosexual brothel in Paris."

Jack Porton was one of the faculty's most popular lecturers
of the time — giving a pyrotechnic display every Friday.
Really, Bo was bursting out into most irregular confidences.
Ought he to stop her?

Paul suddenly remembered how Peter Brown had complained to him about Porton, only a week or so ago.

Brown was a boy from a state school in a provincial town in
Suffolk. He was poor, and had to spend his vacations working
hard in lowly jobs to support himself. So, he had a dogged air,
and his chin asserted itself bluntly in a pale determined face.

"May I have your support in not going to Dr Porton again?"

"Why, what's happened?"

"Well, he asked me to prepare a paper for his class on
Othello, which I did — on the sources. I was pretty nervous,
when it came to delivering it. And he kept saying, 'This is
pretty poor stuff, isn't it?' and 'How much more of this is
there?' "

"Oh dear," said Paul, amazed to learn of such insensitivity
to a young man's feelings: he was increasingly amazed by the
antics of his colleagues.

"Well, I mean, he insulted and humiliated me," said Brown
with a gasping kind of laugh. "I'm not going to him again."

"No, you mustn't," said Paul. "I'll fix you up with someone
else."

"I mean, life's hard enough as it is. . ."

"Oh, yes!"

It wasn't that Porton neglected his students. On the contrary, he was thorough. But he had an unfortunate, lofty manner and he was dogmatic to an obsessional degree. Bo's hint illuminated much: what a lot one learned from one's students he thought!

"Bo!" he said. "You must go, you're corrupting my innocence. You've sunk to the level of undergraduate gossip. It's vile!"

She collected her bags and shoved her note pad into one.

"I'll write you an essay on Donne's attitude to women."

"Good," he said. "Only stick to the poems: prove it, by attending to the words on the page."

He sighed, looking out of the window as a shower of hail drummed into the grass, the white pills bouncing.

"I wish we had just done that. All these revelations about life among the senior members of the faculty are too much for me."

"Oh, there's more," said Bo, from her young woman's wisdom, with a little touch of bitterness even of cynicism in her face.

"Well, I'm sorry, then," he said.

But he wasn't going to ask her about her bruises.

After Bo left, Grimmer reflected on the extraordinary difference there was, between the way the girl regarded him, and how she had responded to him only a month or so before. He was shattered by what she had told him, but he realised that she would only have told him such things because she trusted him. Her earlier aloofness had simply been a manifestation of suspicion and distrust — surely prompted in Bo by someone else: it wasn't in her nature. But now, they met as adults, and she was relaxed enough in his presence to accept that he would leave her free: that he had no urgent personal problem of his own to export to their relationship, to seek to exploit her, as Dixon had exploited her friend.

She could use him, as they all did, as a scratching post — to exercise her newly acquired adulthood — as one used a father.

And then, after Finals, he reflected ruefully, he'd never see her again.

*

Evidence of the sources of the disturbances among his students earlier in the academic year came suddenly out of the Xerox photocopier. The college had a rather primitive machine in the stationery room, that ground away slowly at printing, and was always going wrong. This day he needed twenty copies of Keats's *Ode to a Grecian Urn* for his seminar. The machine began, stopped and coughed: and there was the smell of burning.

He lifted the top and removed a piece of paper, already printed, that was stuck in the rollers. He glanced at it. "Confidential Enquiry into the Teaching of English" he read, and so startled was he that the little room swam as his eyes smarted in the smoke of charred pages. It was like a queer nightmare. There was a summary of the results of a survey of students' views, of his own teaching, with columns and tables: and a critical summary of his own work. At first he was puzzled by references to "The DOS" until he realised it was him. There was a critical muddled statement about what he had done this term, its shortcomings, and its failures to prepare students properly.

"If you put it in a novel, no-one would believe it!" he exclaimed.

He turned excitedly to the signing off book: the last entry for the day before was

22 copies (College)   P. Weekles

So, every English student was to receive a copy of this, and copies had gone to two others: who were they?: a secret investigation of his work by one of the fellowship! With copies to the faculty? Preposterous! And she had had the effrontery to charge the Xeroxing to the college! And she, with a research brief, nothing really to do with English teaching there. Excitedly, he ran off six copies of the singed sheet, and went back to his room trembling with annoyance. He telephoned the master, Sir Martin Blenkinson, who was in his rooms in the Medical Research Council Laboratory, and drove out there at once in his mini.

The master was a big, handsome man with shrewdly intelligent eyes, a kindly face, and a warm sympathetic manner. He, too, wore half glasses, but his face was mobile and his eyes always expressed a benign expectancy. Yet he could look grave, as he looked now.

"What's the trouble?" he asked in his rich and reassuring voice.

"I'm sorry, Master," said Paul. "I'm not a trouble-seeker. But I can't stay in a college where secret investigations are conducted into my teaching by, I suppose, other fellows."

To his relief, the professor received it with serious concern.

"I wouldn't expect you to," he said.

Paul gave him the paper, and outlined the events of his first few weeks. Blenkinson was outraged, but couldn't restrain a chuckle.

"Their security's not very good, whoever they are," he declared.

On the spot, he wrote Paul a note declaring that at no time had there been any official enquiry into his work and that there was no knowledge of any such thing among the fellowship, and that such a thing would not be entertained by the college, and it was hoped that Paul would carry on with his work in the assurance that there was complete confidence in him.

"I've hardly begun, anyway," Paul protested. "Of course," he said, "I'm very happy to have this job, and I will of course carry on. But something must be done about it."

"The question is what?" said the medical man. "I fear you thought it might be the senior tutor," he went on, going straight to one difficult aspect of the case.

"Well, it did cross my mind," said Paul. "But I couldn't believe that. It would be absurd."

"I'm sure he had nothing to do with it," said the master. "But I will ring him."

Which he did: the senior tutor said he was appalled to hear

of such a thing. So, that was it. Petula was hoist by her own petard. Paul felt jubilant, and yet horrified by the whole nonsense. He hated to be involved in such a fracas, in his first term.

"But why should she mess me about in this way?" he exclaimed angrily.

"We must confront her," said the master. "But I think the answer is painfully simple, I'm afraid. She doesn't think you're up to the job: and now she wants to prove us wrong, for appointing you. And there may be others egging her on. . ." he added, looking as if he knew who.

Paul thought of all his sleepless nights, and the cramps and pain they had given him: the misery. Was all this the conse-quence of one graduate woman's strange idealism? Who else was involved? He wanted to die.

"I can't believe she's conducted it all herself. She's been orchestrating my students: but someone's egging her on, and I don't think it stops at the college."

"Someone in the English Faculty?" asked the professor. "That's a can of worms!"

The man's confidence in him was deeply refreshing. And his openness. It was clear he would bring the whole matter out into the open and to Paul this was a blessed relief. His worst feelings were about how Frances would respond. She had wanted him so much to have a place and to have people's respect: now everything seemed to go wrong. He wished he could spare her the inevitable distress. But he still had told her nothing, of course, about the possible action for libel against him, alongside that against Laurel.

*

Not long after Paul Grimmer found himself again in the master's elegant study, facing Petula Weekles. He was much impressed by the satisfaction Blenkinson found — and declared he found — in sorting out problems like this face to face. But it wasn't comfortable. Paul himself tended to flinch from personal confrontation, and to take refuge in letters and memos: in paper. But the master, as indeed he had himself told Grimmer, really liked bringing difficult situations to a satisfactory conclusion, in trying to make human beings behave in a civilised way; and so he always tried to get such things sorted out face to face. After all, he declared to Paul, what else was the place for, but to apply the values of the humanities to people and "life"?

By now the affair had become common knowledge among the fellows, and it was agreed that a fellow who had been so foolish as to involve students in an underhand investigation into the work of another fellow could not really remain a member of the fellowship. It had all risen to the level of a parliamentary crisis over procedure and protocol. Yet there were embarrassing aspects of the matter: Mrs Weekles was one of the college's only two first women fellows, and it would be most unfortunate to seem to be chucking out a woman when the proportion of women was so small anyway. Then, she was a young beginner, and it would seem harsh to ruin her career by such a move. Yet no-one knew whether there were others behind her, in her extraordinary move.

All these difficulties Grimmer was willing to concede. He didn't want to press the issue on principles, or to raise an almighty stink: that would only damage everyone.

"All I care about," he said, "is that my work and my relationship with my students should not be undermined in this underhand way."

Mrs Weekles, he knew, had been in tears at a meeting with the master and the senior tutor, and had confessed to organising the investigation, admitting it was unprofessional. She sat there now, pale and pulling at her handkerchief: and, oddly, Paul felt a wave of sympathy for the woman with her slim, youthful form. But she still seemed to rest on a foundation of self-justification that irked him, as if she were completely convinced that he was inadequate in his job.

"I still consider Paul is not aware of who is working on what specialisation in Cambridge," she asserted, in a shrill nervous voice.

"It isn't as if undergraduates need specialists, for God's sake," said Paul, nettled.

"For their dissertations. . ."

"Dissertations!" he exclaimed scornfully. "These are long

essays for the Tripos, not fit to be called 'dissertations' at all: and too many of them are boring re-hashes of the work of rather dull research students. I've read several. I'd prefer they gave of themselves more. In any case, what use is specialisation, if they can't read?"

"You don't have their interests at heart, I feel."

Paul responded icily.

"It was hardly in their interests to draw out in them disquiet about my capacities, and to make them insecure. I am sure, especially with the weak ones, it has done really serious harm. And you were responsible for that harm."

He was in no mood to be mild about it.

"In any case," he said, "I was given the task of being Director of Studies, and it's up to me to say how things should be done."

The master intervened, with his rich, quiet voice.

"Well, I daresay there are many aspects of the problem to be explored. But yes, what I must point out, Mrs Weekles is that the College has put its trust in Paul Grimmer, and he must be given responsibility. Of course, you were perfectly entitled to put your criticisms to him and I'm sure he'd listen. But a secret enquiry involving the students was not proper, by one fellow of another. As far as the College is concerned, the issue now is whether, because you have carried out this confidential investigation and this has been felt to be incompatible with being a member of the fellowship, we should ask you to resign. I should say, Paul, I don't think that if you pressed for this, it would do you any good, apart from every other consideration of principle and so on."

"I've no desire to press it," said Paul. "All I want is peace, to get on with my work. There must be a solution that doesn't involve anything so dire."

There was a pause: the thin young woman was tense with annoyance and anxiety. Paul was sorry for her now.

The master obviously determined to move on from the pause.

"There was one thing, no, rather, two things which came out at our talk with the senior tutor, Petula. You said you had consulted a member of the Faculty: and you said you had held discussions with another fellow. Can you tell us who these people were?"

There was a long pause.

"I don't think I can tell you who the other fellow was."

To his surprise the master winked at Paul: he was startled to realise that it was assumed that he knew.

"And as for the faculty member . . . if I could use the telephone I could ask them if they minded the name being revealed."

She went out to use a phone in another part of the lodge. The master accompanied her and spoke to the person involved. It turned out to be Mrs Bolton who had been Petula's director of studies. Paul was amazed.

"You mean, she knew that this was going on, and said nothing to you about how inappropriate it was?"

"Nothing."

"Well, I'm sorry," said Paul. "I really do feel sorry for you and the way you've been used by other people."

"I don't see it like that," she said, angrily.

"Well, you may have had your own reasons for suspecting me of being inadequate for the post. But all this nonsense about checking up on lecturers seems to have come from some ass who has some hankering after student radicalism of the sixties . . . I can't think who it might be among the fellows."

"We had enough of that," said the master, "those rootless wreckers."

"I think we need not mention the name of the other fellow: he's going away."

"Ponsonby!" exclaimed Paul to himself. He was a young meticulous modern languages don with whom he had found it impossible to hold a conversation, he was so clipped and cold.

"And as for Mrs Bolton — she should have said to you 'That is wrong: it is not the way for a fellow to behave.' And that she did not seems to me the height of unprofessional conduct."

"I had a feeling," said the master, "there was someone in the faculty behind it. And there may well be others. But to the matter in hand . . . what do we do about Petula?"

Paul sighed. He was exhausted and miserable about the

whole affair. At times he had not wanted to go near the college at all.

"Why, surely, she can get on, and finish her book, and keep her room and everything — and get out of my hair?"

"That's what I hoped you would say," said the master. "Of course, 'they' will say, 'Grimmer got her kicked out'. But that isn't how it will be: we don't have to be uncivilised, do we?"

Paul wrote to Mrs Bolton, but received in reply a cold, blank letter, declaring that his interpretation of events was quite different from hers: she had no doubt that Mrs Weekles had the best of motives. He wished he hadn't written. He knew that in the Cambridge context it was like sowing more dragon's teeth. The Boltons would watch him, and if he put a foot wrong, he would have to pay for his letter as an act of *lèse majesté*.

*

Although Paul Grimmer had the air of an extrovert, he was really very shy, and shrank from encounters about which he was unsure. Faculty receptions filled him with dread, and he noticed, as he stood miserably sipping his glass of wine in a corner of the magnificent long gallery in Godwit college, that there were many members who never went: Peter Blake of Corpus never attended any, nor did Bynne, and from time to time he would remember a face which was never seen at such social events: they smouldered somewhere in their rooms. Those in the true professional ambit of ambition were always there, but they were no bother as they obviously regarded him as a failure and so did not linger in his company: he experienced that bleak phenomenon, of just beginning to dredge up an intelligent answer to a sharp question, only to find the person's eye fixed on a more useful contact, and the person drifting away. The vain and aggressive were there, and those he called the dead: the well-established, well-dressed, confident embodiments of Cambridge as "it", as the place which "knew" and assumed that the world knew it knew. The Marxists and Structuralists didn't seem to attend either, and Grimmer often wondered what the point of the gathering was anyway, and for that matter why he attended. There were one or two young writers there with whom he enjoyed talking, but he felt he could do so much more easily at his home or their home. The professors, of course, were trying to create a genial and agreeable atmosphere, and in a way this seemed to be working: at least no-one said anything cruel or bitchy: the worst thing to bear was the general deficiency or warmth or interest. It was so different from his experiences abroad, in Australia, for instance, for here no-one talked shop and all assumed an indifference to literature and ideas. There was some talk of posts and faculties and universities and one professor always seemed to be using the occasion for various administrative exchanges: but mostly the talk was Cambridge small talk, and people tended to evaporate suddenly if anyone tried to be serious. It was usually a relief to get away, after making a polite appearance to show that one wasn't sulking. Of course, Grimmer had to avoid those who had insulted or bullied his students, and those he suspected of making trouble for him. He was always extremely careful to avoid talking to the reptilian Dixon, and even more so since Bo's outburst.

He was very anxious to see how he would get on with the college fellowship, however, where the mood was so genial. He had been used to working alone for so long, and throughout those days had had no need to make himself agreeable to anyone. However, to belong to a group of men and women with whom one had to work, was now a test, and he must take it upon himself. Frances was deeply suspicious of Paul's problem of fitting into a new milieu, knowing him to be an only child, and a writer whose pursuit of his themes went with a dismissive protectiveness, in the face of opposition or criticism. She prayed he wouldn't make enemies, and her heart sank over his reports of hostility from his students, and the Weekles affair: even more so when he declared one day, "I hate going into that place!" But this mood couldn't last, in the face of the benignity created by Blenkinson.

To his great relief, the atmosphere at meals and in the combination room he found warm and congenial. This was largely, he came to realise, the achievement of the master himself: many of the fellows had come to Pemning to work with the man, and in the relaxed and agreeable atmosphere he created. It was a true fellowship — because at its heart was a genuine feeling for the university as a centre for the humanities. In his own subject, medicine, Sir Martin cherished the inseparability of the mind, the emotional life, and the body, and realised that people gave of their best, in thought and teaching, if they felt at ease and secure. So, in the agreeable family atmosphere, it was possible to talk not only about college administration or one's own family life, but also about "subjects".

Paul, who remembered being occasionally flattened by sharp positivistic scientists at Prince's in the past, was delighted to find that his very naivety was regarded as an asset: the scientists were pleased to be obliged to explain some of their work to others, and to see its relevance to the arts. Paul was often astonished by reports in *The Times* which he read at breakfast, about what seemed to be crises in the scientific world. Then he would seek out Brownjohn again at lunch.

"I read in *The Times* this morning that they have discovered a new asteroid, two kilometres across, heading towards the earth at fifty thousand miles an hour," he said one day.

"Oh, yes," said the young astronomer, unperturbed, and carefully dissecting his grilled trout.

"It says it could collide with the earth in the spring of 1985, if its course has been correctly calculated."

He looked out across the lawn at the master's lodge, as if expecting to see the great stone classical portico dissolve in a fireball at any second.

"Well," said Mark, calmly, "there are various views about that. One theory is that it will come closest to the earth in autumn 1987: but most people think it won't come anywhere near us at all."

"If it did?" asked Paul, thoughtfully buttering his roll: he was almost annoyed the young astronomer wasn't excited.

"Oh, well, it would be very destructive. And, of course, *statistically*, we are 'due' for a cosmic encounter of that sort, like the one in Siberia in the early years of the century."

"The one that flattened all the trees?"

"Yes. But I daresay you'll manage to eat your Fellows' Christmas Dinner first."

Apart from such mild sarcasm, no-one tried to put anyone else "down". Paul would come in anxiously and say to their pathologist fellow, "I see they're snipping up bits of DNA from pathogens, and putting them into that bug that lives in everyone's gut . . ."

"Escherichia coli? That's right."

"Isn't that terribly dangerous?"

"Some people think so. I wouldn't do it myself. But you know the aim is a commendable one — perhaps we can produce antigens by such methods, against all kinds of diseases."

"I tried to read a book once," said Paul, "on *Self and Not-Self*, by someone called Burnett."

"Oh yes, that's a standard work. Or it was."

"I couldn't understand a word of it," said Paul dismally. "It seems all to have moved beyond a layman's grasp."

"Well, that's a pity," said Jack Mentor, "because — well, as you yourself show, the layman feels it's all very dangerous, and he can't understand it. So, he becomes hostile to science."

Mentor, who was a very tolerant man, and an excellent tutor to the young, became slightly resentful, if Paul questioned evolutionary theory, however.

"It's more or less a fact, now, rather than a theory."

"But has there been time," queried Paul, "for something like the horse with (say) its remarkable leg mechanisms, to evolve by *chance*, in the time that has elapsed since life began? Has there been enough time for sufficient random 'throws' of the dice?"

"I have to believe so," said Mentor, and that, rather, was that.

At the heart of the scientist's paradigms were creeds to which they had to adhere, had to take for granted in order to get on with their work. They tended to regard criticisms in those areas as probably lunatic, or cranky, or creationist: and though some were (as Paul found about Brownjohn) practising communicants of the Church of England, their universe remained still strictly materialist and mechanistic. How, then, did they reconcile this machine universe with belief? Where then was God? Why was life in the world? He argued with them over teleological principles, because he could not see that the world could be understood without some enquiry of that kind. What he found was that most scientists left "all that" to the philosophers and theologians, and concentrated on *what is*, on how things work. But when any philosophers or theologians appeared, they were far less willing to discuss such questions than the scientists: indeed, they tended to put on such a professional air that Paul was frightened to raise such issues with them: they made one feel, by a kind of ironic expression in their faces, that even the questions he wanted to ask were absurd, and so unanswerable. It was only when he got home, after an exasperating dinner between tedious small talk and a philosopher's lofty detachment, that he recovered his sense that his sceptical questions had been valid, after all. But then he felt he had been boring and tiresome, and cowardly not to pursue them.

Through all this, he learned most not to idealise. It is the well-kept aspect of the Cambridge colleges that prompts false idealising: the buildings and grounds are handsome or even beautiful, and the architecture is so ancient, and evocative of the distinguished past, that it is easily assumed that everyone there is living on a high plane of intelligence, thought and responsiveness. The colleges are so well run, so orderly, and regular, with their silver and butlers, cooks and waiters with gloves. The companies assembled around the glittering ranges of glasses and cutlery, with all the wine and dishes of good food, seem so distinguished as to be the focus of envy for ordinary mortals. But high table was often boring, and he had seen a waiter with gloves go arse-over-tip with a big silver plate of poussins, at a feast at Godwit: the birds shot along the floor under the tables, and the episode cast an ironic shadow over the pompous spectacle.

Yet at the heart of it all, where the real work is done, there is the hard grind of teaching and learning: and, for those doing their own work of thinking and writing, bafflement and perplexity: sometimes achievement, but often failure. A key figure at Paul's time was the Professor of Experimental Philosophy, an astronomer who had been crippled by some dreadful disease. One of the most remarkable minds in the world ever, exploring the nature of the physical universe through abstruse mathematical concepts and theories of space and time, the man was a pitiful wreck, in an electric wheel chair, unable to move his limbs except with extreme pain and effort, his head lolling like a deformed infant, and only able to speak through an electronic voice-synthesiser. To watch him steering his invalid chair across the street was terrifying and heart-rending. Yet he represented the implacable courage of the human mind, contemplating the voids, and wrote a best-selling book about Time. He seemed to stand for all who strove in the university, to explain the mysteries of existence.

The way to live with it all, Paul Grimmer found, was to be tolerant, and to labour at one's tasks, without lofty expectations or great hopes: but in gratitude for the opportunity and in deference to the truth, whatever that meant: *quaerere verum*. If that role were undertaken in a proper spirit there was no room for spite or vanity or false ambition — and that was the ethos Blenkinson and the fellowship had created. But now, with his reckless involvement in the Laurel Jameson case, whatever would his colleagues think of him? The lawyers simply seemed amused.

*

"What did you say in this article, then?" asked Bernard Drew. "I didn't see it."

He was a young law lecturer at Pemning, very clear-headed and, to Paul, quite frighteningly exact over administrative and legal matters.

"Well, I said I thought it was a shame he was being sued for libel. I was sure he had no malicious intent and that much of his comment was probably misquoted. I said I thought his colleagues should stand by him, and that it was bad for people in the humanities to go to law against one another."

"Do you go further than that?"

"Well, I said that even if he did say what he did about O'Neill being thought a bad teacher, he was probably right."

Drew put his hands together as if deliberating in court.

"Well," he said, "then it seems to me you've made yourself as actionable as he did. Of course I'd have to read it."

"If the case goes against him, you mean?"

"Well, naturally, it is up to him whether he fights it or tries to settle out of court. You say you're a friend of his?"

"Not a very close friend — I know him as a colleague and respect him."

"It's going to put a big strain on your friendship. I mean, if it goes against you both, you might both be ruined. It's the juries have to decide the damages and they've been making some very funny decisions recently, as you know."

"I can't believe it will ever get to court."

"Humph!" said Drew, looking upwards with a shrug, with a strangely cynical expression on his young face. "Having gone so far I can't believe O'Neill would let it lie at that."

"I can't believe it will happen," said Paul. "But if it did, what would it be? Laurel said Charles Hardy, their law man, said it might be as much as thirty thousand."

"Well, if it gets to court at all it will be tens of thousands, you may be sure."

"Oh, lor'," exclaimed Grimmer. "Well I hope I'm right, that it's a fantasy the man will drop before it gets that far."

"You never know," said Drew, again with an old man's weariness on his youthful face. "People get into these cases, become fanatical, all commonsense forfeited. And they can't see how to withdraw. I gather this man's wife is an heiress. If he feels so bitterly about it, he could make the case go on and on — she'll pay!"

"Jarndyce and Jarndyce all over again," said Paul ruefully. He spoke lightly, but a terror of libel had begun to take hold of him. He was beginning to be very afraid of where he had landed himself, and the spectre of unlimited resources on the other side was frightful. He had been in courts on only minor matters, but knew how easily things could go breath-takingly wrong, and he realised he had no money even to defend himself, let alone to pay damages, if any were awarded against him. If this happened, it would destroy any security he and Frances had achieved in the last few years. And it would take all Frances's little estate, and destroy their marriage. He tried to escape the growing realisation of this but it surfaced in the small hours and undermined his sleep. But he still tried to push it away into the realms of fancy, telling himself "It won't happen." So, he didn't even consult a lawyer, professionally — only pestered the college law dons, anxiously.

At the beginning of the Easter term another crisis overtook him.

*

"I wonder whether you can help me?" said John Vaughan one day at lunch.

"Me help you?" exclaimed Paul, laughing. "Well, I'd love to, but you seem the kind of person who can get on very well by himself!"

John Vaughan was a biologist with a big kindly face and a shock of white hair. He had definite black eyebrows, and a big nose, large pale grey eyes and a sensitive mouth which broke easily into a smile. He was a sympathetic man, warm-hearted and dynamic, of about fifty-five. His subject was glow-worms and the chemistry of their light apparatus. He was a reader in the zoology department, and people wondered if and when he would be made a professor.

"Well, I have a problem in my lab which seems to come into your territory rather than mine," Vaughan said, unusually grave. "I've got two people in there who are getting into a hell of a clinch, and it's all becoming like something in a book."

They were talking after lunch in the Senior Combination Room, a large room with big windows looking out at the lawns, with the spire of the Church of St Michael and All Angels rising behind the trees. They were drinking coffee from thin white porcelain cups on a polished mahogany pedestal table standing on the huge green carpet that matched the grass in the fellows garden.

"*She*, Marilyn, is very beautiful, about twenty-five, unattached, and she is doing some marvellous work on the energy systems of insects. Her latest study was of the dragonfly and its flight. I think she's brilliant, and will do remarkable work in the end."

"That doesn't sound like a problem," said Paul.

Vaughan smiled: he enjoyed a good story and he was fascinated by women.

"Ah, but enter the villain. We've taken on a new young man, Atkinson, very ambitious, clever, but as cold as a piece of iced steel . . . He wants to make a name for himself . . . he takes a great interest in Marilyn, the dragonfly girl . . . and she's falling in love with him . . ."

"So?" said Paul, thinking perhaps John was jealous.

"I know — though how I know I couldn't say . . . you know, Paul, though I am a simple guy, I do have uncanny nous sometimes . . . I *know* all he wants to do is to steal her research."

"Well, he may be after something else," said Paul.

Vaughan pulled a face.

"That's a cynical remark from someone like you," he protested.

"I'm sorry," said Paul. "It's my army past coming out. Well, it's natural for a young man to take an interest in a brilliant woman, so what are you worried about?"

"Things are not like they used to be," said Vaughan. "The pressure is on, and people are ruthless. Some do steal other people's work, and in this case I can see disaster ahead. The reward she ought to get — she'll not get it."

"Do you mean," said Paul, "that he's played on her and established a relationship in order to cheat her of her research findings?"

"Exactly."

"I can't believe it!"

There was a pause while Grimmer watched the light and scraps of grey cloud moving behind the spire. He still thought Vaughan was jealous: but he knew the man to be shrewdly aware of people's motives.

"What makes you suspect that? I mean, if a man and a woman become a couple — if they become lovers — they develop a sense that their work is 'theirs'. You don't think he is just entering into her work as a partner, because he loves her?"

"He doesn't love her. He's cold. She's the one who's

emotionally involved. And what does he do? He offers to take her papers and get them printed out properly on my new laser printer. All right, very gentlemanly. But I bet he has a copy made for himself. What I fear is that one day there will be a brilliant paper sent to *Nature* by Mr Ron Atkinson."

"And it will be her work?"

"His work is not up to it. We should never have taken him on. He was supposed to be working on the dynamics of insect movement, too, and this all seemed to fit in to all our work. He does experiments and writes them up — but after a year there's been nothing but woolliness. You can't tell sometimes: he just lacks the ability to define what he's doing, to define his task. So he never comes up with anything."

"Maybe he is learning from her?"

"He's *stealing* from her."

"How do you deal with that kind of thing in science?"

"That's what I wanted to ask your advice about."

"I can't judge scientific matters."

"I'm not asking you to. We can do that. But the situation between people — I want someone who can help me deal with that."

"I'll do what I can," said Paul. "But I'm not all that good with 'real life'," he added gloomily. "I find it hard to believe always, that people can use their emotional life to trick others. But they do, I know — I know it from books. Do you know this girl well, then?" he asked, looking shrewdly at Vaughan.

"We went to Peru together to a scientific conference. I like her company, I admire her. But, no, if that's what you mean, I'm not emotionally involved with her, except I feel like she's a daughter or a protégée. I don't want to see her messed up, that's all."

Paul looked relieved, but still puzzled.

"Well, I mean, you can't shout out about it in the lab or wherever, can you? So what can I do?" he said. "I can only talk it over with you in a theoretical way. And no doubt the affair has its own impetus?"

"But we ought to be able to deal with this kind of thing in a civilised way, oughtn't we?" urged Vaughan, in his naive, simple-minded way. "I'm supposed to be rational and a scientist. You're a literary man, dealing all the time with situations in novels, desperate problems like this. Between us surely we can make a plan?"

"If only life were like that — like a Sherlock Holmes novel, John."

There was a pause.

"Well, the first thing is to find out whether in fact he is planning to pirate her work. Since you are in charge of her research, you can find out from her what originality her work contains, and make sure it isn't stolen. Then you'd have hard scientific realities to deal with. If you were to warn her now it would be disastrous."

"She'd go to him."

"She'd go over to him. The other thing we must do is to prepare a plan for when he abandons her, and she finds out that she has been betrayed, silly child."

"At what point I wonder will he make the break? You see he'll have to plan to get published and then get his next project into the SRC to be sure of funding by next autumn."

"It will be soon, then? So, we must find out if we can what he is organising."

A few days later Vaughan called in at Paul's room with a paper printed out on his laser printer.

"Look at this," he said. "I got this printed out of Phoenix."

The paper read 'Resonance and Energy: Clues to Insect Flight' by R.G. Atkinson, B.Sc.

"It's a clear case of stealing: all these were her discoveries. What I don't know, of course, is what he intends to do with it. It wasn't in my outfit, but in the mainframe computer under his name."

"How did you get it?"

"Richard got it out. Of course, he hasn't printed it out, but it's in there like that. Don't tell anyone. Shall I just confront him with it?"

Paul thought of the master's techniques when dealing with his own problems.

"If you do, it needs to be as open as possible. Sir Martin's good on that. I'm sure you should put the whole question of science and truth on the table, in a situation where there are those present who are able to uphold the criteria. If you see him alone it will seem like your word against his and he'll flannel."

"And she should be there."

"Of course. And surely the master himself? And I'll come, too, if you like — I'm outside the discipline and neutral. In that way, we can surely all stand for something?"

Vaughan looked doubtful.

"She might just bale him out."

"Because she's in love with him?"

Vaughan nodded.

"She'll refuse to see the wrong in him, if we don't produce absolute clinching evidence."

"Must we wait, then, till he can be seen to have really betrayed her: as when it's published somewhere? Perhaps that's happening now?"

"Did she give him the stuff anyway?"

"I've talked with her. I said, 'How are the dragonflies?' She gave me one of her marvellous smiles — I'd do anything for one of those. 'When shall we read your brilliant findings?' I said, all innocent like. 'Oh, I'm not ready yet,' she said. 'I've drafted something. But I'm keeping it locked up in my drawer.' "

"So, he's getting in her drawers first?"

Vaughan grimaced: he wasn't in the mood for joking.

"It looks like it."

"I wouldn't have thought it possible."

"You see — that's why I wanted your help. I don't like to think ill of anyone, and this kind of low cunning seems to me almost unbelievable. This kind of thing didn't happen in the good old days. But if I can bring someone like you in, perhaps I can keep sane," he grumbled.

Paul Grimmer sighed.

"I hate anything like that: gives me sleepless nights. But we're not in this just for comfort are we? Others have helped me — the master, you know, has been marvellous."

"He's a human being," said Vaughan. "We're lucky."

"Well, let's try to be like that ourselves. You arrange

something and I'll be there to support you."

*

In a sense, a good marriage can be taken for granted, though if Paul Grimmer had said as much to Frances, she would have been furious with him. But the strength on which Grimmer was able to draw during crises was given him by what he shared with his wife.

Their marriage had been through many stormy passages, not least when they had had four children at home, and the sheer exhaustion of conducting the normal routines of domestic life had left no energy to renew the emotional and sexual life. Frances had a tendency in those days to sink into bleak depressions, sometimes from premenstrual tension, sometimes for no good reason except some black ghost in her soul. Paul was liable to become cruel or angry, from time to time, for no good reason either. Both had long ago found out the extent and the limits of their uglier potentialities. But in late middle life, by degrees, the strange satisfactions of conflict had lost all interest for them: they became unwilling to spare the energy and pain for division.

To their surprise, they had more feelings of crisis than they expected, over the children leaving home. They clung on to the last child, and he, Simeon, was still living with them at the age of eighteen. But it continued to seem awful to them that these creatures, who had demanded attention hour by hour for so many years, should now be content with a weekly phone call, and belonged now to others, to their husbands, or, in Ben's case, at 25, to a series of extraordinary girl friends, who never seemed quite right. Without children in the house, however, they seemed dolefully without a function, and it seemed uncomfortable to be thrown back on dealing exclusively with one another.

"Well, that's all we had once," said Frances one day, when they were discussing their unhappiness, because the children had gone. "There was you and me, two deckchairs and a bed."

"And the view . . . and the *Complete Works of V.I. Lenin.*"

"No — you made me sell those, you bastard."

"What stimulating evening reading you could still be enjoying!"

When Paul had first met Frances, she had been literature secretary of the Paddington Branch of the Communist Party. They had been given a flat in a street in Hampstead, looking out over the southernmost pond, where swans nested and ducks steamed about all day in flotillas, marking the surface with geometrical patterns. Step by step, Zdhanov 1948, Hungary 1956, they had come to burn their party cards and become moderate labour supporters.

"The sunsets over the top of Hampstead were superb, weren't they?" she said, musingly.

There was a watercolour of one still in the bathroom, by their sometime lodger Heinz Warner, who had gone to be a people's artist in the East German People's Republic. It was in the wild German Expressionist tradition, and when he looked at it every morning Grimmer could remember the hope and excitement of the first days of their marriage, in the bare flat with its shiny "Darkalined" boards, and its white walls on which by degrees they hung paintings and drawings won at Hampstead jumble sales or given them by artists they met.

Sometimes he would catch a view of Frances in the realistic way, and see what she looked like now: her neck was wrinkled, and her skin a little loose with age. But she had taken care of her face, and he found her beautiful and was still deeply in love with her. He saw her as he used to see her in those first days, with her fine-boned proud little nose and her keen green-coloured eyes. Physically, she was very well-preserved and her body when naked was beautiful, her breasts full and round, and her abdomen flat and firm. But she had lost the tiny waist around which he used to be able to put his hands, so that his thumbs and fingers met.

The passionate devotion was there still, and he knew more now, certainly, about her integrity. She was a woman of complete integrity and consistently truthful in all her judgements and doings. Frances moreover, was devoted to the idea of her marriage: not necessarily to marriage in general, but to a concept of what her marriage should be. So, she persisted in believing in Paul and supporting him, even when she secretly believed he had damaged his own career, or when it seemed that there was nothing before him but failure. And she bore his financial disasters with devoted resignation: which did not mean silence of criticism on her part.

But now the one area where they seldom if ever met was that of money. So often had their financial life been a disaster, and so often had this caused menacing schisms, that, by degrees, they avoided the subject altogether. Towards the end of Paul's attempts to be self-supporting, they had sunk to an overdraft of some four thousand pounds. There was little or no hope of ever recovering this, and so, when Frances received a legacy from a rich relative, she paid it off. Secretly, Paul Grimmer promised himself that one day he would repay her. Secretly, she felt sure he never would. They both lost sleep for many nights, in deep and painful anguish about the catastrophe. But from then on, they held their tongues on the subject.

They lived from island to island — the islands of the weekends, and holidays. Their weekdays were intensely exacting, and they spent their evenings quietly reading and drinking good wine. Their greatest pleasure was discussing the novels they had read. Simeon their last son had found this hard to bear, being a practical young man at seventeen attached to everyday reality. He would fling out of the room crying, "You talk about people in books as if they were real! I can't stand it!" He was determined, whatever happened, to have no literary consciousness, in protest.

For the weekend life to succeed, the problem was to get rid of Simeon, once he was adolescent and aware of the sexual life. Fortunately, he took to working backstage in the Cambridge Arts Theatre, so he had to be there for the Saturday afternoon matinee. Paul and Frances liked going to bed in the afternoon, and this was their secret. They would have a simple but delicious lunch, of grilled salmon steaks or Dover Sole, with salad strewn with rose-petals and a French countryside cheese, with a Chablis or Sancerre, and then take their tray of coffee up to the bedroom.

Paul would make an elaborate business of bringing everything out of the courtyard indoors to make it look as if they had gone for a walk, locking the door and even bolting the door of the bedroom. Thus, they could splash and wash themselves, and glide naked in between the cool sheets, in the afternoon sunlight. Frances would make some pretence of resisting him, because he was taking her for granted, or being mechanical.

"But it's not mechanical," he would exclaim. "It is different every time."

"You're a creature of habit," she'd protest.

"You can't call it a mechanical habit going to bed with the fountain of life!" he'd laugh.

Then he would get up and close the window quietly.

"You make such a noise at the end," he said, "and we don't want the neighbours to call the fire brigade."

Afterwards, he would bath and fetch her more coffee. The room would smell of coffee, *Mitsouko* or *L'Air du Temps*, and the flowers he brought her. One wall was papered with an Italian pattern of leaves, and it felt like one of those rooms in cheap French hotels where the ceiling is papered with the same crowded floral pattern as the walls. Frances would lie and sleep sometimes for an hour, and then they would dress and sit on the big white sofa downstairs, listening to Mozart or Brahms.

*

Towards the end of the first term after Paul Grimmer's new appointment, Frances's mother began to decline fast. His wife's mother, a widow, was nearly ninety, and had suddenly begun to become senile. So, all that year they had been obliged to make urgent visits from time to time to South Wales, as the poor old woman was moved from her home, to a nursing home, or to hospital. Fortunately, there was a fully-trained private nurse living in the next street whom Frances and her brother could employ professionally, to care for her, and to report. But every now and then important decisions had to be taken, the doctor seen, and the old mother reassured, and made as safe and comfortable as she could be.

The trips down the M4 motorway over the Severn Bridge were like strange voyages into a faded past, the past of their family album. They always seemed to run into drenching rain that sometimes spread a splashing stretch of water over the roadway, so they often seemed to be floating down to the West rather than driving. When the curtains of rain parted, there were the little mountains with their heaps of black spoil, the clouds of white steam over Bedwas pit and coking plant, and the family house, "Tallylyn", now hanging over a harsh new by-pass and pressed upon by immense new plastics factories, yet already now empty and unused. Economically, South Wales was sinking into disaster again.

Frances remembered the hostile miners pulling up the tulips in her father's garden in the 1929 General Strike: Charles Lewis had been a lawyer, Clerk to the local Council, and so the class enemy. Now the garden was a neglected tangle, and all the objects which were once components of a middle-class curtilage were broken and abandoned — the bird-bath, the sun dial, the crazy-paved paths: while the swinging garden seat with its striped canvas awning was now a rusted skeleton in the collapsing outhouse.

Paul and Frances associated the old stone house "Tallylyn" with the early days of their marriage, not least because it appeared in the snapshots in the earlier volumes of their scrap-books. In even older photos there appeared a neat garden, with smart people sitting in deckchairs with books and tennis rackets. The freshly-painted windows stood open with the curtains blowing. There was Charles, a smart little man with bright intense eyes and slightly balding, with a dandyish taste in clothes. Her mother still preserved the grotesque masonic apron in which he was dressed in one sepia photograph. Charles had died long ago, in 1937, and now the widow was in her last days, in the same house, where they had lived in the heyday of their marriage. Now, most of the windows could not be opened, the rainwater pipes were blocked, the gutters falling off, the paint going scrofulous, the lawn overgrown with thick tufts of couchgrass and weeds. Whenever they went down to his wife's home, Paul would try to put a few things right, but the dilapidation was catastrophic, and they were unable to do much in case it upset the old lady.

Though she was deaf and her sight was dim, she was aware

of the least change in her surroundings. She had been burgled three times in the last year, so that she lived in terror, behind windows that could no longer be opened, with the pantry window completely boarded up, and the house decaying round her. Great strips of wallpaper were pulling away from the ceiling of the landing, and rain-water stains were appearing through all the ceilings. From time to time she would be found in a state of collapse, and would have to be taken in to a nursing home: another long journey from Cambridge would have to be made again, and Frances and Paul would find themselves tossing unhappily in the damp matrimonial bed, solid mahogany but with a derelict mattress, upstairs in the decaying house. So noisy were the huge coal lorries along the by-pass all night that they would have to nail blankets over the rickety window, to get any sleep at all. To make any kind of meal in the grubby kitchen was a nightmare, not least because old Mrs Lewis had refused to do any kind of modernisation since the grim days when scullery maids were the only ones to have to cope with the cracked stone sink and the slate slabs.

For Mrs Lewis had been living more or less in the time of her widowing ever since — ever since Frances was twelve.

When she was able to come home from hospital, the old woman was determined to be in her own place, and they respected this. She was now the image of old age itself, her skin shrivelled and loose, her hair skimpy, grey and unkempt, her eyes weak under the folds of her eyelids, her mouth puckered and pursed. She had shrunk to a tiny, bent, frail figure. Yet, if they took her arm and led her for a walk across the bridge opposite and down the lane, she would wave her stick and cry, defiantly,

"Yes! I want to live here. This is my home — and I shall *die* here!"

Just before Christmas, the nurse rang from Wales to say that Frances's mother had been found on the floor unconscious, having fallen out of bed: she seemed to have had a stroke. No-one seemed quite clear what was wrong. Everyone knew that old Mrs Lewis had brandy bottles and rolls of pound notes tucked everywhere — down the cracks of the arms of the

armchairs, behind her bed, in her cupboard drawers. Sometimes her collapses seemed to be the consequence of the
brandy. But this time there was an ominousness about the
messages, and there seemed no doubt that the hand of death
was upon her.

So, in early December of his first year as Director of Studies,
Paul Grimmer was sitting in the little breakfast room at
"Tallylyn" while Frances went to sit with her dying mother in
the hospital. He had cleaned the ash-clogged fireplace and
kept a good clear coal fire going. All this had to be done with
the maddeningly ineffective brass fire irons and brushes
which the old woman had clung to, while stumbling about
among her clutter of furniture. Paul tried to prepare pleasant
meals for himself and Frances, ready for the time when his
wife would come in pale and distressed from her vigil, but
these were only a pale shadow of the elegant cuisine at home.

The big pendulum clock on the ancient oak linen chest
ticked loudly in the evenings: it had been presented to
Frances's father as Clerk to the Rudry and Pandy Urban
Council, and it spoke to them of a respectable past before the
war, when her parents went to bridge parties and Daddy was
a Grand Master of the Provincial Masonic Lodge. There were
three perspectives of time: there was that distant past of the
house of the successful mining town lawyer: there was their
own early days of courtship and marriage: and there was the
present, the decaying shell and the imminent death. The
tension between these various pools of time in their consciousness was appalling under the strain.

They had never been able to make love in "Tallylyn"
anyway: the parental ghosts were too powerful. So, whenever
they had come down in the past it had never been long before
they needed urgently to get away from it, in order to be
themselves, and to be a married pair. What pressed upon them
at Bedwas was the intense inheritance of the denial of joy:
from the beginning, sexual love had been a horror to Frances's
mother, and her children had come upon her even more
unwillingly. She had been gravely ill with her first child,
Frances's elder brother: then there had been still-born twins,
and finally Frances, who had been told all her life she was

unwanted — though her mother had come to love her and was now closer to her than anyone else. Emotionally, the family inheritance had been a disaster — and then the father had died suddenly of pneumonia, complicated by his asthma, when Frances was twelve.

So, when Frances was asked by Paul to marry him, her mother said, "You won't will you?" And then, when she declared her intentions, "You won't have any babies will you?" Old Mrs Lewis hated babies, and regarded her daughter as insane, when she declared that she loved babies, and produced no less than four, over the years. Yet, she had come to love the grandchildren and insisted on regular accounts of their progress, even when they too, absurdly in her opinion, married and produced yet more babies, to her utter distress.

So, it was confusing, to look at the dilapidated house, and be nostalgic about the days when it was shinier and well-kept, when the antimacassars were well-ironed and there were flowers about the place. When the father was alive, they had had two maids: a housemaid and a parlour maid. Today, it seemed unbelievable, that these women could have been tucked away in backstairs, to labour in the background of the small house. Even in the early days of her widowhood there would be regular callers, for Mrs Lewis owned property and had tenants and was a magistrate. She was a prominent member of the WVS and a trustee of this and that charity. The garden had poplar trees, and a walnut, and roses and cowslips in the lawn. Paul associated it with the days when he was fascinated by Frances's origins, her strange complex of relatives in the farms and mines, and the friends of her youth in the village. She seemed to have an infinite line of cousins. Paul and Frances would wander the country lanes to collect blackberries and climb Bedwas mountain into the bracken, where once they made love, in a hollow deep out of sight: it was miserably uncomfortable, but it had to be done, and, in retrospect, always seemed an act of defiant romanticism, against the doleful sootiness of the little pit village, with its hills of black spoil marring the mountain.

But to reflect on her family world of the past was to evoke the sense of joylessness and hostility to sexuality in the old house. And in turn this made terrible the encroaching death of the old woman, whose life had displayed such a strange and painful rejection of the body. In her own youth she had had to have both breasts removed, because of cancer, and the dread had haunted Frances all her life.

So, now she was dying, Paul Grimmer sat in a kind of guilty dismay and terror, at the table in the decayed house, at the foot of Bedwas mountain — marking his batch of eighty College Entrance Examination scripts. He was glad of those scripts. For one thing they provided a compulsive task, to ease his troubled mind that otherwise would have tramped round the awful reality of mortality. For another, they offered a sense of continuity, to offset the miserable crisis of his term — he would be able to carry on, would he not? And, indeed, when he took them to the village post office he was even able to get a little cachet out of it — a sense that he belonged, even if only in some awkward way, to one of the great universities of the world. He hated the whole thing of examinations: but at this distance it stood curiously for disciplines of the mind — and of the many thousands who had sat to be tested on the three-legged stool.

*

What struck him most was the terrible loneliness for his wife, in her dealings with her mother's last hours. There was nothing he could do at all, to help her. She drove off to the hospital, by herself, caring nothing about food or what she wore, her face drawn and abstracted, and then she would return, exhausted and racked.

"I think she felt the pressure of my hand and returned a squeeze."

"I'm sure she did," he said. She spoke with such amazement about her mother's declining condition, in a strange grotesque excitement.

"She seems so small now, a little tiny woman, just a bag of bones: so thin and pitiful, curled up in the bed like a baby. I can't believe it is my mother."

From time to time in his mind rose remembrances of the trouble his mother-in-law had been, in the past: her strange implacable will. She had a practised capacity, for example, to inhibit her daughter as when they proposed to themselves a manic evening out, at a Chinese restaurant in Cardiff, or an inn, up the mountain in the countryside. She would object to such outings, even when her daughter had been married twenty years, with a cold dogged fury. To what avail, that dominating will? Now it was stilled. And it seemed an offence to recall her powerful attempts to dominate, her powerful negative will and its damaging effect on their marriage. If one has a reluctance to speak ill of the dead, how much more it seems an appalling offence to speak ill of the dying!

Better recall the wonderful time in the early days of their marriage, when Granny Wales, as the infants called her, sat up all night with their eldest little girl, who had bronchitis. The elderly woman had sent the parents to bed, and watched through the night in a room filled with steam from a kettle, while the baby's cough eased and eased. It was heroic, really. There had been so much concentrated into that vigil — a kind of love inseparably mixed with that persistent will.

"She was a demon, really," Frances had said to him one day. "And so unfair: my brother could do nothing wrong, whereas I . . ."

But wrong and fair, love and will were all now dissolving, in the uneasy hospital bed, while Frances sat murmuring to the shrunken old lady, holding her hand as she drifted into deeper and deeper remoteness.

In the end, Frances came back with a mysterious radiance about her, a sybilline quality about her weariness. She came back suddenly.

"She's gone, Paul," she cried. "She died early this morning. She came fully into consciousness in the night, and in the early morning, Sister told me, she sat up."

"No!"

"She seemed to be seeing something in front of her: they do, you know, I'm told, dying people. She seemed to be looking towards something or somebody, and stretched out her arms. Then she simply sank back, and died. That was in the dawn, and so I never saw her again, after yesterday."

As she spoke, a recognition of what she was saying struck

her, and she broke down in sobs, glad to lean forward into his arms. He held her, holding her tightly as she shuddered in spasms of grief. Over her head he gazed at a faded sepia photograph of Frances's mother as a young woman with a mild expression, a kind of weak smile. Her father had been a hill farmer, and there was such strength of character. The strength was there in Frances, and it had given so much to his own life: she had stood by him so resolutely. Now all he could do was to try to ameliorate her misery, by comforting her as best he could, keeping the fire going, setting out meals for her, and listening.

Already, as he laid the table for lunch, she was on the telephone, to her brother, her children, and the undertakers, taking refuge, as people do, in talking — already turning the dreadful reality into a story.

After his lunch of ham and salad, with a bottle of undistinguished Burgundy from the Caerphilly supermarket, she began to feel better.

"I don't think she suffered terrible pain, Paul. She just sank away, really. It was like a complete regression out of the world."

"The hospital sounds as if it dealt with it very well."

"Yes, they gave her a little room off the main ward at the end. Oh, Paul, there were some terrible cases in there."

"Don't talk about them," he said. He was very cowardly about details of sickness and hated hospitals. She had a woman's capacity for concern, and a Welsh morbidity: every morning of her life she began her day by reading the death notices in the newspaper. He tried now to indicate the future.

"I had a peep in the old chest: it's full of junk. Do you realise, now it's all up to us?"

She sighed.

"I know," she said, gazing round the room. There was an unfinished bit of knitting, the needles still stuck in the piece: little piles of bills and cuttings, catalogues, photographs. Where would one begin?

"Mumma lived in the past, too, in a way: there are piles of photographs somewhere of her and Daddy, and local council openings and fêtes and press cuttings about his funeral in

1937. What a time this is ago: and then all the share certificates and dividend statements went on, his business she called it, as if she was managing it all for him. We shall have a job of it!"

He was aware of distinct layers of culture, needing to be kept apart. There were the exam scripts: schoolchildren's comments on poems by Browning and Edward Thomas, desperate and rambling accounts of their meaning and on such fashionable techniques as "enjambement". Then there were the novels he and Frances were reading, and some proofs he had to do of an article on a modern poet. Then there were Mrs Lewis' novels on the shelves, going mouldy — why did she have *The Well of Loneliness* and *Madame Bovary*? There were all the notes of condolence from her father's colleagues and masonic brethren, from his funeral: it was a male-only funeral and they processed past the grave, throwing in flowers. There were piles of the *Geographical Magazine* and some old colour supplements: it was a little like Pompeii, with rather a sense of a life running down: the dates on the magazines showed when last the old lady had possession of her faculties.

Every now and then Frances would give a sob, and pause to dash away her tears.

"At least we shan't have to make that awful journey, month after month!"

"But there'll be the house to sell — you'll have to attend to that."

"And the furniture."

By degrees, the accroutrements of life had to be dismantled. First, the wretched stained fragments of the old woman's nocturnal life, her last nest, were dismantled and thrust into plastic bags. Then, her accumulations of sheer rubbish. For years, nothing had been cleared, because everyone had been so anxious not to upset or offend the once powerful woman, with her residual tenacious will.

It suddenly dawned on Paul Grimmer that the responsibility now fell on him, to deal with the chaotic leavings of a life. Frances, of course, had to be consulted about many matters: ought these deeds to be kept, or were they worthless? Who was this in this photograph? Did she need the accumulated rent books and repair bills of her mother's little properties, in Trethomas and Lower Machen? Most of them, Frances knew, had been sold.

The task was both exacting and yet banal and sordid, but poignant. The elderly, even as their powers begin to fail, cling on to everything, and so the son-in-law found himself disposing of receipts and documents the old lady should have dumped years ago. Yet among these would suddenly emerge a share certificate, or the deeds of a house which were still valid and indispensable for probate. There were shreds of clothing, so torn and wretched that Paul even hid them from Frances, who, if she had seen them, would have grieved and felt guilty, that she had not visited her mother more regularly and sought to persuade her to buy herself new garments. There were the empty brandy bottles tucked down the backs of sofas, and collections of folded newspapers, newsletters from women's organisations, bundles of letters in all manner of hands — it would have taken months to go through all these. He found in a cardboard box all the letters and cards sent and left by relatives and friends, and all her father's masonic contacts, at her father's funeral in 1937, together with obituaries in the local press. There were family photographs, in which he recognised some people, but most of whose subjects baffled Frances, when he presented them to her.

So much had to go, because the house would have to be sold, together with the furniture, and the sale would have to be prepared at a distance. Old pillows, ragged curtains, strips of wallpaper hanging in festoons from the ceilings, ancient bottles and tins of foodstuff, useless accumulations of cleaning materials, broken picture-frames, piles of newspaper cuttings, broken sets of dominoes, minute books and bundles of fuel bills — by degrees Paul filled ten plastic bags of these, making unhappy decisions all the time, and setting aside several boxes of relics which he and his wife would have to take home and sort out in the evenings.

At last, the house was restored to some kind of order, but even so it seemed ghastly — wounded and humiliated. The old mother had hung on to her dream, the postures of her life as the wife of a successful professional husband in the thirties, with their bridge parties and status in middle-class village life. Paul and Frances had worked out that her father's income of over £2,000 a year would have been the equivalent of £45,000 in 1983. The widow had been a magistrate until only ten years ago. Her gestures towards this respectability had been there still, in her lace curtains, her embroidered covers, her sideboard and tantalus, never used, but still, as it were, flying the flag of respectable and genteel dining. But at last, all hung in decay, the surfaces of the furniture yellowed or creased by time, the silver gone black, the antimaccassars in shreds. And now, the polite gestures of her home were stripped naked, leaving only the best pieces — a grandfather clock which Frances's brother would have and a magnificent oak blanket chest from the Cwm Farm.

Now, some relics appeared as good, solid, saleable stuff: a Spode tea-set, with green vine-leaves on it, and some brass fire-irons. Paul Grimmer, having spent weeks in a fog of misery over the death, also became aware that Frances would now share the inheritance of this house and its furniture. This little world of his wife's home would now be translated into cash — and half of it would be hers. His own father had married again, and so he had never expected to inherit anything. To his surprise, he became aware that his wife would inherit a property, and he began to look at the residue of his mother-in-law's belongings with a new eye.

"Actually," he said, exhausted with cleaning out rubbish and broken detritus. "Some of this stuff is very good — that dining table, for instance, and your mother's little bureau."

"I should think so," Frances replied. She saw everything still, of course, as she had known it as a girl. Even the garden swing seat was still to her a luxurious leisure piece, and Paul had to demonstrate that it was now a worthless bundle of old iron, fit only to be piled alongside the garbage bags. But she was right about many things that had not deteriorated — the glass-framed bookcase that still contained her father's law books: the heavy mahogany marital bed and the huge mahogany gentleman's wardrobe beside it.

"What will it all fetch then?" he asked.

"Oh, I suppose the house will go for about forty thousand,"

she said, "and the furniture — well, who knows — five thousand if we're lucky."

He was amazed.

"So, you'll get about twenty thousand at least?" he exclaimed.

"And there's some shares, too," she said, "and a balance at the bank."

Suddenly her face crumpled, and she burst into tears.

"Whatever's the matter?" he exclaimed, concerned for her sudden outburst of sorrow.

"Poor Mumma . . . she could have made herself so much more comfortable, instead of keeping it for Rodney and me!"

"You could never have persuaded her."

"She could have gone into a nice comfortable nursing home and spent it all on that."

"She'd have hated it. You remember she cried — one day when we were down by the river, how she would stay here and die here."

Frances gulped.

"Well, so she did."

"And now," he said. "After all these years of poverty with me, you'll be quite well off!"

She tossed her head.

"I shall have some security at last. I shall buy a little house: then it will increase in value."

"You'll be a *rentier*!" he exclaimed.

"But I shan't vote Conservative," she laughed.

A chill struck him, as he reflected on the trouble he had left behind in Cambridge. If O'Neill persisted, and it came to court, and he lost — could they take Frances's property as well as his? Was this inheritance already threatened, before even cleared by probate? If only she knew! He carefully guarded his tongue and plunged back into his work of clearing out every drawer. What a pile of accumulated rubbish the old lady had laid by!

*

The funeral setting a week later was surprisingly beautiful for the ugly pit village. It was a day of fitful sunshine, and there was a mixture of shadows and gleams under the wet bare trees in the churchyard above the village. Behind the gleaming tree-trunks steamed the coal-pit coking plant. The church was full, and Frances was amazed to be recognised and spoken to by so many elderly men and women out of her parents' past. Dozens of the cousins turned up, and they all kissed her one by one: she had never supposed there were so many survivors. Paul and Frances and her brother had asked for the ancient service from Cranmer's Prayer Book of 1549 because they felt that this would have been what her mother wanted: but they were told, sharply and rudely, by the clergyman that this was now actually illegal. They had to have the Alternative Service Book service. Paul had been asked by Frances's brother to read from the last chapter of *Ecclesiastes*: but this, they were told, as sharply and rudely, was not allowed either: the only readings allowed were those set out in the A.S.B. So, they endured the new service, their hearts sinking at the dull and feeble language imposed by the ignorant committee of the Church in Wales. Frances's brother, Rodney, a quiet, sad man, was far too distressed to help them resist the clergy. He had had much conflict with his father, over his career, and the dark bitterness of it deepened his normal gloom into a deep despair. The shiny brown coffin was lowered into the opened tomb of Frances's father, just by the church path, as they stood miserably by, feeling hurt and alienated, to the language of modern bureaucracy.

Paul held back his anger, until they were back in the house, where they entertained all the aunts and cousins, many of whom Frances had never met. The more distant they were, the higher their plates were piled, it seemed. Frances had bought some specially sweet brown sherry, knowing that this was what the village people and the cousins would like. He was still furious about the service.

"The bloody church!" Paul exclaimed, in the pantry, clutching Frances as she came in for more plates.

"I hate bloody Christians," he added, keeping out of Frances's brother's earshot.

"Well," said Frances. "I don't believe any of it anyway."

"But it's *our* inheritance," he said. "It isn't *theirs*, to tell us we can't have it. Bastards!"

"Oh, come, now, darling: you'll upset everyone."

"All right," he said. "for your sake."

He kissed her, with a great tenderness.

Her sad face was beautiful, among the decrepit ugliness of the unpainted scullery, with its damp-stained walls, and its panes boarded up after a break-in by village youths. Yet it was a brave face, too, for she felt that in the gathering of the Welsh crowd in church, there had been a tribute to her mother. He felt an intense pang of love for her, and dwelt for a moment cheek to cheek on the rich warmth of the living flesh — the first kiss, strangely, since the death.

Her brother was unusually nice to her, she said: he was obviously feeling a devastating sense of loss, and he turned to his sister for comfort like a bewildered animal.

*

All right, he thought, if I can't read *Ecclesiastes* over my mother-in-law's body, at least I can teach it to my students.

For some reason, at the cold beginning of that Lent Term, they had seemed even more suspicious of him. He waited as they gathered: there was an odd tense silence between them, and still again he detected some voice in the background. He noticed that one or two especially the dark quiet little Bo Dibbans, looked at him sadly and steadily, as if summing him up. He had made some remarks in another article, about how much less students had read nowadays, before coming up to the university. He knew that one or two had resented this: but he also wondered who it was that drew their attention to such things? Someone was evidently feeling glee, any time he made a mistake — for it was exploited at once.

As he read the famous verses from the Bible, he could see the students were baffled. For one thing, although it was clearly poetry, it was written in prose. And while it was deeply moving in its resonance, it was impossible to say why, because one did not, at first hearing "understand" it. What was it about? They hated him for asking that kind of question, even implicitly.

"What kind of trick are you playing on us, this week?" — thus Rhees, under his red hair he flashed his wiry glasses. He was actually of a mild and friendly disposition, but somehow he had come to feel he must defend "student interests" against Paul, over whom they had projected such an authoritarian image. He would deliberately provoke at times: when Paul asked him at a supervision why Cordelia said no to King Lear, Rhees declared, "Because she was imprisoned in the language", and he wrote in an essay that Lady Macbeth "was the embodiment of a positive moral energy". Later Paul found that he made these provocative statements deliberately, to annoy him, so he could enjoy the comic effects. All right my boy, he thought to himself: two can play at that game. Rhees was Comrade Ossipon still, he thought.

"You get us all in here, and then you give us something you don't understand and get ready to pick us off when we show that we can't," said Brian Butley, aggressively.

Paul felt annoyed, but tried to smile.

"Look," said Peter Brown, in his quiet voice. "Does it matter that we can't understand it?"

"We shall look silly sitting here for two hours if we can't."

"But there are some things which are beyond the limits of human understanding and we ought to be able to live with that."

"The church can't," added Aschenberg. "And so we have all these 'new' bibles that put it all into language everyone can understand — as though there were no mysteries."

There was a pause: Aschenberg as so often, had established a serious atmosphere for him, amid the tendency to rag, and the underlying hostility.

"It's the almond tree, and the grasshopper that I can't get," said Bo. "I can see that the silver cord and the golden bowl refer to some secret knot of vitality in the living person."

"In the New Bible it says 'When the paunch of the locust is full' or something — that's probably a better translation."

"Yes," said Rhees who was becoming involved in spite of himself, "but it isn't nature notes, is it? It's all metaphysical, about growing old and dying. So, what does the locust stand for, even if we take that reading?"

"Perhaps it means that the person, in his bodily life has taken in as much as he can, like a fat locust."

"I've always read it to mean . . ."

"You mean you *know* this passage?"

"Oh yes," said Rosie Nicols, "my uncle's a clergyman you know. I've always taken it to mean that to an old person even the light weight of a grasshopper is too much: or that the constant zip! zip! of a grasshopper's noise is an irritation."

"What about the almond tree?"

"That's beautiful. But that's the hair."

"Like old Robert Graves's?"

"And all the imagery is about the body — the keepers are the arms: the strong men the legs: the doors the eyes: the grinders the teeth: the music the voice."

So, Aschenberg. The florid Hebrew metaphors came easily to him.

"But the daughters of music and the mourners are the musicians and the mourners at a funeral, too."

"I'm sure that's right," said Paul.

"But is that why you put it to us, to get us to unravel those symbols?"

"There's no right answer," said Paul. "May be, I'm wrong, but I agree with Aschenberg. Only you can't make an exact analogy all through: there's an evocative ambiguity, that leaves you tantalised."

"And that's a matter of the evocative nature of certain words like 'flourish' — for the point about an old man's hair is that he *isn't* flourishing . . ."

Bo was enjoying herself this afternoon. Usually shy, she had responded with astonishment to the passage.

"What about, 'rose up at the voice of the bird . . .' "

So, they went on among themselves now, forgetting him, while he was dwelling on the inner image, of his wife's mother's unkempt grey hair and, long ago, his own mother's once lovely hair, become lank, grey, greasy and ugly, in the end. And then his mother's mother's . . . she had always told him of her mother's beautiful hair, even after her death.

" 'Because man goeth to his long home . . .' "

He found himself saying it: they looked up startled. He realised he had chosen the passage because of his grief: they could feel his involvement. What had begun as a somewhat edgy seminar was turning out to be a healing one.

"Would you call that tragic?"

"It's didactic, isn't it? 'The preacher sought to find out acceptable words; and that which was written was upright, even words of truth.' In its recognition of decay it's tragic: but I don't know if tragedy can be didactic. Or whether the didactic can be tragic."

"I forget they're so young," he said to Frances afterwards.

"Well, I daresay they'll keep their ends up," she said. "If they don't have the experience to draw on, at least they can prepare themselves in imagination."

"They *loved* it," he said with satisfaction.

In imagination. "Let your imagination work . . ." He thought of his work as a discipline of the imagination, but he knew that there were those in the faculty who would not agree with that. Sometimes he got a back-hander around the question: one faculty supervision report, from a Shakespeare class by a colleague, said of a student's essay, "I am rather tired of this thematic/symbolic approach: what a pity there isn't more awareness of textual scholarship." Yet he knew the student in question was capable of writing very sensitive essays on Shakespeare's poetry. So, it was a dig at him really, by some rigid academic: a bibliographer he was, Paul knew. How stupid of the man to declare that he was sick of students who could show they understood the poetry of the plays. He had found a reference to the man in an old letter from Leavis given to the college library: "If people like Bingham can be appointed, then we are in deep trouble!" And that was two decades ago!

Perhaps he, Paul, was out of date? Perhaps the modern faculty was attending to something "else"? But what else was there? He was developing a feeling that his students wanted "something else" — whatever it was, it was not what he was offering — the old-fashioned slog, of reading books and responding to them.

*

He had had a bad night, still worrying about the students' truculence, and whether he would be able to cope. He drove over to college to collect his mail, and found a rather sharp letter from a tutor, pointing out that he had made a decision about a student who was applying to go over to the history of art without telling his tutor.

"Don't let it happen again," the man wrote.

Actually, Paul Grimmer got on well with most of the fellowship. At the moment, apart from one or two old feuds, they were in a benign mood, largely as the result of Blenkinson's talents. One or two had projected an image over Paul, as authoritarian or dogmatic, because of his association with the Leavis following, but those were being modified as they came to know him. But he was upset by Mentor's letter. What right had he to address him like that? It wasn't as if Directors of Studies were answerable to tutors. Then he shrugged, remembering how upset Mentor became over small issues at governing body meetings. Had he made a serious mistake, though? After all, he was very inexperienced, and there was no reason to suppose he was any good at "admin". Frances, who was very efficient and always checked everything to the last detail in her acute grammar school way, laughed at him, over the haphazard way he conducted his planning: yet the students felt he always communicated everything necessary for them, with great thoroughness. He simply Xeroxed every instruction from the faculty, sent it out, and left it to them.

Suddenly, again, he was reminded of the unpredictability of fate. He was agitating over Mentor's note, and wondering again who was behind his difficulties with his students, when, turning round the Jesus College roundabout at the end of Maids Causeway, and driving along towards Newmarket Road, he failed to notice a car which was cruising along against the curb, with its offside amber direction light beginning to wink. Suddenly the car pulled right round from his left, in front of him, intending to turn across the carriageway, to park on the opposite side. Paul aroused himself and braked hard: but there was no chance to stop and he hit the other car hard on its front off-side. It was a big old blue Ford saloon, rather decrepit and rusty in places. There was a crumpling kind of crash, a hissing of water from burst pipes falling on hot engine parts, a noisy clanging of a broken engine fan, and silence. The world stood still and a feeling of ghastly absurdity took him over. One foot was caught between the pedals and a bent panel: horrified, he pulled it free. But there was no other physical injury to anyone: the driver of the other car emerged making dramatic gestures of distress with his arms.

So, there was quite a little drama in the middle of Maids Causeway, where on the one side stood six very staid respectable Regency houses looking at the scene with their big symmetrical windows with lofty hauteur: and on the other two inquisitive horses on Midsummer Common, their shaggy necks bent over the black iron railing.

Paul Grimmer was trembling, however, because for a second he had thought he was dead. He had that awful feeling that "this is it" such as one has in an accident, when the mind seems to leave the body, which is being mishandled by the happenstance, while the consciousness like a startled bird soars away, as if trying to proclaim that whatever is going on is not happening to it. At first he thought he was trapped by the foot, and had a sudden horror of fire, of being burned alive: but with a painful wrench he had managed to get his foot away from the distorted panels.

Shakily, he got out, and inspected the damage. He knew this was the most dangerous moment of all, when the cars were locked in an impossible position, and other traffic could run into it. He thought how ridiculous it was, that the car should be incapacitated like this, only a hundred yards from his own house: that Frances would be sitting there drinking her coffee quite unaware that he had been within a whisper of being killed or injured. A horrible thought went through his head, that if he had died that moment, it would have solved the Laurel crisis, and his wife's savings would be safe.

The other man, in a crumpled blue suit was talking loudly:

he was a Turkish health worker at Addenbrooke's hospital. He was telling Paul he was responsible for the accident and must pay to have his car repaired. Paul tried to remember what you should say or should not say on such occasions, and began to write his name and address and the number of his car on a piece of paper: that was as far as he would go.

"You musta write and say you was-a responsible," said the Turk.

"Oh, no," said Paul. "I can only give you my name and address."

"But I have-ta have my car repaired," said the man, redundantly thought Paul: stupid thing to say. "You will-a have to pay. Pay me now, yes?"

"Here is my name and address. We will leave it to the insurance companies."

The Turk began to circulate his arms.

"It have happen before and I got-a nothing."

Paul shrugged. Into his head came the refrain, "We'll shoot the Turk who invented work," ludicrously. Of course it was the man's fault: but he would say nothing.

"You musta pay! Please!"

Paul tried turning his wheel and was pleased to find it was free. The engine had lost all its water, but would go enough, in a noisy kind of way, to limp round the corner. He parked his car and went back to help the Turk to wheel his alongside the curb. The man was still grumbling about Paul's culpability, but Grimmer was determined he would get no admission out of him at all. He was in dread of financial liability!

It became one of those limbo mornings when suddenly the perspective of life is shifted by such a happenstance. Paul arrived shakily home, to be greeted by a Frances who was first annoyed, that he should have crashed her car, but then pale and apprehensive for him, when she came to realise it could have been worse. They were joined for coffee by a bored and enigmatic policeman whose dark blue serge seemed to fill the small kitchen: the Turkish driver whose name was Suleiman had sent for the officer and had made a denunciatory statement. Instead of getting on with his writing, Paul had to type his statement and draw maps and plans: the policeman had measured the road and the marks on the road.

"Oh, God," cried Paul, "what an absurd waste of time!"

"And we were going to sell the car!" wailed Frances. "Whatever shall we do about that? We were only offered three hundred for it last week: now it's worth nothing."

It was a second-hand red Datsun, now over ten years old with the bodywork going cheesy. Frances had bought it, which made the episode even more humiliating for him.

"And it's not worth repairing." Paul went on, "In any case now it will be in the hands of the insurance company who will also deal with Islam."

Yet even as these considerations were going on between them, another stream of thought was going on in his mind.

About the mystery of time, which flows always, not noisily like the traffic that flubbers along on its rubber wheels all day. Every now and then, at the pedestrian crossing on Maids Causeway near their home, a motorist would make a mistake, and there would be a squeal of brakes. At that instant Paul's heart would stop: was a human being to be torn and bleeding? Or to die? Or walk away, extolling his luck!

So, with him, collecting his post — which, he realised, he had left on the seat of the battered car. Suddenly, bang! And now he might have been in the operating theatre, fighting for his life. Or in the hospital morgue — burned to death, say. One could be burned to death only yards away from one's own home. Every now and then, now that they lived in town, the sirens would go, and an ambulance or rescue vehicle would fly along, dodging in and out of the traffic, lamenting with its siren. Later one would read about the businessman burned alive in his car seat, or old Mrs Phillips hit by a bus on Victoria Avenue, who died later in hospital.

He sat at his desk trying to capture the endless flow of time which sank away: or perhaps oneself and one's desk and typewriter and pen, the carpet, the walls, the glass, all slid into it: and out of the falling film of eternally sinking time come accidents: come the trivial events — or the great dramatic moments. One day, inevitably, the film would dissolve, or fade away, and the sequence would end — for him it would end. The rest of reality would go on pouring on through into the next instant. Perhaps there were only ten years left? Perhaps only one! Or even a day?

What a mystery! And yet one lived with it happily, setting the oven for lunch. It is only when one sits in one's car seat, and the world stops, so you think "Am I dead?", "Am I hurt?" that the way in which the next flowing stretch could be utterly different, that one grasps the mystery.

Still the refrain kept coming into his head: "We'll hang the Turk who invented work!" Was it "shoot" or "hang"?

Every evening for days the health worker telephoned to demand that Paul should admit responsibility and pay for his car. He railed and abused him: Paul stuck doggedly to "no comment". He was afraid the Turk would come round and attack him. "Allah is merciful" he persuaded himself.

In the end, the garage man appointed by the inspector for the insurance company declared the car a write-off and they paid Paul £700.

"You did yourself a bit of good there," he declared.

*

Grimmer would rather have avoided the meeting, but he could not. Vaughan had passed the matter on to the master and so it had moved into an official dimension, with professional obligations in the background, and even the college statutes — though, of course, neither Atkinson nor the woman were members of the college. It was rather that there was in the lodge a sense of the presence of the university, and behind that the tacit adherence to the proper search for truth, with all the legal endorsements behind it.

But Paul shrank from witnessing the suffering of others. He had attended governing body meetings at which students were examined on the reasons for their failures, and one at which a medical student was accused of forging the entries which were supposed to show which dissections he had carried out in his anatomy work. Paul hated the glum tense silence on such occasions, the doleful air of encounter with human weakness, the awful need to punish, since the outrage had been to accepted requirements and to integrity. Of course, he had to endure such responsibilities, but it was harrowing.

But this was worse. In one sense it was positive, since what was being defended was scientific honesty, and if this collapsed, the whole pursuit of truth was threatened. He had heard of a research worker who had painted spots on his mice to get the right results. Of course, he had to go. Once the fraud was exposed, that was the end of his career. But, of course, for the man this was a dreadful moment. What Paul shrank from was witnessing such a terrible episode, when a man came to be exposed, with his life ruined.

With Atkinson it wasn't quite like that. He was believed to be in the process of stealing a march on a colleague, by pirating her work. Yet, at the same time, he had played on her emotions, and had gained her devotion, by subtle persuasions, while remaining cold and detached. It seemed to Paul horrible that a man should be capable of such double-dealing, though he knew from his reading of novels that it could be so. Such inauthenticity must be exposed. Thus, two people were going to be presented with catastrophic revelations. But Vaughan was seeking to avoid the worst professional consequences, by not making a direct challenge within the department. He wasn't even calling on the rules, written or unwritten, of the Zoology department. He had arranged an informal meeting, with Sir Martin, the master of his college, Paul, and his two colleagues, under a specious topic, to do with developments in the printing and publishing unit which he ran for various biological laboratories. Neither Atkinson nor Marilyn suspected the real purpose of the meeting, and both Paul and Vaughan were worried about the propriety of the procedure. Were they being duplicitous? Was this the much-vaunted "openness"?

"I don't know whether it's proper," said Vaughan, his big cheerful face looking glum. "If I did it in the department it would be curtains for him and that I want to avoid."

His shock of white hair stood up distractedly on his head, and his eyes did a characteristic swivel before being brought to bear on yours, as though he was scanning his arguments before speaking.

"But I suppose he could just walk out," said Paul. "Apart

from you yourself, none of us have any status where he's concerned, or Marilyn."

"I'm old-fashioned," said Vaughan. "In my younger days, this kind of thing was unthinkable. So, I'll give him a gentleman's chance . . ."

"Hand him a glass of whisky and a pistol perhaps," said Sir Martin. He could take a detached view, having seen so much in his time. He, too, hated the more painful tasks in his job, but he managed to sail through them, with the medical man's insouciance. It wasn't hardboiledness, because he was much concerned about people who put a foot wrong. It was rather that, since he had managed, in his work between science and patients in medical research to enter deeply into the human dimension, to achieve a sense of proportion, Sir Martin knew human weakness in a stark and real way, and so he was a profoundly kind man. He embraced the pain of moral teething as he had embraced mortality, in the endeavours of his research, to try to relieve human vulnerability a little.

They met in the master's ample study in the lodge, with its mahogany desk and bookcases, and its ancient globe of the world. Armchairs were disposed round the fireplace, but it was a cold springtime, and the sunlight gleamed on the brass carriage clock and the inkwell and the brass rail on the desk. There was an air of civilised thoughtfulness, which calmed Paul and Vaughan, as they moved nervously from chair to chair, and from standing by the fireplace to peer out of the window.

"Perhaps they won't come," said Vaughan, whose face was now grey and tense. As he said it, the doorbell rang, and he hastily moved out of sight his five copies of Atkinson's article, which he had had printed out from the computer.

Paul was interested that the couple came together. Vaughan didn't know whether they were living together, though he felt sure they were lovers. She came in full of charm and expectancy, smiling and looking at each person with intelligent brown eyes. She wore a neat brown wool dress with a high collar, and a frilly cream silk blouse showing under it. Paul and John were in suits, and Atkinson wore a black leather *blouson*. Paul was impressed with the woman's beauty, the bloom on her youthful face, her bright brown eyes and her gleaming dark brown hair. She was especially warm to John Vaughan, to whom, evidently, she owed a great deal.

Atkinson, however, was evidently suspicious from the first. Though he had given Marilyn his arm as they entered, he moved away from her, and went warily out into the open space by the master's desk, shaking everyone's hand automatically. He was a tall man of thirty, with a somewhat swarthy face, a bluish shadow beard, with black hair and grey eyes which were a little narrowed and also somewhat close together. Under his black jacket he wore a black and white striped shirt, but there was no elegance in his manner, and he was evidently tense. Paul was especially struck by his thin ankles, and his socks, which had clocks on. There was a slightly furtive, rat-like quality about him, Paul thought. Marilyn sat in the best armchair and clasped her hands round her knees: she seemed at home at once in the elegantly furnished study.

Vaughan's eyes had become large and the pouches under them seemed prominent, while his big black eyebrows had soared, as he glanced nervously round at everyone.

"We'll have some coffee in a moment," said Sir Martin, trying to put everyone at their ease. Atkinson cleared his throat.

"We don't quite know why we've been asked," he said, suspiciously. He was rather defiant towards Vaughan, as though he suspected him of jealousy.

"You're an English man, you say?" he said to Paul, challengingly, puzzled.

Vaughan now cleared his throat, and took the bull by the horns.

"It's my fault, and I take all the responsibility. Sir Martin here was kind enough to offer us his study and his goodly presence, and Paul Grimmer is here as another fellow, just come to see fair play."

Atkinson virtually jumped at the last phrase.

"Fair play about what?" he said, his voice dry and obviously on his guard. He looked round aggressively, wondering.

"I came here because you said you wanted to talk about your new electronic print reader. I . . ."

He obviously realised that he might give himself away, so he waited. Marilyn was beginning to look embarrassed, and somewhat on the defensive, resenting what began to look like some kind of trap.

Vaughan responded by putting forward his naivety, which wasn't assumed: it was very much of his character, and a great asset, of an old-fashioned kind.

"I'm an old-fashioned chap," he said, "and you two work in my lab, so I'm concerned about you."

"You're not in charge of our moral welfare," said Atkinson, with something of a sneer.

"No, not at all," said Vaughan. "I don't care if you're living in sin, or whatever." He ducked his head and grinned, rather shyly. "I'm talking about science."

"John, I wish you'd bring it out," said Marilyn, who was becoming agitated. "If there's something wrong, for God's sake let's have it."

"All right," said Vaughan, glumly. He produced his five papers, each set pinned with a large paper-clip, and handed them round.

"In a way, I did want to talk about printing and print-outs. This has been extracted from the bowels of Phoenix."

The woman scientist took one glance and put her hand in amazement to her lips, which had gone pale. She could see at once what was wrong.

"Ron!" she cried.

"I can explain everything," said Atkinson. "It's just a trial . . . I needed something to try on the laser printer . . . it's a joke. What are you trying to make of it?"

He was in a dark rage: his face was pale under the blue shadow, his mouth turned down in dismay, his hands shaking. But he was desperately pulling himself together to try to bluff his way out of the situation.

"But this is *my* work," said Marilyn, "look, these are my paragraphs, and I haven't even written them up into final form . . . You've put your name on it."

She was thumbing through the paper.

"And in any case, these figures aren't right — they're not modified properly. And look at this summary! It doesn't pick up some of the . . . Ron, what the *hell* were you doing with this material anyway? I lent it to you on strict trust, you know!"

She was energetically angry, furious: suddenly there was a new awareness in her.

The man began to shake his head and twist his body in an extraordinary way, faced with this exposure.

"Playing around . . . I told you, I needed something to run as a try-out . . . I . . ."

"But this was all locked away in my desk: I was working on it. I told you some of it, but I wouldn't have given it to my dearest friend . . . I *trusted* you," she said, stamping.

"Well," said Vaughan kindly, "you made a big mistake letting him have a look at it."

"Oh, John!" she wailed, "whatever has been going on?"

And at this a great sob broke from her: intelligent and well-organised as she was, her perplexed doubts were beginning to stifle her. Paul could see a physical revulsion rise in her throat and shoulders, and he realised that she was appalled to begin to realise that the man she had been in bed with all night had betrayed her, had been at the same time stealing from her, to his own advantage.

But he did not go to her side. Sir Martin did. He had a theory, from his collaboration with medical research, that it is important to touch people, to understand them. He believed that something, some psychic power passed down through touch, into those for whom one cared. And so, the big man with his genial face and white hair came over to perch on the wing of her chair, and held her shoulders as they began to heave with misery.

"Now, try to keep calm, my dear," he said, "the case has all been put before me and we asked to meet here, to avoid a much bigger detonation as there would have been, had this revelation taken place in the department. This, I may say," he said, addressing Atkinson, who stood rigid and defiant at the window, "was to safeguard you from worse consequences."

"Consequences?" said Atkinson angrily. "It's all a misunderstanding, about a technical try-out: why, you push all kinds of stuff through your print-reader, Dr Vaughan."

"Yes, I do," said John with slow, naive solidity. "But I don't send other people's work to the editor of *Nature*."

The woman leapt in her chair like a furious cat, pulling Sir Martin's arm in an involuntary convulsion.

"Ron Atkinson! You didn't!" she cried. "Whatever kind of a bastard . . .!"

She fell back, crouched in helpless misery, her hands over her face. Vaughan was holding out a copy of the paper with a letter attached, offering it to the editor.

"You see," he said, "there's an edifice of science, and there are proper procedures: and there are certain things you do not do. People nowadays do do them, but it's wrong."

"It's a sort of piracy," said Paul, feeling he ought to say something.

"What have you got to do with it?" snarled Atkinson.

"Oh," said Grimmer, "I'm only a witness. But I understand there's been a serious breach of procedures."

"And what legal status does this kangaroo court have?" Atkinson said coldly.

"Haven't you anything to say to me?" the woman pleaded. She was turning the matter over in her mind, and was evidently wrestling with the awfulness of her intimacy with this man, who had tried to steal her work. Had he only made love to her for that purpose? Her face was that of a woman betrayed, drawn, pale, as she flicked back through her memories, seeing the moments of intimacy, trust and dialogue in a new and anguished light.

"John Vaughan brought me in, to go over people's motives. What we wondered was what you would do if *Nature* had published it?"

"I can tell you, dear Paul," said Sir Martin. "He would have been thousands of miles away, having landed a post in Australia or somewhere on the strength of it."

"And what about her?"

Atkinson actually shrugged. He now seemed to have lost all interest in the woman.

"I never had any commitment to her," he said sullenly.

"You mean you never promised her anything," said Vaughan.

"It was hardly my fault she went overboard for me," said Atkinson.

"It was a bit of luck, though, wasn't it?"

Sir Martin held up his hand, still sitting with his arm round Marilyn, who sat bowed and stunned with her face covered by one hand, her hair dishevelled.

"The question of how these two adults have treated one another emotionally is not our province. But scientific integrity is: it's all part of the very *raison d'être* of a university. Now and then, we have these problems, when ambition gets the better of conscience, and people pinch other people's work. If you, Atkinson, had gone off somewhere on the strength of this paper to join some project, it would have been piracy, and a fraud. But that kind of thing occasionally happens, and all one can do is to stand together to expose it."

Atkinson opened his mouth, but shut it.

"But you have done something strange and worse. You worked on your colleague, found out what you could of her secrets, and instead of doing your own work, you tried to publish it as yours. It was of course absurd, and Paul here was right to say the motives are worth studying. This is an informal meeting, but we choose to invoke the principles of intellectual authenticity on which the pursuit of truth in a university depends. We do not propose to make a professional revelation to the faculty. But you must go: you must resign, give up your grant from the SRC, and leave Cambridge. If you don't we shall have to make an official move. But we don't want to ruin your life and career, though you don't seem to have had the same concern for Dr Langbourne. I suggest you leave now."

Atkinson gave them all a vindictive glance, but ignored Marilyn. His face was cold and withdrawn, and his body stiff with rage and frustration, as he made his way out through the hall. They heard the door close, with an awkward sudden bang, and as it shut the woman broke into silent sobs in her chair, great heaves of her body shaking the master's frame as he sat still trying to comfort her.

Paul and John went out to the kitchen where Lady Blenkinson's housekeeper was preparing a tray of coffee. They said nothing, until, bringing it back towards the study door in the handsome hall, Paul said,

"My God, that was awful!"

Vaughan pulled a face.

"But it had to be done," he said. "I'm sorry. Perhaps you don't have these problems in the arts. But what shall I do with her? It's really cracked her up."

"Wait a minute," said Paul, pausing at the door. "He may have some of his things in her flat. I wonder what we ought to do about that?"

"Hum," Vaughan pulled his face downwards. "I don't think our brief extends that far . . . oh, well, I could see her home, though, couldn't I?"

With a rather gormish grimace he went in with the tray. After they had drunk their coffee gloomily, John took his research colleague home to her flat. There, he told Paul later, they found a trilby hat, pyjamas, a briefcase, some slippers and a dressing gown belonging to Atkinson. Marilyn flung them all out of the window and they lay about among the roses on Fen Causeway for days in the rain.

*

It was a grim winter with cold rain drumming on the windowpanes in the darkness, the streets littered with a mass of rotting leaves, the garden a hopeless mass of dying growth, twigs and debris. It seemed a question of holding on, to survive: they longed for the cold spring to end. Their son Simeon had given up his "A" level course at the technical college and was working as a stage hand at the arts theatre. Because he worked late at night, he had found himself a room in a shared house in Newnham. This meant that Paul and Frances had more time together, especially at weekends. They could take their meals at a leisurely pace, have the house to themselves, and go to bed in the day. It is amazing how quiet a house in the middle of the town can be, with all the doors and windows closed, on a Saturday afternoon. They felt it was their world, and yet strange, with a tray of coffee and their clothes strewn all over the bedroom floor: then after a passionate hour, dozing off in the soft Heal's bed, to be brought back by the sun streaming in, or the telephone ringing or a roll of thunder. These intimate moments felt like a conspiracy. Yet, as they often said to one another, they had a ticket, after all.

When they woke, Paul would fetch more coffee, and they would often check off the family to remind themselves where everyone had got to: it helped to remember birthdays and other anniversaries. So, the contemplation of the family was illuminated by the glow of physical love, though now, of course, it was some years since Frances had ceased to be fertile. Their second daughter was expecting her second baby.

"When is Cressy due?"

"Any minute now, poor dear."

"I bet it will be quick this time: I bet she doesn't even get to the hospital!"

"She doesn't want to!"

"Well, there's plenty of help at home."

Cressy was working as caretaker and cleaner for a practice of GPs, in the upper part of a house in Highgate, in return for a flat on the premises, and answering the surgery telephone. A broad-hipped woman now, she already had one charming little boy of three. Her husband refurbished kitchens doing all the plumbing and carpentry and tiling himself. Cressy had given up her place at Sussex University and had hobo'd round the world, being a motor-cycle courier in London, a chambermaid in Australia, and a hostess at a *Club Méditerrané* in Mexico. She had circled the world from Indonesia, Turkey and Israel to San Francisco, until Paul's and Frances's heads swam over the atlas. They read her letters home with excitement and anxiety. Now she seemed settled in London.

She was still close to her mother, so, when this baby was born, Frances must go up to help. Cressy had telephoned with an account of the birth: it was as they predicted — her waters had broken and had drenched the midwife as she inspected, and Cressy had delivered the baby before any arrangements could be made to get her to hospital. She was into all the latest theories, and the baby was laid on her stomach to help the afterbirth away, while her husband Mike was with her all the way through.

But Frances's visit was not a success. She cooked meals and helped with the first child, Tom, but she found it difficult to cope with the flow of visitors, some of them, she thought, rather hippie types, who smoked over everyone. Frances felt ill, and remembered that someone in her office had had a severe streptococcus throat, called the Cambridge throat, while several of Cressy's swarm of visitors seemed to be ill, too. She came back to Paul drawn and exhausted, not least by the manic excitement surrounding the new arrival. Paul had been up with some supplies, and had found the small flat packed with friends and their children, together with a nurse and a midwife, all milling about on the landing. He saw the top of the new baby's head, and the tip of his nose. Cressy said she was going to call him Hercules.

A day or two later, Cressy rang, and her voice was full of anxiety.

"It's all right," she said, which convinced Paul at once that it was not all right.

"He slept right through the night last night. . . ."

"That's marvellous, surely?" Paul exclaimed.

But when she spoke next there was a sob in her voice.

"I showed him to the doctor here because I thought there might be something wrong. He sent me to hospital at once: by the time we got there he was blue."

Her voice faded away.

"Where are you, then, darling?"

He heard her gulp. Then she said,

"We're in Whittington Hospital. Hercules is on oxygen. I can stay here and sleep in a mother's ward. Maggie is coming over to see me."

The gravity of the matter suddenly struck him and he called for Frances, who was quickly on to her daughter.

"Oh, yes, transfer the charge; what does the cost matter?"

So, they waited until Cressy, who had run out of money, rang back.

"Maggie is going to her — isn't that marvellous?"

Maggie, their first daughter, had two children of her own,

and was going back to work part-time, as a primary school teacher in Primrose Hill.

"It was the same when Maggie had trouble with Jim — she gave her such a lot of help during the summer. You see, they can say things to one another they can't say to us."

"Oh, my poor Cressy — all I can do is to listen on the end of a telephone."

"Is it the flu? Is it a sore throat? What's the matter?" — this to Cressy as she reconnected from the ward trolley.

"They think he choked and got some milk into his windpipe. Then there's germs in there and they get pneumonia . . ."

"He hasn't got pneumonia!"

"In one lung, Mumma. But the doctor says he is very strong."

"He's only two weeks old!" lamented Frances.

"He'll be all right. They have pushed tubes into him. He'll be fed on a drip and they'll give him antibiotics. I asked the doctor how long it took for them to take effect, and he said, 'How long is a piece of string?' "

She laughed, a little hysterical.

Paul and Frances never saw the small infant lying in his oxygen tent, with tubes fixed to his nose. Cressy could hold his hand. She had her milk pumped from her, and it was going to feed the other babies. By calls at every few hours, they knew the ward routine exactly: indeed, their house virtually became an annexe of Ward 3B. Not only did they have reports on Hercules, but on the other babies on the ward. There was one with pneumonia like Cressy's, and others with more serious troubles.

Paul awoke several times in the night, praying that the antibiotic was beginning its work of destroying the hostile bacteria. The darkness seemed more dense than ever, as it can in March. It had always seemed to him a diabolical month, no time at all to bring a new life into the world. March was a treacherous month: and so it was proving. Frances was clearly ill now, and so she had to stay at home. All the joy of welcoming a new child to the world — the fourth boy grandchild, Lord save us — seemed destroyed, and replaced by a solemn dread. It seemed terrible enough that the infant might die: but what would be the effect on Cressy herself? Could she bear it?

As a child Cressy had always been the most mysterious one, the most spiritual one. She used, as a child, to talk quite clearly in her sleep, and her dreams were always extraordinary. They merged and emerged into her imagination, and this would generate plays, stories and paintings of a bizarre and mystical kind. As a little girl she was preoccupied with death: he recalled a long play in which all the characters strove to prevent Granny dying, by getting some badness out of her. Now she lay in a hospital ward hoping that the badness could be got out of her baby. It was clear from the way she talked that she was still in close union with the baby: that he "was" her, in that uncanny way of the nursing pair.

The Ward Sister said Baby Wise had had a comfortable night. But when Cressy rang next the news was not good.

"They've had another look at his lungs and they are both infected now."

"Oh, dear," said Paul. "You mean it's *double* pneumonia?"

"I was talking to another mother," said Cressy. "Her baby was in with double pneumonia last week and she's going home today. So he may pull through."

"May," thought Paul to himself, with a sinking heart. How brave the girl was, in this, her worst crisis ever in life.

"Is he in intensive care?" he said, full of concern.

"No. This young doctor says he thinks that would be a confession of failure. He says he's all on his own, now: we've done everything we can. But he thinks he's not too bad a colour."

That's the oxygen, thought Paul. He didn't know what to say to his daughter, about the possible death of her baby. She seemed to be bravely resigned. She sat by the infant for hours, holding his hand, waiting for some improvement. By now, of course, in the pre-war years, the infant would be dead. But the hospital were taking no chances.

"They're doing tests," Cressy said. "They explain it all to me — to see how much oxygen he's absorbing I suppose. This young doctor took tests yesterday at 11, at 4, again at 11 at night and then 3 o'clock in the morning . . . he'd been due to go off at 10."

Paul had lunch in college, hoping he could talk to some of the medical people — to invoke a bit of their magic perhaps. There was Joan Hepstall, the charming woman pathologist: he told her about the marvellous efforts the hospital doctor was making.

"Ah, well," she said, with a benign smile, "It's a little life!"

They felt helpless. They sat and waited, almost dreading to take up the phone when it rang, so perplexed to be sitting on the verge of mourning, when they had expected only joy and celebration. Cressy's first birth had been successful, but the child had had serious colic for five weeks, shrieking day and night. Its stomach had not been well enough developed. They had hoped so much the second confinement would be happier.

On the third day there was no fresh news: the baby had sunk very low. No-one said anything about his colour and the doctor in charge of the case said nothing about his tests. Cressy had had her sister Maggie, her brother and her husband to see her and had gone out for a meal with them and Tom. Everyone was now anxious about her, to see her through. Everyone now assumed the baby was dying. Paul began to wonder where one got a coffin for a baby that size.

"I can't see him surviving," Paul said miserably. "I gather with small babies the antibiotic sometimes doesn't begin to work for four days or more. It will be too late."

"Oh, poor Cressy!" Frances wailed, her eyes sunken and dark. She was doing her job mechanically, going about her tasks gloomily. She was miserable about having to stay away, because of her illness. At meal times they ate silently, listening for the telephone.

"Why should these bugs eat Cressy's baby?" said Paul.

"After all that carrying about for nine months. She's hardly got to know him. And he's such a perfect little thing . . ."

Frances could hardly speak for glumness.

"He was much hairier than Tom. His back was all black hair."

Paul frowned.

"Don't say 'was' yet, for God's sake," he protested.

Then he thought aloud.

"What do you do about burying babies?"

"Oh, the hospital would arrange that."

"And what does one *say*?"

"Well," said Frances. "I'd be concerned with my Cressy. I don't think anybody would worry about what you said over a dead baby."

"Not nowadays, you mean?"

"A little life," Joan had said. The woman was devoted to caring for human life — against pathogens. He remembered her gloom recently, when she had come back from as conference on AIDS. What was it behind that care: they all displayed it? The scientists showed it, not least Sir Martin, who was a medico ... he remembered the master bursting into tears when he announced John Berry's death to the governing body — for the vice-master whose committee had recommended Paul's appointment had died suddenly from lung cancer, only a few months later.

It was, he decided, a confidence in the human mind, in science as a product of consciousness: and all this devoted to the exercise of love. He knew that his colleagues in the medical faculty went every Sunday to visit sick members of the university in Addenbrookes. Medicine was a profession devoted to thought and to love: its roots in Ancient Greece. Though many spoke of Christian love, that wasn't the main impulse behind medicine, as manifest in the great democratic institution of the British Health Service. It was a far wider dynamic of care: it was a product of the disciplines of the humanities.

Was there, then, a source of values and meanings in this, that he could draw upon, to face the dreadful reality of a dying baby and a mourning mother? Over such problems we were, he thought, by comparison with the march of scientific medicine, still floundering. All he could think of were a few poems:

light as the dust that covers her . . .

and Mahler's *Kindertotenlieder*. Mahler running along the lake when a child was dying, shouting to a colleague, "You ass! I forbid you to ask!"

"I feel totally inadequate to the situation," he said to Frances, who nodded.

"Well," she said, "We can give her what support we can. The rest of the family is being marvellous to her. We must go up, if . . . if it gets worse . . . she *knows* we're behind her."

In her impotence, she wept, for her own grieving child.

The next morning Cressy was quite a different woman: she even spoke with a touch of her wanderer's Australian accent.

"Oh, he's quite a different baby," she cried. "He slept, and he's quite a different colour!"

"You mean a *good* colour," said Frances with a shadow in her face.

"Oh, yes," said Cressy. "The doctor says he's a lovely pink. And later today they're going to feed him some of my milk."

Recovery was slow: and after a few days there was another problem. One baby in a hundred has an imperfectly formed gullet, so that milk may leak into the windpipe. Hercules had been fed on milk for a couple of days and there were no complications. But if he went back on the breast, if his gullet was malformed, it could all happen again. So, Cressy and Hercules had to cross London in a taxi to Mount Pleasant, for a special test and X-ray. He was found to be perfectly formed.

"A nurse had to come with me," reported Cressy. "Then she had to wait: I only found out by accident that she got back here four hours after her off-duty time, because we had to wait. And she didn't say one word about it!"

The nurses in the ward loved Hercules, said Cressy. When the milk was poured down the tube into his stomach — as it reached its destination, he smiled. Everyone in the ward had gone into hoots. Now, the next concern was for Tom, Cressy's first little boy, who had been deprived of his mother for ten days by the new arrival.

Paul called Frances at her office: she was subdued, but really feeling a blissful relief. To both of them, this brought an onset of exhaustion: only now dare they admit how racked and tired they were.

"Let's have a drink on the way home?"

"Just one. I want to get home and think about my Cressy."

Secretly, Paul thought he would try to persuade her to stay out to a meal, for a celebration. After two glasses of wine in Shades Bar perhaps she would relax, and they could eat there, or even in the restaurant upstairs. They made their way to King's Parade and went down into the cellar wine bar. Paul had something of an affection for that basement: he had spent days down there in the war showing films like *Battleship Potemkin* to the Socialist Club, in 1941–2.

A rather sulky beautiful girl poured the two glasses of Muscadet. Paul drew out his cheque-book: so tied to the phone he had been, he had not been able to get himself any cash.

"I'm sorry Sir," said the lean dark manager, bustling up. "I don't take cheques for drinks. Nothing less than a meal."

Paul flung his pen down and turned apologetically to Frances who, annoyed, dug into her bag. He would have stalked out, but Frances was tired and wrought, and now embarrassed. And the drinks were poured.

"This is fucking England all right!" he exclaimed.

"Oh, darling, don't get cross."

"I shall never come here again."

"Remember poor Hercules!"

She grinned, and he mellowed a little.

Miserably, but joyfully, they clinked glasses, drank the contents, and left, glaring at the people behind the bar. At home he wrote glowingly to the authorities at Whittington Hospital, enclosing a cheque for their funds. His letter of protest to the wine-bar manager was answered by an insolent reply that described his response as "ridiculous".

*

"We're rather out of our depth, aren't we?" said Paul.

Laurel gave a grimace and shrugged his shoulders. He looked intensely vulnerable, a thin frame expecting to be broken.

"I can't judge whether O'Neill will go ahead or not."

The thin lecturer spoke softly, with his neatly insistent voice, with a breathless nervous laugh.

"It's getting very frightening. There was this Airey case; the *Private Ear* one. Twenty-five thousand pounds — and some people reckon in my case, if O'Neill wins, it could be even more."

"What would you do?"

Laurel smiled, wanly and weakly.

"Well, we've hardly begun paying our mortgage, so . . . well, I suppose we'd have to sell the house and car . . ."

"I've got nothing," said Paul. "Can they take Frances's money?"

The young man looked agitated, his face full of sensitive concern, his thin fingers agitated and signalling alarm.

"I wish you'd never written that piece."

Grimmer shrugged.

"I was angry and felt you needed backing. I didn't think of ruin. Can't we plead 'public interest'?"

"I've talked to some of our law fellows and it doesn't seem there's a hope. In my case, though, it seems he'll be in difficulties because I was simply quoted, and he'd have to prove I really said what I said. In a way it's worse for you, because you wrote the piece yourself, I'm afraid. I've consulted a barrister," said Laurel. "He says this fellow's lawyers have said they'll draw out the case, reading O'Neill's books out in court for hour after hour."

He looked ghastly.

Grimmer was glum with the sense of an imminent final disaster. It was all very well to be stalwart in Laurel's defence — but he himself only had an overdraft still. The blow might fall on Frances. She was conducting the legal business around her mother's estate, and was looking for a little house to buy, and studying investments against their old age. Now, by his chivalric gesture, he had put it all at risk. Just as they began to climb out of their trough, he had put everything in jeopardy again. Suppose Laurel's case failed and he had to pay £20,000, and costs, perhaps another £15,000 — he could himself hardly fail to be liable for £35,000 too, and this could only come out of

Frances's estate. A deep shiver of cold fear and a tremor of ominous doom went through him.

But then he shrugged. What else could he do? A sickly sense of his affinity with Harold Skimpole ran through him. Of all the characters in fiction, he most loathed Skimpole: yet he knew this because he was like the man himself. Not a villain, but with the same combination of romantic unreality, egoism and the absurd sense of superiority, of being "above" money. To prevent Frances realising the awful weakness of his character, he must keep silent. He couldn't possibly tell her.

"All very well to be insouciant about somebody else's money!" he exclaimed inwardly. Damn O'Neill, he thought: how compulsive he must be. If only, he thought, it could enter the man's mind, that he might lose, that he himself might be landed with ruin, because of the legal expenses: would he really want to draw on his wife's fortune to ruin Laurel and himself?

He tried the case on another law fellow who was in for lunch. His responses confirmed that it was no joke.

"Well," said Herbert Coxe-Wilcoxe, "you never know which way a case like that is going to go. Even a lawyer with enormous experience can't be sure. A lot depends on the judge, of course, and his feelings about the plaintiff and his story: and then the jury's sympathies. Remember Bardell v. Pickwick, old boy!"

Paul picked round his chop silent and gloomy. He had still said nothing to Frances, and this caused him deep dismay. It seemed obligatory, since he had jeopardised all their peace and security, but he didn't have the heart to tell her. If the case went wrong, this very duplicity, this essential disloyalty, would be the worst thing to bear. It would be the end, really the end. How could she go on? With a shiver, he imagined her shocked face as she gazed on the ruin of her home and marriage. And he knew he could not live without her, yet, in the shame of the recognition of his betrayal, how could he stay with her? He was appalled by the way he had landed himself in this terrible miasma of duplicity.

What would he do? He had a vague sense of fading out of life. But then he recalled his horror, when he had wasted her money before: night after night he had tossed and turned until the dawn light. But he had not faded away: he had been there in pain and distress next day. But this time? The horror of libel seemed worse than anything — worse than his mother-in-law's death, worse than the near-death of baby Hercules — because it was his failure in life that it showed up. He rose like an automaton and walked back to his room, mocked by the sunlight and the glad lights of the benign white cloudlets in the blue sky above the stone buildings.

At any time, the sky could melt like wax, and the heavens could pass away like smoke.

To prevent it, he must keep silent, and hope in his lunatic way that the court case would never happen, that O'Neill would think better of his plan.

He must be absolutely careful not to hint anything to Frances. The fact that they never discussed money ever would help. Yet, day by day, he found himself on the verge of madness, even when surrounded by the atmosphere of reason and integrity, when he was in college. He had seen some of the lapses, in which people had failed to come up to the standards of the ideal. But he was now in the worst inauthenticity of all — having ruined his wife's life — but yet unable to confide in her.

*

The annual "examination" meeting of the governing body was a marathon affair, beginning at 9.15 a.m. and taking its way all day through all the Tripos results, and then awarding the scholarships, exhibitions and prizes, or interviewing students who had failed, and deciding their future. It was always fully attended, so a closely-packed rectangle of men and women sat round a long table, old and young, wearing their black gowns and fiddling with their papers. The table was covered with a green baize cloth, and at each place was a piece of pink blotting paper and a copy of the college statutes bound in red cloth. It was all taken very seriously, and rightly so, because so many young people's futures were at stake: and every decision was bound by the law of the land.

There was little that was distinguished in his first year's English results. Paul felt that he had done all he could have done, to try to hold these students together, to see their year out. But he was pleased with some of the classes. At the beginning of the year, Aukland had been incoherent: he had sat and sat with the young man, alone, listening for something into which he could hook a remark, and so demand by interlocution the development of a sequence of coherent words. In the end he had won, and Aukland became reasonably fluent: so he had become able to put forward his intelligent and sensitive responses, instead of burbling. He had come up from a third to a two-one. Rhees, the rebel, had improved on his two-two, by becoming friendly and straight, instead of an irritatingly provocative radical, scrawling nonsense: now a two-one also. Aschenberg, as he expected, had also gained an upper second, in part I, nearly a first. He might have even gained a first had it not been for the exigencies of his love affair. In general, the results showed that the students in his subject had felt more secure, working with the team of people Paul had arranged to teach them.

So, when his results were discussed, he said,

"I've nothing much to say, except that I'm pleased that we helped Aukland to become coherent enough to get a good second, and Rhees to improve himself. The others are very much as I would have expected."

The business worked through, there was a good lunch for them all laid out on the long tables in the hall, of cold salmon with a glass of Alsace Riesling, and then a weary band of fellows dispersed for the weekend. It would be good to get some real work done, and he was looking forward to getting on with his writing in the long vacation.

Sitting in his room, tearing up the papers for the meeting, except for one or two records for the files, he heard a rustle in his letterbox. He picked up the letter and opened it. It read

Dear Grimmer,

Fellows should not at the examination meeting take personal credit for the results of their students: it is

deplorable, and I deeply regret it.
Yours sincerely,
Robert Ponsonby

Ponsonby? The pale young fellow with the slightly pop eyes? Paul had hardly been aware of him, except to note that at meals he spoke with a cold, prissy, meticulousness. But the ass! What right did he have to make such a comment? Was it so? Grimmer began to feel guilty: he was not at all certain what one should say at such meetings.

As he ruminated, he heard another rustle. An envelope of the same size and shape dropped on the mat.

Dear Grimmer,
With reference to my previous letter. Please place a full stop instead of a colon in line 4: to read "students. It is deplorable and I deeply and strongly regret it."
Yours sincerely,
Robert Ponsonby

"He's mad," said Paul to himself.

"If this isn't the bloody end."

On impulse, and really to confirm his own sanity, he telephoned the master's number.

"I'm sorry to bother you again, Sir Martin," he said in response to the cheery voice. "But I wonder what kind of a place this is?"

There was a puzzled grunt. He explained and read out both notes.

"This correction to the first letter — he's mad," said Paul.

There was a laconic pause.

"I'm afraid I've thought for a long time that Dr Ponsonby was mad."

Grimmer gasped at the tactlessness of the remark, but felt a great sense of relief. He was afraid of his own near madness being swamped by madness around him.

"Oh, I'm glad, I really wondered if I had committed some offence."

"My dear Paul," said the voice with a chuckle, "You are

quite normal and you behaved quite properly. We are delighted with your efforts — please let me have those two notes."

As he sat down, quite weary now, he realised that it must have been Ponsonby among the fellows who had been involved in the "confidential" enquiry of last year and Mrs Weekles's nonsense. That was what the master's chuckle had meant! What a sans-culotte generation they were! How old was the man? Twenty-eight: so, he had been a student some ten years ago, at the end of the sixties. It was the last kick of radical student politics, seeking to expose bad teaching, issuing reports on lecturers, checking up on the system. But gone berserk in him — since there was no call for anyone to suppose he, Paul, was ill-equipped or inefficient. It was simply some strong compulsion.

And to call him "Grimmer"! Who was this crazy youth? A wave of fury rose in Grimmer, who had not experienced such an impulse for a long time. He wanted to go and smash something into the man with his pale face and his pop eyes. But then Paul realised in a sickly way the coldly compulsive creature would like that. Dimly, the man reminded him of CICCU men who used to interfere with students, knock on their doors, and tell them they objected to their wicked sex life: how they loved getting beaten up! But he could not altogether ignore him. He wrote

> Dear Ponsonby,
> (Since we seem to be on surname terms). I fail to understand your objection. Had I not known that in fact you were leaving the college I would have raised at the governing body your involvement in the recent secret "investigation" into my work, and would have asked for your resignation.
> Yours sincerely,
> Paul Grimmer

*

This wasn't the only sudden blow, however, from the strange community of Cambridge. The hostility was strangely persistent. He began to understand how the complacency of the Establishment there had infuriated old Leavis. He had hurled himself against it all his life, until, racked and tormented, and scuttling about in a shabby old overcoat, he could be seen running to the post-box in Madingley Road, like old King Lear. Once, in a heavy storm, Paul had nearly run over him.

I'm not going to devastate myself like that, he had decided. I'm certainly not going to take Cambridge on in that evangelical way. But then, compromising here and trying to survive there, am I settling to be one of the damned, one of those "who know neither praise nor blame"? What with that thought and the misery of his involvement in the Laurel libel business, he felt inwardly anguished and spent day after day in a restless state of gloom. Each incursion that revealed the resentment at his presence deepened his sense of foreboding.

He was given to wild enthusiasms, and earlier that year one of those was the discovery of a poem by Browning, *Two in the Campagna*. He had been persuaded by Leavis against this poet: "the effect of his style was that of a frigid bluster" Leavis had declared and Browning had been dismissed by the fierce little man as coarse and unintelligent — who, then, could dare to read and enjoy him? But it was the *sans-culotte* of the third year, Rhees, who said, "You're prejudiced — read some of *Men and Women*: read *Two in the Campagna*."

Paul went home thinking, "I must do some work on Browning and show how coarse and empty he is." But then he felt doubtful: did he really know Browning? Or had he simply, for convenience, just taken over Leavis's judgement? When he sat down to the book, he was amazed by *Two in the Campagna*: why had he never come across it before?

The poem struck home, because of Browning's idealism: "I would you were all to me" — but, he felt, the man had relinquished her, or rather his image of her — allowed her in the end to be a real woman. And accepting with this his own mortality — the sense of being blown like a ball of thistle through time. Already, in the earlier part of the poem Paul had found the historical perspective deeply appealing — the perspective of the Roman Campagna with its feathery grasses, the touches of colour in the flowers and the spiders' webs

stretching from plant to plant, like the stretch of consciousness. He thought the symbolism of the poem magnificently
conveyed the reality of consciousness — the one real experience of oneself that unites what is seen — the historical relics,
the present season, the intimate presence of the other, and
one's own emotional needs. And then there was a hint of
failure that appealed to him greatly at the moment. He loved
phrases in it like

An eternal wash of air . . .

So, he had set the poem for a seminar, and found the
students were as drawn into the poem as a record of a moment
of consciousness as he was. It was above love, said Bo: but the
women were unsure about the poet's attitude to his woman.
Wasn't it still patronising and egocentric? What about her
existence, her freedom? But, protested Paul, didn't he let her
go in the end? To be herself and not just a part of himself? By
close attention to the poem they brought together all the
diffuse elements of imagery and language into a coherent
poetic logic.

So, he used the poem in a number of lectures he had been
invited to give, on poetry and subjective psychology. He gave
one at the Education Department at the University of Sussex,
on subjective disciplines, and another at Whewell's School,
one of those "progressive" public schools, to the sixth form.
He had prepared a lecture on Hardy's poetry but he threw the
Browning in as an extra, saying that he thought Browning was
here doing successfully very much the same thing as Hardy,
following the development of a moment in consciousness.

At the beginning of the next term Paul's turn came up to be
one of the examiners for the GCE examination, the college
entrance, since abolished, for the practical criticism paper.
This exam was conducted by various commitees and the
colleges took it in groups. He was never quite clear how the
exam was conducted, but it was his college's turn to provide
an examiner and he found he was setting the paper in
collaboration with a very energetic young man at Queens':
one of the newer and ambitious young men, very professional,

and challenging everything. He wondered how they would get on.

Surprisingly, they got on very well. They needed a compulsory comprehension exercise on a poem. His collaborator, Eugene Walters, he knew, was anxious to revive interest in the Victorian poets whom Leavis had dismissed.

"What about *Two in the Campagna*?" suggested Paul, looking round Walters' splendid room with its windows giving on to the River.

Surprisingly, Walters agreed at once.

"That's a lovely poem, it's true," he said, hesitantly, feeling himself surprised he agreed so easily with Grimmer of whom he was deeply suspicious and, not a little contemptuous, thinking him dull and stupid.

"It has great depths," said Paul, with great enthusiasm. "And at first glance, it's deceptively simple: looks like a ballad form. In terms of its form it will provide something for them to get their teeth into: its language is simple but needs careful attention. The syntax is all bound up with the subtlety of meaning, and the symbolism leads into a discussion, inevitably, of man-woman relationships and how they are approached. It's a very good poem for a compulsory question requiring comment."

"Well, I must say I agree: it would be hard to think of a better poem."

The summer passed on, and apart from some differences in the wording of rubrics, there were no great differences between Paul Grimmer and Dr Walters. The draft papers were submitted to various other faculty members on the exam committee and to the directors of studies in the colleges. The exam was sat for in schools all over the country and the papers were double marked. The answers to the compulsory question however were not good, revealing how limited were candidates' capacities to understand poetry. But those who could read poetry did well, and so it helped to select those who were suitable candidates for an English place.

To Paul Grimmer's astonishment some weeks after the exam his senior tutor showed him an official complaint from a senior representative in the mysterious structure conducting the examination. It had been brought to the notice of the committee that a headmaster had complained that Mr Grimmer had lectured in public, on a poem which had later been set in the GCE practical criticism paper, for which he was responsible. A serious view had been taken over this, since it meant that certain candidates had been given an advantage. For the future it was suggested that Mr Grimmer was not a suitable representative from his college among the examiners.

At first, Paul felt guilty. Had he infringed some university rule, some professional code of conduct in the conduct of examinations? He checked through his diary. Of course, he had lectured on the poem at various places during the winter, before he had even been asked to examine. Then the question was whether he should have suggested that particular poem, since he had lectured on it, for the paper in question? But he had also been lecturing on Hardy, Donne, Edward Thomas and Shakespeare: did this mean that one should never set any poem on which one had lectured or written? It seemed absurd. No wonder so many examination answers centred on obscure passages from *Timon* or *Cymbeline*: as if there were right answers for which students could be groomed, on the central works! And in any case, he had set the paper with Walters and it had been submitted to umpteen others, before it had been finally included in the printed papers.

Well, technically, it was a mistake. Yet on no occasion had anyone ever told him of the rules professionals were supposed to adhere to, in such work. How was he supposed to know?

But when he took it up with others on the examining board, he found they did take a "serious view" of the matter. What exactly were they getting at? As he told them, he had been at the time a bit obsessed with the poem, in his enthusiasm: and as for the question of having lectured on it, he had never given it a thought. He could not believe that hearing him lecture on the poem would give anyone an advantage.

But then another thought struck him, in the middle of the night, as his deeper insights began to operate at the primitive level. How did the headmaster in question come to write his protest? Again, there grew a sense of a conspiracy, an awareness of people keenly anxious to seize on any error of his to exploit it, so vehemently did they object to his appointment. A man in such a position would be unlikely to make such a connection unless it had been pointed out to him. If he did notice it, he would be unlikely to take it up, unless prompted. The implications about his work and position had again the kind of feel which emerged from all his earlier troubles: someone was trying to demonstrate he was not a suitable person for his job. Who was behind this new incident?

Suddenly, from the depths of his memory, he recalled that certain faculty members had children at Whewell School! And weren't some of them governors?

Now, they had scored a point! They had really caught him with his trousers down! They had really struck home on a technicality, in revenge: to prove they were right that he was not quite-a, quite-a, well . . . *Cambridge*. NQOC. Not only would it embarrass him, but it would get him wrong with the university. It would make him suspect — thought to be unprofessional, careless, unscholarly. If he had had any ambitions to advance his career, here was a black mark!

Of course, it was only suspicion on his part. But, having had the insight, he knew. It helped to explain the dread he often felt. There was a small minority of comfortably dug in people who "knew", who had the power, and used it with such cold deadness. They saw his appointment as some kind of outflanking of that power, that smug system of keeping Cambridge . . . what? Keeping Cambridge dead: sound, scholarly, meticulous, self-assured, efficient, but essentially dead and complacent: they called it, "being professional".

For his offence, he realised, was not so much that he had broken some absurd letter of the academic law — but that he had been untidily enthusiastic, about a work of art. The ghost of Leavis seemed very present: it was this kind of cold opposition to enthusiasm, to heresy, to any unconventionality, that had driven the old man insane. Every now and then, he caught a whiff of the same stifling processes. Well, it was hardly his ambition to be a good examiner. One of them, he noticed, polished off two of the most difficult novels by Henry James in one hour's lecture. A *tour de force*! Ah, the superiority of real intellect! He himself felt baffled by every novel he took up to teach, and could never feel such supreme confidence as was manifest in the faculty lecture list. No wonder they wanted to get rid of him!

Sir Martin was aware that Grimmer was the butt of a good deal of hostility and was puzzled by it. Every time he saw Grimmer he put an arm round his shoulder and encouraged him on. It was a remarkable gift the man had, thought Paul — to sense the need that everyone had to succeed: to know our fear of failure. From time to time he wrote a long explanatory letter to the master: but then he tore it up. How tiresome, to seek to vindicate oneself, in such detail, and be so boring. What did it matter, that one might be wrong! Why did one have to spend so much time on self-justification? Sir Martin had more sense: he always looked positively to the future, and seemed to be thinking of a good way out of every wretched confrontation and shortcoming. His reign, Paul thought, was like some benign dream come true.

We ought, Paul thought, in one of his vigils in the small hours, to be able to apply the dynamic of the university to ourselves — like he does. Hercules had been saved by science. Vaughan had dealt justice on the grounds of truth. But what about himself? Perhaps he brooded too much on the extraordinary undercurrent of spite and hate that lapped occasionally towards him, from his unseen enemies. Perhaps he was paranoid? Perhaps that was the Leavis inheritance? How should he deal with it? Well, he had taken recourse to a psychotherapist colleague, hoping the man could advise him how to avoid making things worse, at the height of the Weekles affair. With his students he saw no path other than patient and painstaking work, so that eventually the students themselves would accept him and have confidence in him. But where his betrayal of Frances was concerned, he consulted no-one, because he knew they would tell him to confide in the woman he loved, and he daren't.

Fortunately, with his students, he had been succeeding, during his second year. One of the hangers-on, of whose work he had been doubtful, was enlisting students in the older years to recruit for him among his first-year students. No-one had told Grimmer. But one day, two men said they weren't entirely satisfied with Butcher, that inadequate supervisor whom he didn't seem able to shake off.

"He doesn't seem to read up the texts before the supervisions."

"But," said Paul, "I didn't even know you were going to him. I don't accept any responsibility for him. I don't say 'Don't go': but if you go to him that's your business."

They looked puzzled. But then Peter Brown, to Paul's great satisfaction said,

"We're going to do what *you* say."

Paul said nothing. He was very pleased, at this declaration, from a second-year man, that at last he was to be trusted. But the way Brown had put it made it plain that other students, still being persuaded that he was not a satisfactory director of their studies, had been organising some kind of alternative pattern of instruction, and persuading others to adopt it. The seeds of distrust, like weed seeds lying dormant in his garden, began to sprout every year. But now the tide was turning: some were beginning to trust him.

With some students it was hopeless for him ever to try to secure their trust. Having been left without a director of studies by the college, they had come to distrust the institution itself, and had developed an angry contempt for it. A wide scattering of disgruntled individuals in one way or another had put their oar into this troubled pool. Grimmer had neither time or energy to investigate all this: he tried to float above it, like an old barge trying to cross a harbour bar, with the currents tugging and knocking at his hull.

Some of this generated its own comedy. Brian Butley, now in his third year, was one of the characters most tormented by the disturbed situation. He was a strange, pale boy, liable to sudden outbursts of fury, during which he would clench his fists and gasp for breath. Paul had never experienced anything like it in an undergraduate, and the nearest thing was a boy in a low-stream in a secondary modern school who would clench his fists until they were white as Paul passed his desk, and who seemed to be taken over with a baseless rage from time to time. He wondered whatever it was that prompted Butley's distress.

As with others in that year, Paul felt that had he worked with Butley from the beginning something might have been done for him — though he couldn't think how he had ever got into Cambridge. He was intelligent, but had as far as Grimmer could see, no particular interest in literature, and an oddly distorted mind. He would come out from time to time with the oddest comment, which Paul would find it hard to bring into the discourse at all. Faced with Blake's *Sick Rose*, he would say, in a gravelly voice,

"It just seems an unhealthy view of the world."

"Why does it?"

"Well, what does it matter whether a rose is sick or not? We're not nurserymen."

Sometimes, the effect would be that of threatening to wreck a seminar. After Paul's reading of Edward Thomas's *Old Man*, Butley thought for a while and then exclaimed,

"All the poems you give us are so *morbid*. Look at this bloke: he sees a little girl picking a flower and he winges on about his own infancy when something 'orrible happened to him in the woodshed. It's unhealthy and mouldy, really: why don't you give us something decent?"

"What sort of thing?" said Paul sharply.

"Well," said Butley, dodging the question. "What I mean is, what makes you think you have the right to pick these poems anyway? What are your *motives*?"

"I'm always ready to hand over the conduct of the seminar to anyone who has poems they like to put before us. Sometimes," he smiled, "I like to give out a poem I don't understand myself."

"Oh," said Butley, for some reason getting quite enraged. "Funny sort of director of studies you are, giving *us* poems *you* don't understand. You're supposed to be helping us get through *our* exams."

One or two of the others were getting annoyed, with Butley and the waste of time.

"If this doesn't stop," said Poppy Beldon, "I'm going. I haven't got time to waste sitting here listening to people arguing about the whole point of this seminar anyway. Not that I've got much time for them."

"Well," said Paul wearily, "I've told you what I think the purpose of the seminar is. And one of the points is to lead us into a situation in which we recognise there are no right answers. Perhaps Butley can't stand that: but it helps if we can."

There was a cold silence. Paul was alarmed: if they all walked out, he would have failed. Again, Aschenberg saved the day. In a cool and collected voice, with a smile, he said,

"Can we go back to the poem, please?"

To Paul's relief, most of them laughed: they delighted in Joel's earnestness, and took a certain sense of mature responsibility from him. They knew he thought they were being childish. He began to talk to the point about memory. And Butley was silent for the rest of the afternoon.

At the next seminar, Peter Brown said jocularly,

"Is Butley coming this week?" It was a mischievous question, but produced no more than a giggle from some.

"Mr Grimmer hopes not, I expect," said Aukland, with earnest loyalty.

The poem was Lawrence's *Man and Bat*. As usual, Paul waited until everyone seemed to be there, before he began: he hated being interrupted. It was a long poem, so he took a deep breath and began.

When I went to my room, at mid-morning.

The poem is very dramatic, and took hold from the beginning:

> . . . A bat!
> A disgusting bat
> At mid-morning . . .
>
> Out! go out!
> Round and round and round . . .

Just as Paul reached the 19th line

A bat, big as a swallow.

Brian Butley gently opened the door, and his pale face timidly entered.

> *Out, out of my room!*

cried Paul Grimmer. Butley looked startled, but couldn't believe his ears. So he paused, his eyes fixed on Paul.

> The venetian shutters I push wide
> To the free, calm upper air;
> Loop back the curtains . . .
> *Now out, out from my room!*

Because it was italicized, he declared it loudly. Paul was oblivious of Butley, so involved was he in his dramatic rendering of the poem. He was gesturing, and the last line was accompanied by a dismissive gesture at the door. Slowly, the astonished Butley began to retreat, showing a dismal pale face.

> So, to drive him out, flicking with my white handkerchief:
> *Go!*

Butley went. Paul could not understand why the students were sniffing with suppressed amusement. He took it that they were enjoying the comedy of the poem: which they were. But even more comic was the embarrassed retreat of Butley, who was feeling regret for his rudeness the previous week, but now took it that Grimmer had finished with him. They couldn't help bursting out in laughter when Paul read

> Hastily, I shook him out of the window.

At last, in the silence that followed the end of the poem, Peter Brown managed to say,
"I don't think you noticed, but Butley poked his nose in, and daren't come in. Afraid of bats, I think!" he added with quirky laugh.
It began to dawn on Paul what had happened.

"Oh, poor fellow," he said. "Do go and get him!"

Peter Brown went out to fetch Butley.

As it turned out, it was one of the best seminars they had ever had. The women began to discuss with enthusiasm their dread of mice, spiders and even butterflies.

"But you can see from this," said Aschenberg, "what he's afraid of is something in himself, that he's projecting over the bat."

"Don't talk nonsense," said Butley. "How can anyone project something out of themselves over someone else? What does it mean? You're not a magic lantern, are you?"

They all laughed, and there was no need to say anything, because it had become clear that they had all been projecting a good deal over Paul Grimmer since he arrived on the scene.

*

An important break in his academic life came when Paul Grimmer was invited to go as a visiting professor to MacMaster University, near Hamilton, in Canada. It was a significant response, he realised, from two people there who knew his work.

"Shall I go?" he asked Frances.

"Of course," she said. Then, like the business woman she was, "how much do they offer?"

"Two thousand dollars."

She gave a gasp.

"Canadian?"

"That's about a thousand pounds."

"For a fortnight's work! There's no question, surely?"

"We'll go on a Swann's Hellenic tour with the money."

"Humph!" he said, thinking that the libel damages he might have to pay would be ten times as much.

He had heard nothing from O'Neill's lawyers and it was now half-way through his second year. He could just manage the trip to Canada in the vacation at the end of the lent term.

It was not long before he sat alone in the Canadair jumbo jet, as the huge machine rushed forward with a thunder of engines, and the ugly airport buildings fell away. That was what amazed him most, the way in which the soft bumping

ceased, and the earth fell away. Then he remembered it from
long ago — the intoxicated kind of joy that comes over an air
traveller, when he leaves the ground: he had known it,
cadging lifts home in the war by bomber. Past the small oval
window flowed grey cloud: they were into another space and
time. Then, at last, after a long fast climb, the machine levelled
out into brilliant sunshine, the illuminated messages about
seat belts went out, the cabin crew got up to wheel out the
drinks trolley, and everyone relaxed.

Out of the window he could see the enormous circular
engine nacelle was faintly drifting about, in relation to the
fuselage and wings. As the whole three hundred tons of
aeroplane shot through patches of slight turbulence, the body
would float up and down a little, and the engine would shift
about like the blade of an oar in the water. A few hundred feet
below was a layer of broken white cloud which moved quite
quickly past, but below that was a lower milky layer, all ribbed
with froth, that seemed at first not to be moving at all. If he
fixed his eye on it, he could see that it was creeping steadily
past. But then it gradually cleared — and now he could see
right down to the sea. The sea was a very dark blue, but with a
glitter on it, and across it faint long lines of waves. He knew
these were moving across its surface, but they could not be
seen to be moving, and so the ocean looked like dark glass
with a shivered mass of cracks in it. Once he saw a ship, a tiny
shiver of light, with a fan of wake stretching out in an arrow
shape behind it. He felt a great elation, over the meaning of
being there, over the mysterious savage sea, approaching the
wastes of Greenland and Northern America — in the service of
learning and culture.

"The waters upon the face of the earth": it was impossible
not to feel god-like. Yet this act of traversing the wild wastes of
the world had become commonplace. Not for him: he gazed
and gazed, as the hours passed and the long stretches of cloud
and water slowly swung under the high machine. At last he
saw what looked like twists of white curds between the
clouds: it was the frozen sea off Newfoundland. And then
patches of full green and a pink rock colour: tundra or Arctic
waste. At last, in between woolly banks of cloud, the waste of

land, covered with snow. The plane swung around a great lake, and began to lose height: they were approaching Toronto.

He had been in a dream of white cloud and pale blue air, and he was surprised as the heavy machine sank into grey mist, the engine notes changing. After a while he began to find the fast passage through dark mist alarming, and he felt a last feeling of utter dependence on the skill of the pilot. Eventually, he saw what looked like a great expanse of concrete, with crack lines on it, and he supposed that the wheels would soon touch down. But then, getting his bearings, the earth dropped away: the "concrete" was snow-covered fields and the cracks were the roads. Dizzily, the perimeter of the aerodrome rose to meet them, now the great hangars, and there were thuds and bumps as the wheels were lowered. The plane began to sway a little, and the solemn detachment of the world of the sky was broken. At last, with a wild braking, the plane sank among the rushing buildings, the undercarriage bounced and rolled, the great engines roared terribly in reverse, and they came to a rest, trundling about now like an awkward bus.

For a time he was lost in the confusion of the great airport, but at last he was recognised by his host, a thin-faced ginger-haired man in a duffle-coat, and his wife, who wore her hair pulled back smooth from her forehead, and so had an archaic look, a North American farm wife look, with her pleasant sharp countenance and her thin gold spectacles. The couple looked out of place in the airport, like villagers: but then Paul, in his fresh aeronautical excitement, reflected that he was much of a villageois himself.

The Croxtons drove him in their big estate wagon down the main ugly highway from Toronto to Hamilton, and Paul became depressed, at the drab ugliness of man's earth, or at least this conurbation, compared with the beauty of the Arctic wastes he had been watching. But his mood improved as they drove off into the hills in the countryside, and it began to snow a blizzard.

The Croxtons' home was sparse but handsome, like, he supposed, a home in New England. It had a conservatory full of plants and in the plain, fine rooms, with honest pine furniture and books, there were wood fires glowing. Ann Croxton was preparing a meal, and they talked over a glass of French white wine: Paul was a little confused — he had left England at two o'clock: in his bones it was now about nine o'clock as in Britain, but only four o'clock in Ontario.

But he was also startled by finding, after traversing all that cloudy distance, people so close to his own interests: the books on the shelves, the articles Mark thrust at him, the language they used was so familiar, as the blizzard pattered noisily on the window panes. There were some of his own books! He felt he had come home, to another home. At last, after a long talk and supper, when the blizzard had stopped, Mark drove him over icy roads to the campus, where he was to stay in the president's house — a house reserved now for visitors among the pine trees. There he had a huge suite with a private bathroom and a great brass double bed. As he sank to sleep the bed drifted downwards in air pockets, and then soared back upwards on powerful wings.

*

The two weeks at MacMaster were exciting and stimulating. Paul Grimmer could hardly move without being hailed by someone who wanted to talk to him, about his work. If he went to the staff canteen for a quiet lunch on his own, when Mark and the others were occupied, he would be called at once across to someone else's table, and there would be two or three people who had heard him talk, and wanted to discuss this point or that.

The staff social club was a handsome building tucked away in a woody corner of the campus with a big hall, rather Scottish baronial, and a restaurant downstairs with waitresses and a counter display of cold foods and salads. Paul, as a visitor under the Hooker Foundation, was able to put down all his meals and wine to the institution.

Grimmer found the campus, which was arranged in a simple grid pattern, very sympathetic. MacMaster had once been a Baptist foundation, and its oldest building was in ecclesiastical Gothic stone, of the turn of the century. The rest had been built in various modern styles around big squares, now covered in snow. There were some grim modern scientific buildings, soulless and daunting, but some of the buildings were of a very human scale, with sculptures around them, groups of trees, and pleasant paths. Behind the campus the ground fell away into a forest, and just away in this forest was a large frozen lake where there were wild geese and animals. From the forest came an occasional squirrel awakened from hibernation: one day Paul and a girl student stood entranced while one of these sleepy creatures loped about on the path.

But the weather was bitterly bleak and froze severely at night. Paul was glad of his fur hat and gloves. In the evenings he ate dinner with members of the English faculty. Their talk wasn't small talk and it wasn't thought bad form to talk shop: they questioned him and answered his questions, with an openness and enthusiasm that excited him. He recognised again that openness he had experienced in America and Australia — so different from the sense one was often given in Cambridge about what was "right" and "it".

Here were people who sat together three or four times a week, exploring together difficult concepts from subjective psychology and trying to apply them to the humanities. Some of these people had worked in American universities, or in Berlin and Paris: some were practitioners in medicine and therapy: and they responded with generosity and excitement, to whatever insights he could offer, from his response to poetry and to the investigation of human nature: to his interest in consciousness.

After lunch in the club with two philosophers, one an American, he had the afternoon off. After checking through his papers he made his way to the end of the road where the president's house stood among pine trees, to a tall structure of pylons which hummed intensively, and then turned down a path towards the lake behind the campus. After only a hundred yards or so he found himself in another world. There was a foot of snow on the ground, crisp and blinding white in the sun, and it lay in smooth forms over the broken boughs and shrubs at the base of the trees which grew thick and tall in the wood. A trodden path led down to a wooden walkway across a neck of the lake, and along the shore. But the streams leading into the lake were high and the walkway was half submerged: so, he could only get across by hopping across some fallen logs and getting his feet wet on sunken slatways. There was no-one about, and the bright spring sunshine shone on stretches of pure white snow. Only half a mile from the campus he was utterly alone in a bleak desert of whiteness. A large stretch of the lake was ice-free, dark blue, with sparkling wavelets: then the rest was covered with cream-coloured ice. Three large white geese flew slowly over against the blue sky, and away in the distance he could see a flock of them like tiny white dots on the ice. Although there was no noise, and no signs of spring, there was just a hint of expectancy, as though the grip of winter was about to be broken.

He sat on a log overlooking the lake and basked in the sun. He was filled with a sense of his own good fortune, a deep sense of satisfaction. Every morning he had managed to get down to the sitting room, to a new silvery radio set, and listen in to the world service of the BBC, to hear the news bulletin. When one heard of events in Ireland and the Middle East, the world seemed torn by insanities, and events seemed to be about to decline into some cataclysm. That morning there had been a debate about the acid rain caused in industrial fumes blowing over the Canadian border from America. There was an assassination attempt here and a bomb outrage there: one could easily lose hope.

But then, he reflected, one crosses the earth, all that frozen sea, just because one has attended to other human voices, and brought them together — only to find that others are following, into the exploration of new insights. Here was the possibility of hope: that one could speak of Fairbairn on schizoid states, or Melanie Klein on envy, or Winnicott on symbolism, and be understood three thousand miles away. Here, surely, he was experiencing hope for the world, if only in the attentiveness, of one to another, as the agreeable Canadians listened to him and he listened to them, in excited openness. Last night he had had a detailed discussion with Croxton on the exact nature of John Donne's perplexed mixture of devotion to women and hostility to them, around insights he had learnt from Bo Dibbans.

He wanted to talk to Frances now: somehow the white geese had reminded him of her. With cold hands he drew her a sketch of the lake, and then climbed the hill. The path up the slope was slippery, and he had to walk in the deep snow to get a foothold, and he broke himself a stick to get a better purchase on the patches of ice which had formed where the sun had melted the snow in the day, and where it had frozen in the bitterly cold night.

What time was it? It was lunchtime in Britain. He rang her from the pay phone in the president's house, using his credit card, a phone unit placed in a kind of cupboard under the stairs. At last he heard her familiar voice. Not only did she sound as if she was speaking from a phone in the next room: he could hear chatter and the clink of glasses in the background.

"I'm giving a lunch party," she explained. "All my colleagues in the university offices. I can't talk now, really."

She sounded so formal, he was quite upset. He wanted to tell her about the great sheet of ice, and the geese: and about the meeting of minds.

"I'm having a marvellous time," was the best he could do.

"So glad for you. Ring me again tomorrow, sweetie."

" 'Sweetie'," he snarled to himself.

She sounded quite dismissive: he felt within his breast a burst of jealous rage. How could he convey how lonely he felt, so many thousands of miles away. How absurd, what a waste, he thought, casting round for some word he could use, to establish some kind of intimacy with her.

"There are white geese on a frozen lake here," he said. "They reminded me of some goose-girl story, but I can't remember what."

"Darling, I must look after my guests: I can't moon on about frozen geese."

"You're my goose-girl," he said, frantic.

She laughed, but in such a way as to show off to her little company, who were obviously listening.

"And you're my duck," she said. "Goodbye."

But she was so anxious to get rid of him. He was furious. But then he laughed at himself. And then jealous and angry again: who were all those people? Who was she flirting with? Squadron-Leader Barton, he supposed, that pompous ass who was Bursar of Winchester?

And then a strange time change came over him, developed out of the great distances he had travelled. Feeling his need for her, in a fit of homesickness, he had tried to get some kind of reassuring response from her, but she had been caught up in her own world — and the tinkling of glasses and chatter in his own home seemed evocative of her own world to which she belonged, quite apart. So, he found himself back in the situation he was in, when he first met her, and believed she belonged to another man, and had her own entourage. He remembered exactly how he felt, when he rang and, among a chatter of voices, found her having a party to which he had not been invited, belonging to a milieu from which he was excluded. And he remembered the long hard struggle by which he had brought her into a world which they could call theirs.

"But I've been married to her for thirty-five years," he said to himself, when he re-entered his splendid bedroom. He wished she were there, to share the huge brass double-bed, and to splash about in the luxurious bathroom. With two hours to fill before supper he went down to the saloon to play the big black grand piano, through Schumann's *Scenes of Childhood* and some Chopin *Nocturnes*, sadly.

That night, after his last lecture, he gloated on the fee he was to receive. A thousand pounds. But then a dismal thought overtook him, again that he might be liable for thirty times that amount! What a disaster! What a thing to bring down like a collapsing house on Frances's head! Now, he mourned for her, because she was three thousand miles away. But then, when she found out, she would be beyond reach for ever! She would be more estranged, really estranged, than she seemed just then by three thousand miles of cold distance! What had he done?

*

He heard nothing about the threatened libel case all that summer, nor well into the winter or the next spring. It was now May, and a new Easter Term, the exam term, had begun.

He crossed the road at the lights with care and chose his path carefully to avoid the patches of dog dirt on the grass of Parker's Piece. At Hobbs' Pavilion he was hailed by the figure of an unemployed derelict in a crumpled brown suit, sitting under the porch, already brandishing a bottle of cider. There was a row of them there, sitting dismally along a bench, prepared to begin their day, spacing out their swigs to fill in the vacancy of the May morning. Sometimes Paul saw them on his way home, sleeping on the benches or the grass, on newspapers, with their caps or a plastic bag stuffed with newspapers for a pillow.

By the time he reached his room he had had some interesting reflections on his role.

As he walked up Fair Street, a newspaper fly-sheet had come into view: DESTROYER SUNK IN FALKLANDS WAR. On the newsagents' stand were all the papers displaying a striking photograph of a ship exploding pyrotechnically, streaks of flame shooting into the sky.

He would rather be walking into a college to be teaching Shakespeare's *Sonnets*, he thought. But could he justify himself?

Poppy Beldon, however, did not appear. She had made a special request to discuss Shakespeare's *Sonnets*, and so Paul had spent two evenings reading them, and essays on them by L.C. Knights, Derek Traversi and William Empson. Now the wretched Poppy had stood him up, and, he supposed, was still in bed lying in the arms of some sporting oaf.

He sat down to write an angry note to her and her tutor, though he was also happy in the knowledge that he would be paid for the hour, and yet have nothing to do in it except catch up with marking essays. He sat down with satisfaction to a long one by Aschenberg on Nietzsche on Tragedy.

However, there was a knock on the door and at his call, appeared the wild figure of Dot, another awkward second year girl, clutching the pages of her dissertation.

"Oh, I'm so glad you're free!" she exclaimed. She was tousled and flushed.

"Well, I shouldn't be," he said. "Bloody Poppy has stood me up."

"I've been up all night," said Dot, who had curly fair hair and a rather doll-like face, her complexion usually peach-like and fresh, but today a bit grey. "Or, really, well I did sleep a bit. But you see — this is due in to the faculty office on Friday, and I have to get someone to type it, and I can't get it right . . ."

Dissertations had to be in by the third day of the Easter term.

She looked at him appealingly. She was not one of the hostile or difficult ones. But she was having such a good time socially Paul couldn't imagine when she did any work. She was one of those women students who leave a note apologising for not being able to get to a supervision because they have a headache, but then even as you read the note you see them out of the window hanging round some male student's neck outside the porter's lodge, having something better to do than reading mouldy old literature.

"You're not a wise virgin, in short," said Paul.

She pulled a face and looked annoyed with him, pouting rather. But then, realising he wasn't criticising her for behaving wildly, looked miserable again.

"Look," he said, "there's only one thing for it. Sit there, and I will sit here looking over your shoulder, and we will do it. I have an hour, which ought to be enough."

She wore a brown wool skirt and a grey pullover and looked almost as if she had slept in them. Because of her dismay, he felt towards her as he did towards his own daughters.

"You realise," he said, "if you don't get it in there on time, you stand a good chance of failing altogether? No-one ever *really* fails at Cambridge: but it is an awful disgrace to get a 'special'. You have to go before the governing body. I wouldn't wish that ordeal on anyone!"

Her eyes became wider and she looked remorseful.

"Perhaps I'm wrong," he said. "I don't nag people. This

isn't a grammar school. I expect students to pull themselves together, to organise themselves. But maybe I ought to badger people more. Maybe I'm a soft touch and I'm letting everyone down? Anyway — let's get at it."

It was a long essay on the "Narnia" fantasies of C.S. Lewis, about which, fortunately, he knew a great deal, as he had made a special study of them himself. The girl had some good ideas, trying to relate the symbolism of the stories to Christian mythology, but then showing where they didn't seem to square with it: where this happened, what pattern of myth was being followed?

But the essay was a mess. She wandered off, interpreting one story, then losing herself in a thicket of Jungian interpretations, switching back to a consideration of Aslan as Christ, then developing a theory of Lewis's attitudes to children. As he read quickly through, Paul broke out into a cold sweat on her behalf: how could it be organised in one or two days?

It was still early in the morning and he was suffering rather from his own laziness. If only he could have a morning in bed! But then, again, he summoned his resources: this silly young woman's career was at stake!

"The first thing to do," he said, "is to decide what you want to say. You have never decided what this essay is *about*."

She looked frightened. But then she said, "Well, I suppose if anyone asked me it is about whether these are Christian parables."

So, he took a piece of paper and drew a scheme, drawing out from her how she felt this page and that page related to it.

Damn, he thought to himself: I thought I was going to have this hour off. I've never worked so hard in my life. Damn, damn, damn, he reflected: here I am plagued with girls who let me down, girls who don't apply themselves, hostile men students — and in the background, sabotage: yet I've never worked so hard in my life! Sod the lot of you, he said to himself remembering a poignant scene about a failed comic, in a stage play, who turned to curse the reluctant audience: "Sod ya!" How could he say "Sod you!" to the whole distinguished set up of the Alma Mater?

By the end of the hour there was a scheme, which drew out

of the essay what it was she wanted to say.

"I'd leave out that page on Christian love: or reduce it to a sentence. And I'd cut down the cross-reference to *Perelandra*. Keep to the theme of Christian mythology."

"But don't you think the bit about his view of childhood is good?"

"Yes, it is good. Well, that's right — yes, you can relate his attitude to children to his Christianity. What is sin? Eating Turkish Delight? What does he mean by that? Becoming so attached to the pleasures of the world that you betray people — that makes sense. "

"I could end with that?"

"Yes, and then ask how Christian it is, to urge children to fight the good fight so, to be so aggressive."

"I suppose it depends on what you mean by the good fight?"

"Well," he said cynically, "look at the front of today's newspapers."

Someone else was knocking on the door. But Dot's dissertation was on the way to being organised into a condition which at least would earn her a third.

*

They were approaching the Tripos examinations, and Paul Grimmer was praying that no-one would be overcome by a personal crisis. Would Rosie manage? She ought to get a first. The trouble was that she had got in with some odd supervisor who was shoving her nose into a rich dose of nihilism — Sartre, Beckett, Jarry, *Crow*: but then she was intelligent enough to detach herself — she wasn't cynical, despite all her suffering. Only with Aschenberg the crisis was real — having given up the Jewish religion and Roman Catholicism, he had been left with nothing but a thousand pages of Nietzsche and Patty Blossom, but then Patty Blossom had given him up. Would he be able to hold everything together through May?

"We must go on playing the game," he said to Frances. "That's our way out. I hope, at any rate, I shall never have a student who will commit suicide because of the examinations."

Her face grew troubled: as the Secretary of the Lodgings Syndicate, she came closer to the problem at times than he ever would. To her it was no joke.

"How absurd it is, to destroy one's life, because of a mere examination!"

"Listen who's talking," he said. She had walked out of the Old Norse paper at London University, during the Blitz, and so ruined her chances of a degree. She had thought then of suicide, at twenty, she had told him. She had never got over it: and so, when it came to her driving test, she had had to take it seven times before she passed. Well, now the thought of suicide had returned to his own thinking. Yet still no word came from O'Neill's lawyers.

"It's a test of oneself," he said, "that's what's so awful. And at this stage, late adolescence, this is what it really is, it's the worst time to be tested, before one really knows who one is."

"Do you know who you are?" she laughed.

He gave her a quick scrutiny: had she heard something? Did she suspect? He poured himself another cup of coffee and drank it standing up. She was sitting at the round table having her breakfast with *The Times* propped against the marmalade.

"I play a game too," he said. "But I know who I am enough not to get them into my hair. I'm too old now,' he added ruefully, "to get wound into their crises."

"You're very much concerned about them: you're always worrying about them."

"Oh, yes, do you know — I wake up at three o'clock and I have to put the World Service news on, to prevent myself thinking about them. But I've also professionalised it: I kept myself out of it in a much clearer way than I ever did."

The conversation stuck in his mind and he remembered it throughout the day. Out of doors it was a bright, clear, hot day, with the fresh green leaves just coming on the trees. So everyone was restless, and it seemed unfair to have to sit in the rather dark room talking about literature, rather than walking in the countryside or sitting on the steps in the sun. Yet the young were excited by the spring weather and full of lively ideas.

Rosie Nicols was now in the throes of exploring the later

works of Doris Lessing, and here he found himself on more complex ground. Since she had begun work on it, he had read *The Four-Gated City* and loathed it. How was he going to be able to challenge Rosie's enthusiasm for fashionable modern novels? Who was he, to attack established reputations?

"This woman is called 'Quest'," he said, "and yet she mooches and groans about in post-war London, never enjoys anything — with one exception — but grumbles and grouses, drifts into sex with this one, and work with another. Life really isn't like that."

"Well, it must have been for her," said Rosie, who was pale with overwork and tension. Her badly ironed skirt hung on her in a pathetic way and her jumble of plastic shopping bags full of books leaned dismally against her chair.

"The one thing she enjoys," Paul went on, becoming heated, "is this act of depersonalised sex with 'Jack'."

'Yes," said the anxious girl. "She feels it is exceptional in this man, that he can live so in the body, and separate his body-life from his other faculties."

"But she *humiliates* herself," cried Paul. "She knows this man is in bed with another woman when she rings up, and will be in with another one in the morning. Yet she knowingly goes to him, and finds it 'marvellous'."

Rosie looked sad but somehow complacent, even with a touch of cynicism. She looked at him with a challenging wise stare.

"People do behave like that. They behave like that *here*," she said, making a gesture towards the college.

The boot's on the other foot now, he thought: she's trying to get *me* to recognise human potentialities for evil. Is she trying to tell me that this kind of behaviour isn't evil, or that there's no such thing? But why does every venture into modern literature have to be so disgusting, so perverse, so essentially destructive? But I must go easy on this. It was, after all, standard fare in that middle-brow world of the modern novel.

"I marked Jack down as a pervert," said Paul. "I use the word diagnostically. He seemed to me, from all I've read in case-histories, a man who hated women and sought to triumph over them, to exert a malignant power over them."

"But she *approves* of him."

"Yes, she idolizes the separation of sexuality from emotion, and there's a remarkable chapter where she attributes this to his war experience. . ."

"Being torpedoed."

"The most exciting thing in the book. But later. . ."

Rosie looked glum.

"Yes later. . ."

"Later he is shown to be acting out a fantasy of the most perverted and bestial forms of humiliation on women — and she still remembers how 'marvellous' he was."

"She doesn't altogether approve."

"She goes back to him, with the author's approval."

"I can believe she might."

"But where does the author stand? Is this the solution, depersonalised sex?"

"Do you expect authors to offer a solution?"

"I expect them to 'place' human behaviour. Certainly I do if they're trying to offer us possible solutions to 'the modern world'."

As he argued, he was aware that he had ammunition in his armoury which he couldn't use. He tried to keep their noses into the novel. At times both of them wanted to talk about their own experience. But he didn't want to know about the callousness or recklessness of the young. And he couldn't speak to her of his own experience of love: it could only be tacit, in his attitude.

To himself, he said, that kind of idolisation, of being taken by a man who has a number of women on the go, with no commitment to any one, or any consideration of love, is the idolisation of hate-sex. To anyone who has known love, in its embracement of the unique other, the spectacle is pathetic. But he couldn't speak of how in his own marriage love had risen to heights once unimaginable, a tremendous secret richness, which had all their suffering behind it, and all the effort of home and parenthood, as well as the good experiences of life. The richness was at one with the depth of the commitment, and behind it lay the triumph over fear of giving. And it went with the impossibility of speaking about it. So he could say nothing. Yet, today, he felt now beneath it all the chasm of his own treachery.

And as for her, poor girl: he knew she had suffered terribly, because her man had suddenly left her, to go back to another woman. She had given herself and, like so many men, the partner had reacted in sheer terror against the reality of the commitment. So, the idolisation of impersonal, "mere body", sexuality had a strong appeal to her. But he wasn't here to psychoanalyse Rosie — he was here to teach her the novel.

But why, in any case, he thought balefully, were they "doing" Doris Lessing rather than *Middlemarch*? He was aware again there was someone else, another of her supervisors, pushing her into all the latest trendy fashionable nihilism. She had been bringing along Genet and *Who's Afraid of Virginia Woolf*, Alfred Jarry and some terrible modern plays. Someone was doing it deliberately, that was what disconcerted him: they were using students as pawns, to challenge him, to reject his taste, his canon, his traditional stance. Even Aschenberg had come along with a brutal modern play, full of spurious nihilism ("We gotter get deeper than hate") — which Paul had tried to demonstrate was thinly sentimental when looked at carefully — despite its coarse language. By contrast *Who's Afraid* had a certain sophistication to it, and in a strange way had been valuable, as a picture of Western man and woman wanting love, but being terrified of it, and substituting hate for it.

"Well, I suppose they think I'm old-fashioned," he exclaimed.

Rosie had been packing her files away.

"Who's 'they'?" she said.

Paul pulled himself together.

"I was rambling," he said. "I was thinking of all those who bring in such nihilistic works to try on me."

"Like I do?" she asked.

"Well, some Doris Lessing isn't nihilistic: she seems to me desperate in a different kind of way. Like all that stuff about telepathy and space fiction."

"I like that," she said.

"Does it give you hope for the future?" he asked.

"She seems to think that we — we human beings — have potentialities as yet unfulfilled."

He mused for a moment.

"I want to think that, too," he said. "But I don't think it's in the area of depersonalised sex or telepathy. It is in coming closer to our human reality, not getting further away from it."

She looked very young and vulnerable as she picked up her floppy bags and left.

"Are you going to be all right?" he asked.

"Oh, I think so," she said, taking his meaning that he hoped her boyfriend crisis wasn't going to wreck her finals. "I'm pretty tough," she added, smiling.

"I'm sorry to disagree so strongly with you over Doris Lessing," he said, "when you're finishing off your dissertation on her."

"Oh, no!" she grinned, looking lively and charming. "I find it stimulating. I've really enjoyed talking about that novel."

So, he thought, as the door closed: we stick to the novel: it makes a third ground. Somewhere in the background to all that, there are big divisions. She's a bit neurotic, a bit vulnerable, and I bet that man treated her badly while he did stay with her. And then she's a sucker for the world of black, spurious, fashionable art. But then, so long as we keep to the novel, we can avoid being personal! If only I can get her into Edith Wharton!

He reflected on what Frances had said. He felt he was somewhat reluctant about learning of students' personal problems. Rosie had wanted to talk about the way she had been treated, but he had gone back to the novel. But even so, he knew in general. And he felt sure not one of his students could ever be in serious trouble, or on the verge of breakdown or suicide, without his being aware of it. They'd come to him surely?

Well he hoped so. He hoped he wasn't tempting fate, by thinking like that. But he was going to preserve his game, his impersonality. It was a form of love. The master was quite right: "We must love them even if they fail." None of them would fail, but they would have terrible life experiences. I do, he reflected: I fail. But it doesn't help people to deal with failure or pain, to promote cynicism or a sense of the worthlessness of people and values. I owe them a lot: they come in on a May morning with such fresh faces, I want to live for ever. In exchange, I shall not try to drive the smiles from their faces, and undermine their joy in life.

*

Terms at Cambridge are short and intense: eight weeks of hard slog in the two winter terms, then the Easter term, with its brief last period of teaching, and then the exam. Just as the season begins to smile, the "season of somer with the soft windes", students have to barricade themselves indoors, glued to their books, rummaging through the year's essays, ticking off subjects for revision. The end of the four teaching weeks comes as a severe shock.

"Is this the last supervision?" they say, rising reluctantly to their feet.

To some, in their last year, Paul would say,

"It's the last ever!" — causing dismay rather than delight. Instead of puzzling over the meaning of a poem, or discussing the exact nature of Grandcourt's treacherous treatment of Lydia Glasher, they would soon be tramping around for jobs, or serving in a pub or pizza restaurant, or coping with thirty difficult children in a noisy classroom, or fending off an publisher's amorous editor.

The Easter term is also the worst term for crises. Though people are as careful of mentioning it as actors are of articulating the dread name Macbeth, it is the suicide term.

Paul hoped his students would be able to place the examinations in a wider context. The important thing was their grasp of literature and their response to it. Leavis, in those years, had uttered a continual stream of bitter and sarcastic comments on the futility of the "stand-and-deliver against the clock", and had advised his students to study well the stupidity of examiners. Paul didn't take such a caustic line: but he tried a little to deflate the intense anxiety. Once he circulated a cartoon, showing one student helping another out of an atomic crater: "Are you a two-one or a two-two?": in the face of the reality of the world, what did it matter? He found relief in being sceptical.

Yet he could see that for the young men and women, it was a test, a test of the self and its capacities, just at the moment when the self was most vulnerable — just as the tender adult self was forming. One couldn't pretend that the test didn't matter. And for many it was a source of satisfaction — a pitting of the emerging new self against the strongest powers of an intellectual challenge.

He was aware, however, that this term brought out the weaknesses in some. One of the most difficult problems among his young charges was that of bereavement. In his psychoanalytical studies he had first of all explored sexual problems and then the inheritance of early infancy and the relationship with the mother. Now he was coming more and more to feel that loss by death was one of the most terrible human experiences, and he noted especially that those young men and women who had lost a parent suffered badly under stress. These, too, needed him more than the others.

There were those who came and went: they would participate in a supervision hour or a seminar, then leave happily to take their reading further. Their essays would drop neatly through the door a few days later. But there were others who lingered as the hour came to an end: could he explain this a little further? Some, like Peter Brown, a sad serious boy with big eyes, who lived alone with his mother, never seemed satisfied. He would invent reasons for stopping Paul in the college court, or as he came out of lunch. It was no good being irritated: it was important to offer what one could, in terms of the offered reason. But Paul knew very well that the demand was really an emotional one.

"I sometimes think it's a good thing," he said to Frances, "that I've taught kids in school in the bottom stream and encountered the really dickey ones."

"But you haven't so many this year who are really difficult?" she said.

"No, but at least it stops me getting stuffy with the unhappy ones. At the moment I can't move without Peter Brown pouncing on me. What with him and Aschenberg!"

"Aschenberg's different, surely? His is a crisis of belief."

"I thought so, until Wilkinson, the senior tutor, gave me the low-down on his emotional life. He has been having what William called a 'torrid' love affair with a girl who's a practising Anglican. That was why he was sitting up all night discussing nihilism and authenticity. Now she has given him up, he's into Nietzsche. . ."

"She hasn't given him up *this* term, surely?"

"If you got sick of *me*," he said, putting his arm round her, "you wouldn't care what term it was."

Sally was another, a warm-hearted easy-going Yorkshire girl, who would suddenly turn gloomy and disappear to Richmond without warning. Her mother had been left a widow just before she came up, and she sometimes couldn't bear to think of her mother being alone. Paul knew that she needed him more than the others: she would ask for a meeting with him, to discuss her progress. She couldn't get this essay organized: so, they would sit together and work through it, paragraph by paragraph.

"Look," he would say, the pages between his fingers. "On page one you set out a programme as it were: you're going to discuss the episodes in which Paul's mother exerts her power over his independence. . ."

"Her double bind," she said, in her rich Yorkshire voice.

"Well, that: by the way, if you're going to use that phrase you must explain it, and give your sources."

"Ronnie Laing."

"Ronnie to you: 'R.D.' to the examiner."

He laughed: Sally always wanted to appear so avant-garde and modern, and he played being the old fogey.

"But then you don't get to the point for five pages. You go off about the effects on the mother of the loss of the other son. I'd bring forward the excellent discussion of the episodes, where the mother's presence intrudes."

"Right," she said.

"And you ought to say more at times about the symbolism: the burnt bread, the moon."

"All right. Do you mean I should leave out the bit about William?"

"Oh, no. You're right. Think about the novel: Lawrence was writing it while he was grieving for this mother. So, in exploring bereavement he is coming to terms with his own grief. And there is something here, by which the mother's grief for William makes her attach herself too closely to the other son: and while he is working on his grief, Lawrence sees how this ghost, with that strong need, attaches itself to him."

"Aye," she said, very Yorkshire now, and thoughtful.

"But I'm running away into my own hobby-horses," Paul said, laughing. "Even if you agree, you haven't the space in this essay to explore and explain it."

I'm glad, though, he thought to himself, that it came up. On this impersonal ground, they had been discussing her, so haunted by the ghost of her father. But they had been exploring it, in supervisions on the novel, on the third ground of art, in a detached way. In that respect, he could take on the father role: but as a mirror. How easy it would be, he reflected, to cross the boundary — to hold her hand, to confide and become intimate: and so, to use a phrase a student had used, about a lecturer who had exploited her friend, to "fuck her up". Sally would often materialise, in an uncanny way, in the town, or the college grounds as if she needed to meet him: but, he knew, she could do so, because she felt safe, to use him as a surrogate father.

This kind of risk he could take, he knew, and so he could join a student in the explanation of the deepest themes of art. How long could he go on doing it? Did people tire of it? It didn't seem to pall on him at all. At times the intense sense of sharing would be at its strongest with the men. Aschenberg would say, "Look!" and then "Right!" Peter would say, "I thought. . . " And out would come some insight which was the product of many hours of work. So thrilled would Paul become that he felt he was in some male-to-male intensity that had a rich emotional quality: but then he remembered how he felt when he put his arm round Simeon, or even kissed him when he came back after a dangerous hitch-hike.

Only sometimes did the parental role become exasperating: occasionally it was comic. One Saturday afternoon in April, he and Frances had gone to bed after lunch, after a superb meal of grilled salmon and Pouilly-Fumé. The sun had sparkled in the bedroom, and theirs had been the lovely enclosed silence of having a world to themselves. He rose to wash.

"Fetch me some coffee," she murmured sleepily, lying naked in the glow of the sun through the leafy curtains.

Paul pulled on his trousers and shirt and padded downstairs in his socks. He unlocked the door and rearranged the deck chairs in the yard to look as though everything was normal. He was strangely surreptitious about his sexual life, and liked to establish a complete secrecy around his lovemaking.

To his astonishment, suddenly appeared Rosie Nicols, the girl with a pale face, the streaks down her cheeks revealing that she had been crying.

"Oh, hullo!" he said loudly, partly as a warning to Frances upstairs.

"I hope you don't mind me coming to see you. I'm having a bit of crisis."

"You look a bit like it," he said. "No, no, come in. I'm just making some coffee. Frances didn't feel very well, so she's having a rest in bed."

Afterwards, Frances said to him he needn't have said anything. The girl would hardly want to inspect the bedroom. She wasn't secretive like him and didn't care a damn.

"Does she often do that?"

Paul felt he was blushing.

"Oh, well, if she gets fed up," he said. He felt the girl was studying his state of half-dress and his sock-clad feet.

"Frances!" he called. "Here's Rosie come to coffee."

He heard her bump out of bed and begin to splash in the bathroom: thus, it became quite clear to everyone what had been going on.

"I'm sorry to interrupt your weekend," said Rosie.

"Not a bit," said Paul, filling the kettle. "You haven't interrupted anything." And a good job she hadn't, he said laughing inwardly.

Rosie was a little adenoidal, having cried so much.

"Only my boy friend has thrown me over again . . . I don't know if I can face the exams. . ."

"Oh Lord," said Paul. "Well, let's go out in the courtyard and have some coffee."

He was sad, because he liked to watch Frances washing and putting herself together, drying herself and powdering herself, and brushing her hair into shape, grumbling "I've done all this once today already." Now she had to appear all neat, in her dealing-with-the-students mood: and she would feel it was work again. The island of Saturday peace was broken.

"I wish you'd take down that notice outside your room," she would say, "telling students how to get to our house."

"Well," he'd reply, "I wouldn't want to put the girl off till Monday."

"You've had a bad year," he said to the girl, when he and she were sitting outside with their coffee under the patio umbrellas. "You were rather pale and miserable all the autumn term."

"Yes," she said. "He was bad to me then. You see, he double-timed me. He went off to Paris with someone else. But I went back to him."

"He might have chosen a better moment," said Paul. "Is this the man at Shelford?"

She sat there sipping her coffee looking pale and drawn. She had been a bright-eyed happy young woman in her first year, but this year had seemed drab and crushed: she dressed in black a lot, and seemed to have become unsure of herself. Her work had been lively and promising in the first year: now it seemed boring, and he wasn't getting the responses from her he had last year. But this kind of phenomenon he knew: the changes in growth often meant that the school child brilliance wore off. Peter Brown had been like that in his second year last year, and kept getting drunk and damaging himself walking into lamp posts — a state of affairs unthinkable in this his third.

Paul Grimmer was not anxious to draw out details of students' private lives from them: he sometimes blamed himself for not being more accessible in that counselling way. But he also knew that the tutors liked dealing with personal problems and weren't keen on directors of studies intervening. He also knew from Peter Brown himself that Rosie wasn't altogether blameless. He had heard about some of her provocative behaviour, and how the man, a graduate student, had two-timed her in revenge: he mentioned it to Peter.

"Huh!" he said. "I wonder what she means by two-timing?"

But he wouldn't say any more.

"For God's sake," said Paul now, "don't give up the exams."

Last year a girl student he hardly knew, another orphan who had lost her father, seemed to drift away into an unhappy haze. She had become what he could only call "spacey". He worried that she was on drugs. But she degraded — the Cambridge term for having a year off — and because the continuity was lost, she didn't seem to "belong" any more. She fixed up all her own teaching, and never came near him. He didn't want to lose touch like that with Rosie.

"I don't want to," moaned Rosie, pressing a handkerchief to her mouth. Paul hoped she wouldn't cry.

"Can you hold yourself together until the Tripos is over?"

"Only," she said, with a sob, "if I get out of here. I can't bear to be where I can see him. . . On the street, every day."

He thought of Polixenes' outburst, and poor tormented Othello: he remembered dimly those long past days when Frances had gone back to someone else, and he was gripped with the evil horrors of jealousy.

"Go home, then: go home for the whole fortnight. I'm sure the college would allow it. I'll speak to the master."

"I didn't think it was possible. . ."

"With Sir Martin, all things are possible," he said. "I mean, if the vice-chancellor can't fix it, then I'm a Dutchman."

It gave the girl something to do, to telephone her parents.

"When shall I go?"

"Now," said Paul, "if you like — I'll drive you."

"Oh, I can go on the train: it's only Royston."

So, Frances came down to a slightly brighter Rosie: by now the girl had become aware, by womanly intuition, that Paul and his wife had been in bed. She was a little envious, but also fascinated by the discovery. Frances, a little *de haut en bas* in her manner, as if to say what's-it-got-to-do-with-you —

I-shall-go-to-bed-with-my-husband-whenever-I-like, comm- iserated with the girl. She looked like Criseyde: "Then may I not stand here?"

"I always remember my daughter, Maggie," Paul said, "at her training college. She found this student had another — a *real* — girlfriend for the vac. She was just a stand-in."

"Oh, it wasn't like that!" protested Rosie.

"I don't say it was," said Paul. "I only mean, one becomes aware of the pain people go through."

"And how badly people can treat one another!"

"The men are brutes," said Paul.

"Not only men," said Frances.

They both had in mind the pronouncements of a psycho- therapist: "Psychopathology plays a part on both sides." Paul thought it was clear that somehow the girl needed to have a man who would treat her badly: it seemed like one of those cruel things that therapists say in case-histories. But it was often true. So, he reflected: she would go back to him: and so one must be careful what one said. All he was concerned with was that she should not ruin her career by packing the whole thing in, just at the crucial moment of the final test.

Frances was now going into closer detail, in a close conver- sation with the girl, while he clipped some dead rose-heads off the Albertine. At last he drove the girl to her digs and then to the station.

"We'll see you, then, on day one — the Tragedy paper."

"Sure," she said, dim-eyed and unhappy.

He sighed.

"What a gulf there is," he said, "between how wise we all are in the supervision room, and the world outside. We were all being so knowing I thought, last week, about Wyatt's problems over women!"

She gave a wan smile.

"The trouble at Cambridge is that you have to try to live up to this ideal of being wise and knowledgeable and you feel you ought to be 'successful'."

"Oh, I know," he said. "I've known that to destroy people — among senior members, too, I mean."

She was keen to expand on the theme and her pale face became eager.

"You're overlooked so as a student. Everyone knows everything. Well, not everything, but you're always being summed up and talked about. People are trying out their ways of dealing with things. And if they go wrong, well, there's that image of glittering success: you must be a success."

He thought of saying, "I'm not a success." Leavis used to say that, and he remembered being shocked by it — not because it acknowledged a truth, but because in a way it was hypocritical: old Leavis knew his strength as a critic and was really boasting about it: he meant "I'm not a false success," or "I'm not a worldly success" — but that made a claim to success *sub specie aeternitatis* and that was hubristic. How very vain Leavis had been, really! But he himself was really no success.

For some reason, today, students couldn't bear one to be a failure. He knew Rosie would be upset if he tried to say to her, "I'm a failure — look at all my unpublished books — I don't own a house — I can't pay my bills — I've ruined my wife probably and she doesn't know it — nobody thinks much of my work — I'm getting old and will soon have to retire on a pittance and then die."

But as he inwardly recited this to himself, he thought how comic his miserable sense of himself was, and chuckled. She gave him an odd look, wondering.

"I'm sorry to laugh," he said as they turned by the tall and ugly Catholic church. "Thank God one doesn't get a class mark for one's success in family life: or for being an author. I'd get a special! I'd have to go before the G.B.!"

"It's hard enough for students to do all the reading and the written work that's required, without aspiring to that television-inspired, boater-bedecked image of successful living," he added.

"But we women, *have* to be successful. We feel it ourselves."

"I'm not prepared to do anything about it," he said, "but I think that's why it's so good when students go out on voluntary work, in a battered wives' hostel, or the town family planning clinic, trying, as they said, to dispel ignorance. Of course, it helps them relieve their guilt at being privileged. And it gets them a bit out of the hothouse, and — that's what's so good about the young — they get satisfactions in such work, and this makes all that May Ball nonsense look trivial: that television-glittering-prizes image of Oxbridge."

"Poppy went to one of those job jamborees — it wasn't Hatchi and Hatchi but it was like that: advertising."

"Oh, God, she would!" he said.

"They were all swanning about in this posh room and one of the undergraduates went up to one of the smartly dressed men, very ambitious type. He said, 'I suppose you get tired of interviewing silly students!' 'No, sir,' the man said, 'I don't actually — I'm the waiter.' "

They laughed immoderately, in relief that they could laugh.

She left him in quite a good mood and waved recklessly if a bit wanly. But he felt exhausted: it was the listening, he decided: the need to listen carefully, for just in that attentiveness lay the clue to what they were seeking. He felt sure Rosie would be back with the same man after the examinations. Would he always mess her about at a crisis? He thought ruefully of some of the dances he had led Frances, and drove into Pemning to fetch any post. Its wide expanses gave off a solid and calm air of continuity. There was no-one about: everyone was glued to their final revision.

*

The Alps were astonishing, snowy in July, the great black folds of their bulk soaring up towards them, the folds with puddles of lake in them, and tiny green patches. What an immense excrescence on the face of the earth! Paul Grimmer stared transfixed out of the plane window into the chasms below. Frances leaned over him heavily, to look out of the same window. She had never flown before, so she hadn't chosen the seat next to the window in case she was frightened. On land, she was sometimes terrified of cliffs and sheer edges. But nothing alarmed her on the Tristar trip from Gatwick to Venice, and she spent the journey in a state of wild excitement.

At last the plane descended to the Italian coastal plain, and then turned east along the sea coast to Mestre. As it lost height the strange lung-shaped island of Venice swung into view, attached to the mainland by its long thread of causeway. It was an astonishing sight, this completely man-made city, thrust out into its lagoon, its colour from the distance the earthy red of baked tiles, criss-crossed with interstices where the canals divided it. Soon they landed at the Leonardo da Vinci Airport where they boarded a bus in a dusty corner.

At last they gazed out once again across the Giudecca Canal to the Redentore. There were the mooring posts, the launches: here were the work boats pushing to and fro. And there was the Pensione Accademia, the Salute and the Rialto bridge over the Grand Canal. It was all like a well-loved stage set.

And at the ocean terminal was the stubby little Greek cruise ship, the S.S. Orpheus, on which they were to spend the next fourteen days on a Swann's Hellenic Cruise. It was painted a strange ochre colour, with a white superstructure, and its flags fluttered vibrantly in the sea breeze. Already, they began to feel the sensation so well known to them, from their Australian trip round the world, of a slight panic in case the ship sailed without them. They had to be on board by four thirty: but this gave them just time to absorb the sun-baked sleepy feeling of the Venice alleyways and pizzas in the afternoon, and to spend a few minutes in some of the dark church interiors peering at the sacred paintings.

At length, they stood at the rear of the ship alongside the small swimming pool, listening to a cultivated English voice of a lecturer over the Tannoy, talking about the history of Venice and the Venetian empire, as the vessel gathered speed down the Canale della Giudecca. A tubby red tug, the Geminus, had helped nose it out of the mooring S. Basilio, and the little liner had glided slowly along Zattere where they could see the moored platforms used by the cafes and restaurants.

The afternoon sun was just beginning to sink in the sky, and the light had taken on that pearly, milky quality which is characteristic of the sky over the magic city. There were tugs and waterbuses fussing about in the canals, and boats rocking gently against their mooring posts. And along the shores stood the ancient buildings, their stone fronts to the water, making it look as if the city floated on the sea. The two lovely domes of the Salute offered their perfect forms to the soft light of the sky behind, and beneath them the wavelets sparkled fiercely as the sea shimmered in the afternoon breeze. At the end of the point stood the little square tower of the Customs House, with its gold globe on top, and the sculpture of a human figure — Fortuna! — standing high above it against the pearly sky.

"One sees it," Frances mused, "*through* all the paintings and literature: Desdemona was here, and Othello: Thomas Mann and Henry James: Little Dorrit even!"

"Don't make me into poor old boring Arthur Clennam," he said, laughing. "I'd like to paint it."

"You'd have to hurry!"

"And then it would just look like another imitation Canaletto. . ."

"Well, Monet made the Houses of Parliament look like Venice."

"Look now! Look now! That's quite unearthly!"

The water seemed to darken as they drew away and turned towards the exit to the sea. Sadly, the great buildings of the Salute shrank into shadow, too, against the sun and now they gathered pace still more with St Mark's and the Doges' Palace receding away behind on the port bow. In front was the wooded shore of the Isola di S. Elena, and they began to turn towards the Punta Sabbioni.

"You remember how we walked and walked, along the coast, to Jesolo — and then got that express motorboat back to the hotel? We felt so lost — and then, there we were, sitting down inside the hour, to our veal and Chianti."

There was a great stir of feelings, as a liner leaves a port, such a sense of occasion. Now, approaching the open sea, they remembered their long walk along the beach, from the Lido to the point, and the strange sadness of those lost hours, when they seemed likely to be stranded: how welcoming seemed the enclosed courts of the city as they swept back to it! But now they were going the other way. The city was sinking into the sea, and this brief glimpse was all they would have of her this time. With her went all the massive crumbling palaces, with their air of decay, corruption and evil, and the magnificence, of the tombs and sculpture, the scrolls of masonry, the Tintorettos and the Veroneses: the whole amazing concept of a city of the sea. According to the lecturer its glory ended in the fourteenth century.

"You realise," said Frances, "last time we were here, we had an overdraft of several thousands. This time, we aren't here quite so much in defiance of fate."

He tried to disguise his features as his heart sank. Little did she know what she was saying: she knew nothing of the potential ruin still facing them. He was glad he had kept it from her. But what a mockery it must make of this voyage! They had decided to put his £1,000 earned at MacMaster towards this Swann's Hellenic Tour. Well, he would try to enjoy it while he could: it would be like some unbelievable dream — and then, when they got back, he would have to face the music: the ruin music.

And then what? If he lost, she would leave him, wouldn't she? She'd have to. it would be the straw that would break the camel's back — after all her efforts to put their affairs on a sound footing, after all her sacrifices for his working career.

She would go, and he would be left. Could he live without her? He didn't think he could. But, what would he do? Whatever kind of love was this? How could he go on talking about love?

Frances had gone below deck, supposing he would follow. The domes and façades of Venice had sunk under the sea and a dark cold wind was blowing as the ship steamed out into the Adriatic: he roused himself and went off in a gloom to follow her.

*

All next day they sailed on through the blue Adriatic, swimming in the little pool and resting on the lounge chairs on deck. There was a lecture by a white-haired professor from Dublin, on Greek symbolism: the Greeks, he said, saw light as a divine manifestation. Going up and down the stairs Paul noticed that the notices said in Greek, biblically, EXODUS.

There was also a talk on ancient Mediterranean shipping, and an account of a warship of Ptolemy's with a crew of 9,000. They met a young woman teacher from Long Island, travelling all by herself, and an aunt from Bishop's Stortford with two young nephews. Frances brought out a white lace Mexican dress for dinner and her silver Mexican enamelled earrings, and looked beautiful. They danced after a dinner of poached salmon and turkey, in the lounge of the Muses and then walked out on the top deck under the full moon: the air was calm and balmy.

"It's like a reward for something," he said.

"Well," she said, "think of the blizzard in Hamilton and all those bicycle trips to nine o'clock supervisions in February.'

"And Mark Pointer got a first, Aschenberg a two-one, and even bloody Poppy Beldon got a third! And Rosie got a first too — that's marvellous! Two firsts in one year."

"You can forget them now," she said. "We're on holiday."

"That struck me this afternoon," he said, mischievously. They had come down to shower and change after swimming for the third time, and it had become inevitable that they should make love.

"More like crucifixion," she said wryly, "on those hard narrow beds."

Making love on the small ship's beds with their raised wooden sides had been a new experience. It had been wildly romantic, with the sea slapping the iron plates, and the sea's slight movement obvious. But Frances's thighs were bruised and Paul had had agonies when cramp stuck him, as he tried not to fall off the bunk.

"A very comic kind of crucifixion: a good job no-one could see us."

"I should think not."

"It must be very hard. . . No, I oughtn't to say it. . ."

"Go on!"

"Well, we can manage because we're old hands and we know one another, but some of these young fellows who are chatting the girls up — however do they manage?"

"It's supposed to be an educational tour, after all," he said, hugging her, tenderly. They were beginning to enjoy themselves, and had become relaxed at last, though he remained tormented by dark thoughts.

"Will it help you, do you think, with the Tragedy paper?"

She looked so earnest, he couldn't help laughing at her.

"I've only heard four lectures so far, and it seems to me much more perplexing than ever. These temples and even the Parthenon — apparently they weren't the by-products of an extremely efficient city. They *were* the best they could create: next door to them, the sanitary arrangements were primitive, the houses hovels. It was all quite different from the Romans, with their plumbing and hot baths. So, you have to look at those flutings cut in the columns in quite a different way."

"That effort went into the . . . what was Henry Morris's word. . .?"

"The numinous. And the same with the sports at Olympia, you see: it was a *divine* activity. I never realised that."

"You mean you can't understand the drama at all, unless you understand the whole civilisation?"

"Already I feel it's absurdly parochial, for us in the English department at Cambridge to lay such an emphasis on Greek tragedy. What can they get to know of it?"

"I hope Simeon is all right."

As soon as they relaxed, she began to think of her children.

"And Hercules."

"You can ring them all up from the ship you know, for five or six pounds a time."

"As if I would!"

"Then you'd better forget them!"

"Soon I shall be an old woman, like some of the old widows on this trip," she reflected sadly. "A lonely old woman," she added with Welsh enthusiasm.

"Steady on!" he exclaimed. "Have you got rid of me, then?"

"I suppose I do think of myself like that. . ."

She was surprised.

"A widow elect. Well, the boot might be on the other foot old girl!"

She looked sad.

"We'd never used to talk like that," she said. "I only meant to say I was glad I was going to Greece at last — it has always meant so much to me."

"At Bassaleg County Grammar School, that centre of classical culture? You're identifying with your mother, I think," he added: "She was a widow long enough."

"Poor Mumma!"

She realised she wouldn't have been able to afford to come, if it weren't for her mother's legacy: and she, poor neurotic old woman, had never got further than Llantwit Major for a holiday.

"Anyway," he said, pulling off his tie, "we've had enough of real tragedy and near tragedy. That is always sordid: old people dying in hospital is ghastly and mundane: adolescents in the agonies of broken love: babies struggling for life with tubes in their noses. It's all commonplace. In fact," he added, "it isn't tragedy at all. It isn't even myth."

"Yet the myth belongs to a place. That, I thought, was what was so marvellous about Professor Stanford's talk: the Greeks attached a myth to a place — Apollo here, the gods on Mount Olympus there. Of course, they belong to the inner world, the subjective life: but they attached them to mountains and islands. . ."

At night, they went through a rough patch and Paul dreamt of a huge Centaur, kicking the side of the ship, a great beast trying to burst out of some confinement: it was the sound of big waves striking the plates by his head. He had enjoyed their excited talk: but a horror had grown in him, even over her sadness. Once she knew about Laurel's libel action, and the threat hanging over her, she would indeed be a lonely woman — by her own choice.

*

Next day was clear and calm and the sea was smooth. They went out very early, as the ship was approaching Ithaca, sailing into the Ithaca passage. Paul Grimmer began to feel better: perhaps the horror would never really catch him up after all?

What is the connection between art and life? As the ship

sailed on his perspectives on the question opened up into new vistas. It must surely make a great difference to human life, he thought, the setting against which it is played out. What a difference there is, between the featureless housing estate and a farm in the Lake District: or a Liverpool slum and a coastal settlement like Laugharne or Portsmouth. To recall the Lake District was not a random choice, he decided, for surely the capacity of Wordsworth, Coleridge and Dorothy to see their lives with such clarity and so dramatically has much to do with the scale of that country, and the special relationship that seems to become established there, between human beings, the lakes and mountains, and the sky?

In Greece, there is this human scale: but in its significant place something more: in the beauty of the scene there is inherent a dark mystery, a deeply disturbing sense of looking through the scene, into another world.

Their first experience of this extraordinary landscape was the Ithaca passage. It was misty and the early morning light was slightly ominous because of the intense shadows: the ship was moving slowly, gliding towards the islands. At first they looked like Scottish Islands, the inner Hebrides, say: but then it was obvious they were not. The sea here was a dark indigo blue, and yet full of luminosity. The islands rose steeply from the sea, very dramatic in shape, big breast shapes, covered with dark woods.

The islands began to play tricks with the eye: at first they seemed near and familiar. Only by degrees did they come to see little lines running along the cliff-sides through the trees — roads. And so the islands could be seen to be more immense than the eye at first allowed. So they seemed to be living things, peopled as with some curious mystery.

On the right was the island of Kephallenia, rather lower and more stark than Ithaca. As the boat entered the channel they could see the village of Phiskardon and a few tiny boats. On the dark side of Ithaca itself they could see little houses perched on the slopes, and tall dark cypresses standing high among the other trees. And there, at last, as they looked back along the curved wake heaving slightly from the ship, the beach from which Odysseus is reported to have set sail.

It was all so dark, so lonely, so mysterious, so ancient, and the hills of the dark island seemed to be brooding over incalculable stetches of time: still waiting for Odysseus to return. And Paul, as he stared at the little beach in the cove remembered the sombre horror of the slaughter of the suitors. That seemed to belong to a very ancient primitive world, where certain acts had to be done: certain obligations had to be carried out. Revenge was ordained. Blood must be answered by blood, to expiate a curse. The shadowy green island sailing by them seemed like a gaunt and unrelating backcloth for appalling deeds: sailing to the conquest of Troy, obeying the gods, being a butt of the gods' whims, surviving, returning, to claim the estates stretching over the hills, rejoining Penelope with Telemachus: and then, in the end, executing the treacherous women, even: and so purging that island. Now, from its peaceful dark green bulk in the morning, it seemed to embody a dreadful fate — in which man could be caught. For miles, the ship passed through the atmosphere of a deep grave myth, looming in the lovely shapes, between the brightening blue sky and the dark sea that mirrored both sea and island, in a rich reflective harmony.

*

S.S. *Orpheus*:
just beyond Ithaca.

Dear Laurel,

I was deeply disturbed by your letter, of course: it reached me at Venice, fortunately, and was given me when I called at the purser's office for our passports, and so I was able to keep it from Frances. She has been longing for so long to get to Greece, it would be awful to spoil this holiday of a lifetime. It seems more than a holiday to us — more like a pilgrimage, to examine the whole question of the relationship between art, thought and "life" (sounds, doesn't it, like the title of a Leavis book?).

But to the matter! I was hoping the O'Neill business

would have faded out. Surely, I thought, he couldn't really bring a court action after all this time! But now you tell me it is all made worse by some scurrilous stuff in *Private Ear*, which quotes me, and then goes on, as if relaying gossip from the same source, to say outrageous things about English lecturers at Cambridge.

What I have to say will surprise you. I have not spoken to anyone about this matter at all, and have not even discussed it with Frances. I have (on your lawyer's advice) kept mum on the whole business. What can have happened?

Can you possibly send me a cutting or a Xerox? We shall be in Athens on Sunday 22nd July, surely a letter would reach there by then?

*

He had to put his notes carefully away in his case, to hide them from Frances. They seemed like a detached fragment of some distant past, like the ancient bundles of cuttings he had jettisoned at "Tallylyn" last year. Yet a horror attached to them: only, now, too, a nightmare — an unreality, in which he began to see a gleam of light.

*

"No wonder," said Paul, "it was here they began to ask about the origins of the world. And what are things made of."

"Who made the world?" said Frances: "Faustus didn't get an answer to that one."

"Thales thought that the fundamental property of things was water: or were all things derived from water? You can see why he thought like that here — everything is related to water."

"You're talking as if it was the geography that determined the thought. Nobody knows why it should be Greece, or Myletus, or Asia Minor: why should Ionian culture be so influential?"

"It's something to do with the drama of the situations of these places — it is the perfect world for self-reflection, and for the teleological."

"*The axis age*, Karl Jaspers called it: the world's mental history changed at that time. So the man said, in the lecture this morning: you didn't come," she said accusingly.

There was more dramatic setting, of course, at Olympia. Buses took them from Katakolon along a country road with maize growing and olive trees, to a small and scruffy town and then into the hills with cypresses and scrub oak. At the site it was tremendously hot, like standing in front of a furnace, and it was a relief to stand in the shadow of one olive tree, with the cicadas fluting. Paul Grimmer had brought his black umbrella, and he was glad of it. The finest of olive trees and tall cypresses behind the site with its rows of stone pillars was an intense misty blue in the heat. The site was covered with hot dun grass, and a dusty sand here and there. There were dark green fig trees growing in a scattered way. The arena itself had sand so hot it hurt the feet: it was inconceivable that anyone would run, even naked, in such heat.

The rows of columns and the pavements spoke of a gracious order: an orderliness of devotion — for it was a shrine. Perhaps most impressive were the stone slices of the fallen columns of the temple of Zeus, which an earthquake had toppled. Europe has been imitating such columns for hundreds of years: Pemning college exhibited its copies. But the broken state of the fallen glory, with its tremendous podium, and the unbearable glaring heat, revealed the great intensity, the primacy of the devotion. It was as if the whole purpose of life was to compete here with the holy body. The flutes on the columns were simple curved troughs: erect, the columns would have soared to the eye, in perfect conjunction. But to cut that stone and drag it there: to assemble it into a handsome temple — from the site one could appreciate the devotion to a great meaning, the huge transcendent meaning of the spirit breathed into the human force. The columns of the Palaestra were more elegant, against the retiring thickets of heat-baked trees and the blue shadows; but the thrown down columns of the temple of Zeus spoke of an act of consciousness that belonged to that emerging moment, when ideals, values and meanings were beginning to develop their physical expression.

Paul tried to people the place, first with the statues, melted down or burned for lime in the Middle Ages: and then with the athletes and the 40,000 spectators. For a moment he heard the noise of the populus, like some distant echo from Keats's "Ode to a Grecian Urn": but then the cicadas triumphed, and he was glad to enter the cool museum, a new building, to gaze at Praxiteles' "Hermes holding the infant wine-god Dionysus." Frances was fascinated by the strigils, the scrapers which the athletes used on their bodies.

Back on the ship they sat at a Greek dinner with a whole roast lamb, and a bottle of Hymettus, as the ship raised anchor for Knossos.

*

There was a breeze at Knossos, and while the sunlight was blindingly intense, the wind provided a relief from the heat from time to time. The buses had only taken ten minutes or so to reach the site from Heraklion.

The mountains of Crete had appeared at breakfast and had brooded at them from the edge of the sea all morning, bright and pale grey in the strong sunlight. At first they seemed part of the sky. As they came to be perceived hanging above the sea, their immensity was incredible. Later they brooded behind the city of scruffy concrete and the docks. There was a big white ferry from Piraeus, the *Candia*, and air liners were roaring overhead at regular intervals. The landscape seemed dusty, the hot wind blowing around concrete boxes, all very hideous and scruffy. The museum was packed, but they did manage in the scrum to see some brown tablets with linear "B" script on them, before catching the bus.

The site of the Palace at Knossos had a shady entrance, overgrown with olive trees and shrubs. Beyond stretched the hills also covered with olives and a few tall cypresses. They plunged down into the dark interior of the palace, to the throne room and the queen's rooms. The Greek guide, an intelligent woman called Ellen, described the plumbing arrangements, of the queen's boudoir and her private lavatory, which had some kind of flush system. Water had been brought down in clay pipes from the hills, and at points on the platforms of huge stones they were shown the underground conduits: the waste had been taken away by a long circuitous route so as not to foul the stream. There was also a separate system for the rainwater.

At the side of the rising walls of the palace was a wide flight of steps constructed in pale stone, and below it ran between high stone banks that sloped back a long paved street. Rising above it here and there were dark cypresses and at the top of the banks were shrubs. Once, in the Minoan city, this had been a street of shops. The steps led up to a stepped theatrical area, which had tiers on both sides.

This seemed to Paul Grimmer the most exciting and dramatic place in the palace site, and there he watched Frances, in a straw hat, holding it on against the breeze, meditating in her excited way. The changes from sea to land, the shifting of the ship's time as they sailed across the Mediterranean, and the heat, especially the change from the shadowy interior of the Minoan palace to the intense sunlight of the stone platforms without, had given him a strange feeling of suspension of consciousness, and so a feeling of being out of time. Some of the mural paintings, meticulously based on the originals, were so modern: there were twisted ribbons in the designs that could have been done in the last hundred years, whether in William Morris's Victorian England or the period of Nouveau Art in England and America, or even in today's optical designs. It was impossible to stretch one's mind back, through forty centuries, to the great Minoan age. He tried to think of his grandfather, who had lived eighty years ago, and then multiply that time by fifty: but the mathematics simply slipped out of engagement with any reality. And when he looked up past the sculptured form of the double horn, echoing the double axe, out to the hill from whence the water ducts flowed, the engineering feat seemed as if it had been done yesterday — though the Greeks, a millenium and a half later, had not the same ingenuity and concern with plumbing.

Here were found stored the linear "B" scripts, and this provided a link back to Cambridge, for one of the fellows of his own college had helped Michael Ventris to decipher them: and yet they were only inventories of the stores, the contents of the jars, the armour, chariots and sacrifices.

Everywhere they went, they toiled round human attempts to off-set the great ruins of time. He was still thoughtful about the great slabs of stone at Olympia, thrown down by Poseidon. And here, it seemed, the whole had been burnt and buried by some vast cataclysm. All that they now wandered so freely around had been painstakingly dug out, under the direction of studious Western minds.

So that Frances could stand there, enthralled, holding on her straw hat, gazing down the long stone pavement which seemed in its sunlit emptiness, to be waiting for a procession. The small slight woman wore a simple white cotton frock with bare shoulders that billowed in the breeze, bare legs and pink canvas espadrilles. She looked like the frailest of butterflies, against the broad stone steps leading to the theatre platform: and yet he knew her to be a tough and determined woman, with something of her mother's will. She went swimming a great deal in the summer, and so her upper arms and shoulders were well developed. He knew he had been attracted to her by her apparent vulnerability, yet he knew that really she was not vulnerable at all, but a woman of remarkable resources. Why it had to happen at this moment in Knossos, he could not think, but because of the expansion of his perspectives of time, he was able suddenly to see her more clearly as a person in her life totally apart from him. Usually, he projected an image over her, that threw over her the image of the women he loved: but they had tried to learn not to idealize a long time ago. In the heat and deep shadow of Knossos the projected image was torn away. He didn't love her any less: indeed, he felt he was loving the real woman more, since to discover her in her time revealed to him the mystery of her existence. The more mortal she seemed, that butterfly figure in the stone arena, the more he felt he knew who she was. And now, though he felt her mortality more keenly on this trip, a slight ray of hope had appeared, to illuminate the darkness of his deepest fears, even as they seemed to have justification to get worse. Thank God, the visits and talks took his mind off his obsessions. But have I destroyed her, he thought?

*

She turned to him with a bright happy glance, his heart leapt.

"Oh, I love it here, this causeway!" she said, "isn't it marvellous — so dramatic?"

"But what can you see, coming up the way to the theatre? What kind of a procession?"

"We shall never know. But I can only see it as joyful: to do with sunlight and wine, and the gaiety that's in those friezes. . ."

"But then the volcano blew its top," he said. "It must have been like several hydrogen bombs."

She sighed.

"Did you see in the museum: the survivors tried to imitate the Minoan artefacts, the sculptures and figures, after the devastation. But they couldn't do it! They were grotesque gestures only!"

"It wasn't only that there weren't enough of them. It was as if consciousness itself had been wounded: as though some overpowering forgetfulness had overtaken them."

"And the delicacy had gone. That lovely gold earring with the two bees at a drop of honey — a lovely piece of life. It's on the museum ticket, look!"

He took it out of his pocket. He sighed, and put it back. It would go into the family scrap-book like his photograph of her holding her hat on the causeway.

"It could happen to us, of course. After the nuclear war, only a pathetic mutation of civilisation."

Oddly, the great edifice of human failure, in the face of the devastations of time, which the palace of Knossos was, and which she could have taken as a symbol of the looming failure of her own marriage, excited Frances. Here she was, as a happy butterfly, feeding on the bright gleams of the perspectives, against the pointed cypress trees and the olive groves, against the pale brown and white sterile hills beyond.

"There was a day of strong south wind, and the throne room was left in confusion," he read.

She nodded.

"Then they tried to pull a little of it together. The tiny

shrine of the double axe belongs to this period."

"The tiny shrine of the double axe," she said, wryly.

He knew she was thinking of her mother's death, and the dismantling of her own family home. But he also knew, having reflected on time and property, that she was preparing herself for widowhood. He had noticed her fascination with the widows on board: and at home before they left with widows of their acquaintance. After meeting each one for lunch she would talk about the woman's loneliness and sigh.

"I'm not going yet," he said to himself. But every site they visited spoke to him of the doom that can overtake man . . .

*

Dear Laurel,

I was glad I was able to get through from Heraklion: it was so hot in that telephone cabin, and I had a terrible feeling of imminent disaster, as though another Santorini was going off. Which in a way it was.

I shall have to wait until I get home, to see what legal letters are lying on my mat. But your report horrifies me: are O'Neill's lawyers now thinking they'll get more out of me than they would out of you? You say you rang them and they told you that they had issued writs against me "with even greater confidence that they will win their client's case and win recompense". But does that mean they've dropped the action against you?

"Dr O'Neill's beliefs on revolution were felt by the faculty to be outrageous"; "it was common knowledge that he carried a picture of Joseph Stalin in his wallet". These were the two extracts you quoted, but they are things I could never have said, since I know nothing about the man. If they are true, I'm amused; but I never said them because I have not spoken to anyone. But how can I prove this?

I ought, I suppose, to fly home and face the music. I suppose I must consult lawyers myself, damn it: all libel is a minefield and there could be a hell of a bill. But how do you prove that you were never interviewed by a journalist when he reports you were? Is *Private Ear* being sued? The things you quoted were nonsensical, surely?

These are rhetorical questions. I don't suppose there's anything I can do from the Aegean. Do get all the advice you can to pass on to me.

*

As the ship left Crete for Alexandria, they enjoyed a Greek dinner, with blue and white flags strung round the dining room and the waiters in Greek costume. There was taramosalata on the menu, with dolmades, rice patties in vine leaves, youvalarkia meat balls, fried chicken livers, kalamari — little octopus, and tiropitakia, cheese pie. These hors d'oeuvres were followed by arni souvlas parmassos, baby lamb roast in the country style, which the cooks brought round on a spit to Greek folksong with a concertina and bells. There was a honey sweet, baklava, and feta cheese. They drank ouzo, then a bottle of Hymettus and later some more ouzo.

Their company at table was the lady from Bishop's Stortford, who was a recent widow, travelling with her two young and timid nephews. Her husband had been a colonel in the 7th/8th Royal Hussars and he had been 24 in 1914: so, when he died the previous Christmas, he had been 94. She was thirty years younger, and had obviously adored him. She told a long tale over dinner how she had arranged horses for his funeral and a bugler from Colchester Barracks. It was a real tale of devoted widowhood, but Frances didn't respond sympathetically at all to this tale of life-long girlish devotion to a male ideal.

She had had too much ouzo, and began to glower: Paul could see trouble was coming. They moved off after dinner to the lounge for dancing, and tried to foxtrot: but he couldn't manage it and was clumsy. He felt her go suddenly stiff and hostile, and she slid away from him saying nothing. He shrugged his shoulders and sat alone for a while watching the others. At last he made his way down to the cabin, but she was not there. The corridors were deserted and quiet, with only the vibrating sound of the ship's movement.

He became worried. What if she was unsteady with drink and had slipped on a stairway? She could cut her head open or break a leg. Or — horror — she might even slip overboard? Sure, they weren't going to re-enact *The Family Reunion*? He ridiculed the thought, but then in his mind's eye he could see her, unsteadily moving along the rail hand by hand, and then perhaps coming upon a gangplank entrance not properly fastened, and falling, with a cry, into the sea. He grunted and rose to his feet at the awful thought. He was angry with her, for slipping away from the table in such a rude way, obviously snubbing the cavalry widow, but now he broke out into a sweat at the danger he supposed his wife to be in. He was overwhelmed by guilt, too. Perhaps she had found out his secret? What nonsense! But she might have suspected from his manner? She might well have divined that, in some way, he had a secret which was inimical to her? His secret horror, that he would lose her anyway at the end of this trip, welled up and gripped him. He began to panic and run about the ship.

She was not on the starboard promenade deck, nor in the swimming pool area: as he came round towards the port side he gasped, for there was a huge orange moon hanging over the sea where Crete and its immense mountains had receded a few hours before.

How can one describe the way the moon and stars hang in the sky, over calm seas nearer the Equator and in the tropics? In England, they seem to be away beyond a great sheet of glass, the stars remote white fire, the moon a distant stone face. Here in the Mediterranean towards Africa, they hung close in an intimate way, warm and glowing fires, as if one could touch them. They come forward, as if to hand, while the moon looks like a huge lantern put out to light the ship on its course. Both the moon and stars seemed much bigger than the Northern ones, and the stars were not white but multi-coloured, pale pinks and blues, and they winked voluptuously rather than glittered. At last, there beneath them, looking over the prow, beyond the screen beneath the bridge, on the passengers' foredeck, was the dark figure of Frances, strangely statuesque. All her anger had evaporated at the spectacle of the hanging fires. Behind the ship to the port side was a long line of watery fire too, the reflection of the moon. All the fruits of the night voyaged with the ship, as if to accompany her.

The beauty of the night, which was warm and balmy, with a faint smell of Africa, was only to be compared with a scene from some ancient odyssey.

Paul Grimmer knew enough about Frances to be careful not to refer to her rudeness or her giddiness under the influence of the ouzo. He could see from the dark glow of her eyes in the starlight that she was responding deeply to the mystery of the African night, and he had no wish to spoil her mood. For a dreadful moment, he thought he would have to confess to her. Now she had recovered, there was no need. He simply stood beside her, silently. On the foredeck it was just possible to see the prow darkly urging forward over the dark sea like a thrusting shadow.

"It's like sailing to another world," he said.

"If only one could," she said bitterly. "No, I'll not say that. I won't . . . No. We are all dead, and we are sailing to the land of the dead."

So, he thought, she left the table because the widow's account had upset her: it wasn't that she was protesting that the woman was boring, was of a dull social class. It was somewhat morbid: but he had found it fascinating. Never mind.

"Where shall we wake tomorrow, then?" he asked.

"In the tomb," she said, darkly.

All next day, which was at sea, they swam and sunbathed in the sunshine. But both had slept badly, tormented by the sense of imminent death that had come to them under the hung lamps of the Mediterranean night.

The sea was calm, and all that could be heard during the night was the light slap of little waves on the hull. But Paul, catching her metaphor, heard these noises as the moments of time rapidly passing. How old was he now? Sixty. How long had he got? Perhaps ten years, perhaps fifteen. He felt it was a voyage, the ship coming to land eventually: but then he would be dispersed into that blackness between the stars. He would never again be able to see such a beautiful sight. There would be a time soon when he would see no sight at all. He tried to imagine it, but failed. All he could think was that there was once a time before he existed: he didn't after all, grieve about that. Where was he at the time of Knossos? So, what did it matter that he would not be here when New York was a ruin? All that was needed was some trick in consciousness with time, to distance oneself from it, and be glad that one had existed.

But then, the last years! Suddenly, a cold draught of realism flowed over him, as if it came through the ventilator, quietly blowing cool air with a hiss over him. A little passage of successful service, ending in ruin. Before long, he would have to retire! He had never really thought about it. Now, what would they live on? For so long he had put nothing away for his pension: then, a few years' contribution to a small pension. Now, imminent ruin, and final penury. It was absurd to have spent so much on this voyage. He should have put the money he had spent on this cruise towards his pension. So, he began to reproach himself. Now, there was nothing but stark ruin left.

"Oh, God," he groaned inwardly turning over.

He went in detail through his own failures. Not that he felt he should have done anything else. But he had invented this life for himself as an author, and it hadn't come off. The same was true of many of their friends: the Andersons and their market-gardening venture; the Simpsons and their pigs, which all got swine fever. What no-one budgeted for was failure. He thought of Sir Martin's dictum: "Even if they fail . . ." But how if one goes on failing?

And then, smiling into oblivion as now they sailed eastwards into darkness, there again came a sense that it no longer mattered whether one was a failure or not. One took nothing away from this world anyway. At one point, he broke out into a cold sweat, thinking of the burden he might leave Frances. But he wasn't leaving Frances, something in him protested. Suppose he did, though? He had made a list of all his unpublished books before he left and had deposited it in a drawer in the study. But who would cope with all that *inédit* work? Each would be hours and hours of work for him, seeing them through the press. No-one else could do it: no-one should be asked to tackle such a problem. It would be better to dump it all in the sea.

The vases and little figurines — the Heraklion museum, the terracotta tablets of linear "B" — merged with the manuscripts piled on his study shelves, his files of letters and his paintings. He wondered which of his children would have the grand piano, and which the sofa? Frances's mother's grandfather clock and linen chest were being moved into a museum, while tourists tramped through their little house in Cambridge.

"But we are not emperors and kings," he said to himself.

"We are nothing!"

"We are nothing!" he whispered to himself.

Frances grunted and turned over in exasperation in her narrow bunk.

"For Christ's sake, darling," she growled, "stop saying we are nothing and go to sleep!"

He felt a great wave of love for her, half awake in the night. But then he remembered how he had secretly put all their belongings in jeopardy, by his rash article in support of Laurel. He broke out in another cold sweat and went down further into a tormented engagement with his dread of the future and the weaknesses of his own character. The ship now seemed to be sailing on recklessly, into some appalling danger.

*

The desert was beautiful even from the window of a tourist bus. Grimmer fell in love with the desert. It beckoned from its enormous inhuman sea of golden sand.

At first there were one-storey buildings with high towers full of holes for the birds. Every now and then there was a squalid factory yard. There were occasional palm trees, and an occasional donkey or camel with a figure sitting on it. All along the desert road were bill-boards, advertising insect sprays, tyres and oil.

But then the desert began, and although it was only a corner of the desert, Paul knew that one could march across it to Libya, and to cross the whole of the North of Africa, into the Sahara. There was a heavy mist, and the sands only appeared fitfully at first. But Paul loved the pure aridity of the desert as he loved the sea: it stretched and stretched away under the morning sun, pink and creamy, marked with its own waves and natural wind patterns, beyond the long line of telegraph poles. It beckoned, the desert: but then what it offered was a different kind of purity — one's white bones bleaching in the sand. Here and there was a cluster of small low skin tents, of desert dwellers, Bedouins perhaps?

But then they drove into the twentieth century again: after two hours' travel across the naked sand, army camps, with thousands of men. Thousands of men in serried ranks, doing exercises in the barrack yards, weapons, army cars: and on lorries pulling on to the roads, great missiles strapped and bolted. To the merciless sweep of the desert sand was added the fever and fury of preparation for fire and death. Only one of the rockets strapped to a lorry could have turned acres of that desert into fertile land, where at present the Egyptian government strove to transform it, here and there, with a few scrubby patches of shrub-planting.

Cairo at first seemed richer and more civilised than Alexandria: but this was Gizeh, with its palm-trees and tourist hotels. The pyramids were astonishing, rising snub-topped and geometrical behind the apartment houses. They drew up beneath them at nine o'clock, while the camel boys in their blue smocks were still sleepy and the tourists had only begun to arrive. The camels were richly decorated, and smelt horrible, releasing wind noisily, while the air became full of flies.

The first pyramid rose above them like a mountain, the huge blocks of stone burning in the early morning sun. Only the rough immense squares of stone were visible, tier upon tier: the white marble had all disappeared over the millenia, except from the top cap of the largest pyramid. Obediently, they went down into the Mastabas, and listened to a lecture on the lower shelves of the massive Pyramid of Chefren. They visited the Solar Boat of Cheops in its new museum, putting on special big felt slippers. And there Paul picked up again the image from Frances's moody gaze into the darkness of the sea. Everything they saw seemed now to speak of the final journey — the desert, the massive tombs, the boat made of dark cedar wood in which to sail to another world. The boat was huge, built of massive planks sixty feet long, tied together with ropes. It was to be impelled by immense oars and there were small pavilions on the great decks. Yet all this had been lain buried, dismantled and ready for assembly, in a pit at the foot of the pyramid, for six thousand years.

To go where? Across the sky? Across the desert? Across the sea? Only to an imaginary destination. There seemed to be a primary need in man, to seek to voyage to some other life, beyond this one. Oh, curse of consciousness, that one should be aware of one's dreadful fate: to be able to see and know the world, its curved surfaces, its vapours and skies, its sun, moon, and stars: and know that one must leave it. But then comes the protest — the desire not to leave. And so, with the great ones, the power is expended, so that thousands upon thousands of slaves, whose lives do not count, and whose death is not worth a kick, pull stones up immense inclines, to form a pyramid that shall last for ever: shall create boats never to be used except for the last voyage — to that "other" state: by the existence of which the present mortality can be denied. For the great boat was buried, in pieces, ready for assembly, in a huge stone pit in the ground until now.

So, into the dark tunnel of the interior of the pyramid. They descended through a gate, and began to clamber about inside a dimly lit tunnel. Some of the steps were very high, and some of the older visitors with them became quite hysterical. At one sloping and suffocating tunnel some turned back. Paul found himself comforting them, calling out, "It's all right! You'll be all right!" to the older women. But it was not all right: it was horrible. In places the rickety electric lamp system had failed, and they clambered in total darkness. At last, after stumbling down and down, under a million tons of stone, they came to the burial chamber: a grim, undecorated, ugly, horrifying stone hole, lying under six thousand years of dead weight: meaning nothing. There was no other world, only this: in the face of that blank, robbed chamber there could be no delusions.

Then they had to climb out, not knowing where they would emerge, or whether they had to push back by the others, or not. Paul was now in a panic, but kept control of himself. He slipped once, and hurt his knee. Suddenly he thought —

suppose there are scorpions? Or snakes? He suddenly realised he was in Egypt, a country utterly foreign to him, in the most dangerous continent of the world. So, he kept his hands out of the dark corners. Had he lost Frances? He heard a cry and a curse: she had entered a tunnel which was a little higher, in front: had stood up a little higher, and had walked into the stone roof, crashing her forehead against the stone. For a moment she was silent with pain, while he did what he could in the cold darkness to comfort her, before they clambered upwards. At last, the glow of hot bright day appeared like a blessing at the end of the stone channel, and they emerged on a ledge half-way up the side of the pyramid.

"We're out of the tomb!" he gasped.

"This time at least," she said, a little sob in her voice. "I did it," she added, proudly. "But I wish I hadn't. It was horrible in there."

"I felt it was going to fall on me," he said. "It's weight was on me — and the whole horror of it, the decades it took to build, and the futility of the hope it expresses. The hope of eternal meaning — which is nothing because it all comes to nothing."

He shuddered. As they waited for the bus, he looked down at his feet: and there was a big black ant, carrying a piece of wood in its jaws, making its way in the hot sunshine persistently and awkwardly along a crack in the stone floor. Indifferent to the legs tramping round it, it staggered on with a sense of purpose, undaunted. Against every obstacle it met, it banged its load, but then retreated, and went round, persisting in some blind brute way, at its pointless task. It was a relief to touch Frances's warm arm.

*

Turkey was cleaner and more fertile: water ran down from the Taurus Mountains and was channelled about the fields in concrete troughs: every now and then these troughs fed into square concrete well boxes a little bigger than rainwater butts. Suddenly in these cisterns the heads of children would appear, bouncing up and down in the water. Beyond Alanya there was a big fertile plain, where grew fields of bananas, sunflowers and cotton in flower, olives and peppers. Here and there were bright pink flowering oleanders, bougainvillea and a shrub-like jasmine with white blossom.

At Side was a huge dusty stretch of ruined agora: here the slaves were sold for buyers all over Asia Minor and the Eastern Mediterranean. In the centre was a big round base of a pedestal in white stone, where there had been a temple to the God of Luck. Beyond the agora were the ruined walls of streets of Roman villas with mosaic floors. The theatre at Side was not built into the side of a hill, but constructed upon massive arches of stone. The vast theatre with its tiers of stone seats must have been the most important building in this city, built on the agricultural wealth of the plain of Pamphylia.

But it was the theatre at Aspendos that made the greatest impression. They reached it down a side road through fields of cotton and sweet corn. The theatre stood by itself, and they entered it through the immense proscenium. This was a huge wall with galleries at three levels, with columns and the ridges where there must have been friezes of mythological scenes. Before the proscenium was a huge semi-circular space paved with stone. Before this rose semi-circle after semi-circle of stone seats, twenty rows to the first gangway, and another twenty to the top where, above the top-most walkway, rose high arches on columns. The theatre must have been capable of seating 50,000 people. Paul climbed to the top of the seats, and so high was the auditorium that he felt light-headed and dizzy. Yet he could hear clearly the voice of one of the lecturers who was reciting Sophocles on the platform below, in a voice only a little louder than normal. It was like being inside a huge stone ear, so clearly resonant were the acoustics.

". . . never to have been born is best . . ."

The collective force of consciousness, among the tens of thousands of spectators, had left its mark on the stones, so that they seemed to echo still the wails, the shrieks, the howls and sobs of the crowd, at the imaginary woes. Yet to them they were not "imaginary" as we would call them: no construction could arise like that unless the devotional drama had been a primary activity in this civilisation: what they saw and shared there must have been more real than anything else in their lives. There was nothing in our world to parallel this kind of theatre, that basked grey now in the sunshine, feathered here and there with tufts of brown grass withered by the sun. All that, which was so painful, to do with ultimate meanings, was unreal. It lasted, and now we study it. What was real was the price of slaves in the market, and the goods dealt there. They are gone for ever: they are nothing.

In the night the Melteme wind began to blow hard, up the Aegean to the North: "but the wind that blows from the Strymon, rotting ships and cables, shredding to nothing the flower of Argus." It was the same wind to which Agamemnon sacrificed his daughter Iphigenia: thus enabling the Greeks to go to Troy: thus beginning the bloody sequence of the Oresteia.

*

To Laurel Jameson: a post card

Just to say that it struck me, in this Greek theatre ruin, that if I took some kind of action against Private Ear for maliciously implying that I was the source of those scurrilous things, and you declared that you were misquoted, the whole impulse of O'Neill to pursue libel might be so complex that it became doubtful? The thought made me feel much more cheerful, even among the fallen prosceniums and stages of ancient tragedy. My perspectives on the whole Cambridge petty malevolence is extended by 6,000 years! Salutations from Asia Minor!
P.G.

*

The Parthenon was in scaffolding, as was the Erechtheum, from which the caryatids had been removed because of damage by acid rain. Looking along the base of the Parthenon to see the curvature of its line, Grimmer noticed the cracks in the structure caused by an earthquake in 1981. There had been an earthquake in England while they had been away. He tried to ring Laurel but couldn't get through.

In the early morning the sun was already intense, and a hot wind blew dust into their eyes and noses. They gazed down for a moment at the theatre of Dionysus among its cypresses, and then began clambering down the marble paths against the mounting waves of tourists. So much marble! And so much litter!

When he went up on deck, as they passed Ithaca again in the dawn, there were little gleams of glinting light all over the sea. When he brought one into focus, he realised the sea was covered with beer cans, as far as the eye could see.

They were on their way home.

*

When they got back, there was still a period of vacation, as Cambridge sank towards that peaceful stretch of September, as the milling tourists began to go, and the students are still far away. Petula Weekles had gone: Ponsonby had gone: there was no post to deal with, and no-one wanted to know about anything to do with university work. Paul Grimmer set out to put his garden into some kind of order, which meant mostly pulling out weeds which had grown since he went away. The essence of gardening is the huge amount of rubbish one continually accumulates: and in Cambridge it all had to be bagged up in plastic farm fertiliser bags and taken out to the municipal dump on the Milton Road. Frances went back to her office, to deal with her correspondence, and for her there was no rest, for students and visiting scholars were still clamouring for accommodation for the new academic year.

They felt very close to one another and at peace, and they celebrated this by listening to music together. They would sit close on the sofa and hear a Mozart piano sonata on Radio Three, or put on Mahler's Ninth Symphony, or the *Kindertotenlieder*. Some new and deeper note had entered their hearts since the Hellenic cruise, and they found the best way to cherish it was to enter into the shared musical experience. Even to discuss a novel seemed too explicit, and to lead to considerations with which they did not at the moment want to engage. The dread in his heart was evaporating, as the libel threat seemed to be dissolving into indifference.

Paul felt he should bring himself round to preparing for his winter's teaching, so they began to discuss *The Awkward Age*. Paul put it down, angrily.

"This is the third time I've read it," he said, "and I still can't understand it."

"It's too subtle for you," she mocked. "It just isn't your kind of novel — that subtle structure of differing perspectives. You're too mundane."

"Thanks," he said. "I understand more than you allow, I hope. And if I re-read every page three times, I can begin to get to the heart of the situation."

"Like what?"

"Whether Vanderbank is Mrs Brookenham's lover, in physical terms. I believe now she is, and they go to bed on Friday afternoons, when Nanda is prison visiting or whatever."

"But it says, 'we don't even have the excuse of passion'. How do you explain that?"

"I had a great argument with Rhees about that."

She smiled.

"You'll be glad to get back with them, won't you?"

"Yes," he admitted. "I grumble at the time. But with intelligent young people like that, they drive you, to persist at problems of culture and value — and that's perhaps our equivalent of the Greek theatres, and the way they took myth with such gravity."

"No doubt the Greeks had their Poppy Beldons, too."

"She'd be for the satyr plays," he laughed. "I saw her on a punt yesterday, with a young man and a bottle of champagne: people take that for 'Cambridge'."

"Well, why shouldn't she, you old puritan: what about you and your Hymettus and your Mavrodaphne wine and the rest. You've still got a touch of the Leavisite you have!"

He blushed.

"*He* thought Nanda's final situation made that novel a 'trage-doi'," he said. "I can't see it as a tragedy. There's no doubt the promise of her youth is blighted by her mother's corrupt sophistication, and she can't have Van because he's her mother's. And she loves him so there's pain. But she has got Longdon."

"He's too old! James would have supposed he was past sexuality."

"Like himself."

"He was never not past it: I mean he never *began* it."

"But Longdon is old and will die — and then she'll be free — to begin again."

"You want another book!"

"No, the point I'm making is that tragedy is about the predicament when you *can't begin again*."

"Because you're dead?"

"Because you're dead."

He reflected a bit, over the great theatres: in his mind's eye he saw the crowd of tens of thousands weeping uncontrollably over the death of Agamemnon at Side, while, in the agora nearby thousands of slaves had been sold the previous day.

"Leavis wasn't, in the end, very good about tragedy," he said. "He could see what it *wasn't*, such as Bertie Russell's posture."

"I'm not sure he was good about art," she replied. "after all, all we're concerned about is *art*, which — like that lovely Mozart we just heard — yields a feeling of joy: that's its first purpose."

"Because it makes you feel so much more alive: and that life has a meaning. It's the recognition that one is up against death that generates the joy, funnily enough."

"It has something to do with love, doesn't it?"

"Love took a new dimension out there, under those African stars," he said. "You seemed so vulnerable and dear to me! But back here, a certain narrowness has come over me again: I can't hold on to my vision."

He clamped his jaw sadly on it.

"Just now, it all seems so provincial here, so 'Cambridge'. " He said in a Fenland accent "Kymebridge". "Out there in Greece, Cambridge seems a great centre of intelligence, from which the relics and scripts, the texts and artifacts, are illuminated. But when you get back, the long perspectives of history make Cambridge seem a funny little Fenland place, that takes itself so seriously."

"And thinks it is *it*!" she laughed. "The pity is it doesn't have those terrible gods."

"Like Poseidon."

They were thinking of the bronze statue in the Athens museum, a green figure with a spear — a piece dragged out of the sea: the god who had shaken their ship so often in the night.

"Well," she said, "this spring and summer have helped, haven't they, to get Cambridge and even the ghosts of *Scrutiny* a little off your back?"

"Oh yes," he said. "I am Duchess of Malfi still!"

"And Simeon survived," she reflected tenderly.

"Interesting, isn't it," he said. "It was *The Alchemist* that saved him."

Simeon had been in the throes of a crisis with a new girlfriend. Happily, he had been asked to fly scenery in the Marlowe Society production of *The Alchemist*. It had been a complicated set, and it had been made to collapse, so it had had to be rebuilt every night, and the fireworks of the exploding alembic re-wired. Simeon loved the manic life of the theatre, and worked in there until the small hours. The experience had taken him out of himself — and had given him a sense of a future: he wanted to be a stage designer. In his misery at being jilted, he had displayed a deathly sense that there was no future in which he was interested at all. Now, he was restored to the world.

"That's another use for the theatre," said Paul.

"Therapy?"

"Yes, but art isn't therapy. I'm devoted to psychoanalytical theory, but it won't do to be reductive."

"Well, what is it?"

"That would be telling," he replied. "I suffered terribly over all that Petula business, you know," he said.

"I know," she said, gravely.

"I don't know that you do know," he said. "I really wanted to die. There was a time when I wanted to smash up everything, and die, in a last failure."

"Like the old days," she said, wryly.

"Oh, worse than that, really. But now it takes its place: I've placed it — against all those ruins we tramped over in Greece. But it isn't therapy I've had: it's a look at time and death: and that long struggle man has, to try and believe that his existence has a meaning."

He shrugged.

"Aschenberg would say that — at times, at any rate. But my students save me from scepticism and despair: how could I not believe in the future, with them around?"

"So Aschenberg, in his nihilistic mood, won't win?"

"We'll go at it hammer and tongs: but in a way, that's his answer. Since we take it so seriously, since we attend so gravely to the subjective realm, to consciousness, to the search for meaning — it isn't delusion: it's true and real. There is something there, some principle of order, some creative dynamic in the world . . . I glimpsed it, didn't you?"

He thought of her holding her straw hat on, in the winds of Knossos, on the tiers of Aspendos, in the dark tunnel under the pyramids. And the long woe, of his intense love of her at such moments, in anguished conflict with his sense of culpability, for the unseen threat he had brought upon them.

"Yes, I suppose I did," she said. "Faintly and far away."

"You've never found out who it was, who was mucking you up with your students, did you?" she said sadly: she was deeply distressed, still. Having hoped for so long he would find a place appropriate to his efforts, she had been appalled to see him in such pain and despair at times.

He shrugged, unhappy. He felt they were on dangerous ground. He hadn't yet seen Laurel.

"It's been such a shabby episode, so characteristic of the pettiest side of Cambridge, that provincial meanness. I don't want to enquire: that would be to compound it, somehow."

"Perhaps it was the gods?" she said evasively.

"They were pretty mean," he laughed. "And you must have mischief-makers: Thersites, Judas, Iago: they make the big dramas possible."

"You sound very resigned!"

"Well, I suppose I still could fail, but I don't think I shall.

Except, of course, for the big failure, that wrecks the theatres and tumbles the temples. I've got to get all these books done before I die."

Was it all futile? What did writing words count, against the erosions of time that tumbled the great stone blocks everywhere? Or against one's inner weaknesses, where the little pinpricks brought the whole edifice down.

"Oh, the typing costs!" she moaned.

"Would you rather I used clay tablets? Or a word-processor?"

It was a relief, to get back to his desk: he had at least thirty days before the students came up again for the new academic year.

*

He waited until they had settled down for the evening, with a bottle of Gamay rouge from Sainsburys. Frances was yawning over *The Times*.

"I was vastly relieved today," he said, "to hear that O'Neill has dropped his case against poor Laurel."

She put the paper down and took her spectacles off to look at him, sensing some underlying gravity in his voice.

"Has he? Or is he just delaying and playing cat's paw?"

"Oh, there's no doubt. He had a proper legal letter."

"You've seen it."

"Yes, I had to. He has been in a great misery over it, for months you know."

"I know. And so have you, haven't you?"

Paul looked sheepish. He realised she knew by intuition that he had been in a deep crisis about the affair, even though he had told her nothing.

"I've been in misery, too," he said. "I wrote an article in the *Sunday Press* which was just as libellous. Then there was a scurrilous piece in *Private Ear*, quoting me, and making it look as if I was the source of all these imputations and worse. Fortunately, we got them to apologise and they withdrew the allegations. So, the case has all collapsed. But there was a grim time all last year. You see I made myself as liable as Laurel, because I was in such a fury and felt I must support him."

Frances gave a gasp and her face turned pale.

"So that was it!"

She looked angrily incredulous.

"You did *what*?" she gasped, furious.

"Yes," he said, going on reluctantly. "I wrote an article saying O'Neill shouldn't have sued him, and confirmed that it seemed his appointment was not renewed for other reasons."

"And was that libellous?"

He nodded.

"Did you realise what you were in for?"

"It was most embarrassing. For one or two lawyer fellows got on to this, and warned that we could lose."

"What, and have to pay damages?"

"And the costs, too, if we contested it."

His face was a picture of misery, and now he could hold nothing back.

"And did this *Private Ear* business make it worse?"

"For a time . . . but then it all became such a muddle I suppose he couldn't be sure he'd win his case. The whole thing fell apart, because *Private Ear* went too far."

She began to turn pale, as the realisation sank in.

"But Laurel would have been ruined. He would have had to sell his house and everything."

"That's right."

He hoped she wouldn't take her realisation of the possibilities further, but he knew she would.

"And what about you? You might have been liable for *thousands* too," she said, appalled.

"Well I wasn't," he said, rather sulkily. "It all fell down, thank God."

She was extremely angry now.

"I hope you aren't playing Galahad anywhere else with our money!" she said loftily. "*My* money it would have come to in the end," she choked.

He shrugged.

"You realise," she went on, "if things had gone wrong, *you* don't have twenty thousand pounds or more. I have, from my mother's estate and through good housekeeping, despite paying all your bloody bills: but that's *all* we've got. And since

I'm married to you, it would have been really *my* money that would have had to go to O'Neill and the lawyers. How dare you put our property, our whole life, in jeopardy, and without telling me — without even *consulting* me. How *dare* you! How dare you keep it from me, for month after month — for *years!*"

She was pale with rage.

"We could have . . ." But he stopped. He didn't know what they could have done. He felt shivers of cold sweat running down his back, at the horror of what he had done. Apart from the sense of the rectitude of his support for Laurel, he hadn't thought about the real consequences.

"All very well," she cried, "all very well to be moral. But it is stupid and hypocritical, to take up such high-minded and generous postures, at other people's expense. Why did you not ask me? Did you suppose I wouldn't have backed Laurel — morally? At least I have enough sense to accept we're too poor to jeopardise all our property on such a public and reckless gesture."

"I didn't want to jeopardise your funds . . . but I can see now of course that *I* did, I suppose."

"You knew very well you did."

He looked miserable.

"I suppose I never thought it through."

"You're such a cunt about money," she said, exasperated, with a big explosive sigh.

"You're like Harold Skimpole!" she added, scathingly.

"Oh, I *hate* him," said Paul, pained.

"You don't live in the real world of hard realities. It's all very well to think of yourself as a great friend of this unfortunate young man. But what were you going to live on, in your retirement, when you've got no pension to speak of anyway? You're going to live on *me*, aren't you, like you did for years before you got appointed at Pemning! Well, don't jeopardise it, bear that in mind. You haven't any other schemes for spending my money have you?"

He had never seen her so furious.

"I can't help it. I'm married to you," he said, lamely.

"You're lucky!" she exclaimed, caustic. "You'd be in dire

straits otherwise. I always thought a husband was supposed to keep a wife." Then a thought struck her.

"Do you mean that all through that lovely trip around Greece and the Mediterranean, you knew about this?"

"Yes, I did," he confessed.

"And when you earned that thousand in Canada and we decided to blow it on going to Greece?"

"Yes," he murmured.

"That when we were so happy together you were thinking secretly that you might have ruined me? *Ruined* me!" she shouted, her face hard with rage.

"It was wrong of me," he said, humbly.

"When will you change!" she cried. "When will you learn not to be such a fool, a hopeless, romantic, inadequate fool!"

"How can I go on living with a man," she exclaimed, "who is so fundamentally disloyal to me, so untruthful, so duplicitous, so insane!" she raged.

"I never thought it through," he said again, bitterly, depressed about himself. "We never talk about money matters ever, anyway," he added lamely.

There was a pause. Paul Grimmer could think of nothing more to say. It had been wrong: she kept her property so separate and secret from him, afraid of what he might do. He had no idea how much she had now by way of savings. He simply hadn't taken it in, that if he put himself in jeopardy, she might have to spend from her estate to get them out of debt. He had been careful not to get into debt. But when he backed Laurel, he had simply not thought that this might rebound on him, and so on Frances. He had never believed Laurel would lose, and he had regarded such an end as unthinkable. But he had failed totally to realise that he was gambling, in a sense, with his wife's property.

"Well we haven't lost any money," he protested. "The case has been dropped. So that's all right."

"All right!" she mocked. "Never mind the libel case. What I've got out of it is a glimpse of what a *fool* I have as a husband — when it comes to property. You're a babe! Who else would do such a thing? I never move without advice! Did you ask one of the law fellows?"

"Yes, well, no," he said. "I asked about the case in terms of general principles and expectation."

"You never asked them, 'What will happen to me if Laurel loses?' "

"No."

"And you never said, 'I have no money, no home — where would I get the money to pay my share!' "

"No," he said.

"You never said, 'My wife has a little — *will this take that?'* "

"I never thought of it," he said.

"Too bloody true you didn't," she cried.

There was a pause, while she looked exasperated at him. Despite her rage, she still loved him. It was not the end. She was appalled by his foolish treachery: but she could see he hadn't calculated to risk her money.

"There's no other mad scheme to ruin us, I trust?"

He shook his head.

"The never-succeeding-author business is enough: there I've always some hope something may come of it. But this — well, I shall have to take some steps to protect myself."

Inwardly, he gave a sigh of relief. She wasn't going to leave him then: he had been appalled at the thought she might leave him for ever. She spoke as if she was going to go on living with him, defending herself against his foolish romanticism, his egoism, his impulsiveness.

"I *could* get a divorce for it," she said, reading his thoughts. "I'm sure I could. Risking my whole estate! You must be mad!"

"I was sorry for Laurel," he said, doggedly.

"Well, in that case you should have gone out and worked to earn something to help him pay his costs . . ."

The storm was beginning to abate. But he knew a deep chasm of distrust had opened between them: and worst of all was that the whole charm and excitement of their Greek cruise, all that shared attention to the civilisations of the past, and the beauties of distant cultures, was now marred for her, because all that time he had known that he had put everything she owned — everything she had wisely put away for their old age — at risk, without even one word to her.

She was deeply wounded and afraid of him, and it would be a long time before any sense of confidence and trust could grow between them again.

*

"I'm sorry I was so angry," she said.

Paul was amazed. He ached all over, with a sense of guilt, which was bound up with a new discovery, of the truth of reality, its cruelty, and the dreadfulness of the consequences of one's actions. He had slept only fitfully all night again. Now in the morning, she had come to him in a different mood.

"I don't think any less that you were wrong to jeopardise my savings. But I have thought a lot about it, and I could see how, step by step, you got involved, when you didn't really mean to."

He licked his lips. Perhaps he had been feeling more guilty than he really was?

"At first," he said, "I only wrote generally in support, and supposed that it would all appear reasonable to O'Neill and he'd drop it all."

"And you never thought it would happen?"

"Well, it didn't, did it?"

"No," she said, sadly. "Promise me you won't take risks like that again."

"I'm always full of dread every time a book comes out," he said, "in case I've libelled someone."

"I ought to divorce you," she said, not meaning it.

He sighed.

"I hate the world," he said.

She scowled at him, annoyed.

"It was good of you, in a way, to stand by Laurel. But when you do that kind of thing, don't fancy yourself as a millionaire."

"They're all round us, you know," he said, brightening. "Larry told me the chaplain is a millionaire. And Jeffrey Archer's wife was *almost* next to me at last week's feast."

"So near and yet so far," said Frances grimly. "You can't catch the success by rubbing shoulders, alas."

"No Midas effect?" he grinned.

"She's a very attractive woman," he reflected.

"Off you go then," said Frances. "Then you can both write novels about it."